Rekindled

BOOKS BY BARBARA DELINSKY

Rekindled
A Woman's Place
Shades of Grace
Together Alone
For My Daughters
Suddenly
More Than Friends
A Woman Betrayed
Finger Prints
Within Reach
The Passions of Chelsea Kane
The Carpenter's Lady
Gemstone
Variation on a Theme
Passion and Illusion
An Irresistible Impulse
Search for a New Dawn
Fast Courting
Sensuous Burgundy
A Time to Love

Rekindled

Barbara Delinsky

HarperCollins*Publishers*

HarperCollins*Publishers*
10 East 53rd Street, New York, N.Y. 10022-5299

Flip Side of Yesterday copyright © 1983 by Barbara Delinsky
Lilac Awakening copyright © 1982 by Barbara Delinsky
All rights reserved. No part of this book may be used or reproduced in any manner whatsoever without written permission of the publisher, except in the case of brief quotations embodied in critical articles and reviews.
For information concerning *Flip Side of Yesterday* address Simon & Schuster, 1230 Avenue of the Americas, NY, NY 10020.
For information concerning *Lilac Awakening* address Dell Publishing Co., Inc. 1 Dag Hammarskjold Plaza, NY, NY 10017.

ISBN 0-7394-00681

HarperCollins® and ■ ® are trademarks of HarperCollins*Publishers* Inc.

Cover photo: © 1998 by James Randklev

A previous edition of *Flip Side of Yesterday* was published in 1983 by Silhouette Books, a division of Simon & Schuster.
A previous edition of *Lilac Awakening* was published in 1982 by Dell Publishing Co., Inc.

Printed in the United States of America

Letter from
BARBARA DELINSKY

Dear Reader,

This volume contains two of my early books. *Lilac Awakening* was originally published in 1982, *Flip Side of Yesterday* in 1983. Both have been out of print for years. This is their very first reissue.

These books were initially written as romances, with the primary focus on the love story. That hasn't changed in this volume. The plots are exactly as they were in the original versions. I have, however, slightly edited these books to reflect the growth in my writing style that has occurred since their first publication.

We are calling this two-book volume *Rekindled* because each story tells of a relationship that is, indeed, reborn. In the case of *Flip Side of Yesterday*, the story opens with Chloe and Ross meeting again for the first time, eleven years after a brief affair. In the case of *Lilac Awakening*, the relationship between strangers, Anne and Mitch, is renewed each month with repeated visits to a secluded Vermont cabin. Since neither book is as long as my current books are, my publisher agreed to put the two together and thereby enhance both your reading and your fiscal pleasure.

I do love these books and sincerely hope you will, too!

My best always,
Barbara Delinsky

CONTENTS

Flip Side
of Yesterday

1

The evening breeze was gentle, softly whispering "Chl...ooo...
eeeee..." as the long-legged vision in white whisked across the dusky
lawn, her dark hair streaming behind her, and ran lithely up the broad
stone steps.

"Chloe! There you are. I was beginning to worry." A man stepped from
beneath the deep brick overhang and fell into easy step beside her as they
passed through a large oak door into the high school and headed down a
long corridor.

"I'm sorry, Howard," she said, meaning it. Howard Wolschinski was the
state senator who had first sought her services. After three meetings, she
had come to like him. "I'd hoped to be on the road by four, but, I swear,
there was a conspiracy against me. First the phone, then my car."

"Anything major with either?" he asked.

"No on both counts. But I didn't clear Little Compton until five, and
by that time the rush-hour traffic was horrid. I drove as fast as I could. I
hope I haven't messed things up."

"You haven't. The meeting was called for seven thirty. You're only five
minutes late. It's given the crowd a chance to settle down." He guided her
around a corner with a light hand at her elbow and began the climb as
soon as they reached a staircase.

At the first landing, Chloe asked, "How's the turnout?"

He grinned sheepishly. "I only wish we did half as well at political ral-
lies. This is a welcome change from apathy. The auditorium is packed.
There must be several hundred people in there."

Chloe was surprised and decidedly pleased. "Several hundred? Not bad
for a county meeting in New Hampshire." She smiled, lowering her voice
dramatically. "But which side are they on? Are they for us or agin' us?"

Her humor drifted unanswered into the stale schoolhouse air as
Howard ushered her into the meeting hall, led her onto the stage, and ges-

tured her into a seat. He took one by her side. As though on cue, the crowd silenced and the moderator began.

"Ladies and gentlemen," he said in a voice made flat by its broad New England slant, "on behalf of my friends and, uh"—he cast an encompassing glance backward, then turned a cough into a snicker, bringing chuckles from the audience—"adversaries here on the stage with me, I would like to thank you for coming tonight. It's a rare pleasure to see so many of you gathered at once. We realized that the issue of the Rye Beach Resort and Condominium Complex would stir a few of you to action, but we had no idea how many. I don't believe we've had a response like this since that talk of a state prison here a while back."

Chloe was wondering who the man was when Howard whispered, "He's Felix Hart—town manager, commissioner of public safety, President of the United States in his dreams."

She smiled at the quip. Nodding her thanks for the information, she refocused on the speaker.

"... and they listened to us then, just as they listened to us when they mentioned a hazardous waste disposal center six miles from us. And before that, there was the matter of a state sales tax ..."

The monologue went on, freeing Chloe for several seconds more. Bending forward, she drew a notebook from her bag and prepared to make notes on the opposition's points. That opposition sat to her left, occupying two chairs on the far side of the one vacated by the moderator. Her peripheral vision took in two men, one significantly taller and darker than the other. They would be the state representative in favor of the complex and the owner of the development company. Chloe knew neither of their names, a situation that was about to be remedied.

"As for the others here tonight," the moderator said, "let me begin with Howard Wolschinski. You all know Howard, our distinguished state senator." He gestured from Howard to Chloe. "Chloe MacDaniel, geological consultant and one of the founding partners of Earth Science Education, Inc., out of Little Compton, Rhode Island." His hand went toward the other side of the stage. "Bradbury Huff, your state representative"—she jotted the name in her notebook—"and finally, the president of the Hansen Corporation, Ross Stephenson ..." R-O-S-S S-T-E—

Chloe stopped writing mid-stroke. Ross Stephenson? Ross Stephenson? She would never forget that name. Heart pounding, she glanced at the fourth member of the panel. He was the taller, darker one. Was it the same Ross Stephenson? This man was nattily dressed and impeccably groomed. The Ross she had known had been bearded and wore faded jeans, high boots, and a peasant shirt of Indian cotton. Eleven years had passed. He might have changed. How could she know?

His eyes. They were the same memorable amber. Eleven years ago they had cut through all pretense and snagged her in the space of a breath. They were just as striking now—and they were looking at her. He knew.

As all else faded, she felt shock, remembrance, pain. Then she tore her eyes from his and lowered them to her paper. P-H-E-N-S-O-N. Ross Stephenson. Un-believable.

"Are you all right?" Howard whispered, seeming to sense her distress.

She contemplated lying. The society belle of New Orleans would have done that. But today's Chloe was too honest. She whispered back, "I knew him—Ross—a long time ago. I never expected to see him here." Or again, for that matter, she added silently, struggling to keep her thoughts from racing back in time.

"He shakes you up?"

She smiled ruefully. "He shakes me up."

"Will you be able to go on and speak?"

She took a deep breath. "I'll be fine once we get going." Unfortunately, Felix Hart continued to talk, gesticulating more emphatically than ever.

"He's been sidetracked on the background of your pal. Listen."

Chloe had no choice.

"As many of you know," Felix drawled with an air of self-importance, "Mr. Stephenson has been behind the building of two successful mall complexes here in the Granite State. His company has left its mark from coast to coast in factories, libraries, educational facilities, and office buildings. The reputation of the Hansen Corporation precedes him here. It is with great honor that I present to you, for an explanation of his plans and hopes for the Rye Beach Complex, Mr. Ross Stephenson."

Chloe's heart was hammering again. When it was momentarily drowned out by the applause of the crowd, she dared another glance at Ross. Again, he was looking at her. She held her breath, barraged by memories that gathered and surged. A slow pallor spread beneath her ivory skin. She was thinking that she had to get out of there fast, when he finally faced forward, pushed himself from his chair, and approached the dais.

"Whew," came a whisper by her ear. "That was some greeting."

Chloe felt the color rush back to her face. She realized her misunderstanding when Howard went on. "Felix introduced him like he was a visiting dignitary instead of the man whose blueprints we plan to tear apart."

"Please keep reminding me," Chloe murmured, to which the senator chuckled. Then they both settled back to listen to Ross Stephenson's presentation.

For Chloe, listening was an awesome challenge. The sight of him standing straight and tall before the microphone was a distraction in and of itself. She couldn't help but admire the breadth of his shoulders and the slow tapering of his frame toward narrow hips and long, lean legs. To her chagrin, she couldn't help but remember the skin beneath, firm and drawn taut over the muscles of shoulder, chest, and arms, its dark matting of hair a cushion for her head, a playground for her fingers.

She forced those fingers to work now, making notes of words that she barely heard, that her mind could barely assimilate. Still she made herself concentrate, jotting down thoughts with increasing rapidity in an attempt to keep her mind on the present and off the past.

But was it the past that brought her head up again and her gaze back to Ross? Was she intrigued for old times' sake alone? His dark hair was thick but well-trimmed and combed into as much submission as she guessed it would go. Eleven years ago it had been longer and even thicker. With the beard, he was like a bear—large, overpowering, dominant, but cuddly. Now there was a refinement to him, a control in his stance, a purposefulness. Addressing his audience, he conveyed competence and intelligence.

And that audience was enrapt, some nodding, others shaking their heads, all measuring his words with the keen interest that had brought them out on this mild September night.

His voice was deep and resonant as it flowed through the mike and filled the room. "The benefit to your community would be multifold. We're proposing to use a parcel of land that is presently underused. The resort will attract guests who will patronize local businesses. Food outlets, entertainment houses, restaurants, real estate establishments—all stand to gain from the Rye Beach Complex. The condominium complex will bring untold tax revenue both to state and local purses. Given the easy access to this area by the federal highway system, the condominium units will be in high demand year round."

Chloe found herself listening closely, wondering how this could be the same man who had once chosen to live on a communal farm in Kentucky. That free-spirited Ross was a far cry from this entrepreneurial one. Trying to reconcile the two was impossible.

Howard leaned close. "He's a powerful speaker. What do you think? Will he have them sold before we even present our side?"

She answered without taking her eyes from Ross. "Lord, I hope not. I often work with groups of shoreline residents. They feel strongly about the land, which is their finest resource. I'll be appealing for the preservation of that resource."

"You're a powerful speaker yourself, Chloe. I heard you address that group on Martha's Vineyard on the subject of natural erosion patterns. You had them eating out of the palm of your hand."

Chloe gave a crooked smile. "Many of the issues are the same here. Let's hope they buy it, too."

Ross finished his formal presentation and opened the floor for questions. A podium and microphone had been set up in the center aisle of the auditorium. One by one, those residents with questions came forward. Most asked about specifics, all of which Chloe noted on her pad: the price range of the condominiums and the subsequent tax revenue; the time projection for the erection of the units; the capacity of the resort complex; and a listing of its self-contained facilities. At length, Felix Hart stood and joined Ross at center stage.

"I'm afraid we have to move on now," he apologized, eyeing the large clock on the front face of the balcony. "There's still another side to consider. Thank you, Mr. Stephenson. You've been very direct and a great help. Perhaps we'll have time for more questions later."

Chloe watched with growing excitement as Ross returned to his seat— and that excitement, for the moment, had nothing to do with him. She liked talking to groups like this, and did it often. Though she loved the scientific end of her job—the sample-taking and analysis, the computer work, the intricate calculations of ground composition, weather-related components, time predictions—she found the presentation of her findings to be heady.

Felix Hart made the introduction. "I have the delightful task now of giving you Ms. Chloe MacDaniel. Ms. MacDaniel has been retained by the county to study our coast with an eye toward the environmental impact of the Rye Beach Resort and Condominium Complex as proposed by the Hansen Corporation. She has already spent a good deal of time on the project. Ms. MacDaniel?"

After lifting a neat folder from the floor beneath her chair, Chloe rose to her full five-foot-eight-inch height and approached the podium. Her appearance was understated; she worked at that. Still, the curiosity of the crowd yielded to a murmur of appreciation when she stepped forward. Tall and willowy, dark haired and light complected, she was the image of grace. Her dress was of a soft and simple white eyelet fabric, lined through the bodice and skirt, the sleeves hanging free and loose to her elbows. A wide sash of contrasting aqua enhanced both the slimness of her waist and the porcelain of her skin.

Her voice was steady and well-modulated. "Thank you, Mr. Hart, for your kind introduction. Let me say how pleased I was to have been approached by your representatives last spring. Not only do I have a professional interest in your coastline, but I have an emotional involvement with the entire New England coast, since it's my home of choice. In keeping with this, let me begin by saying that I am not opposed to the Rye Beach

Resort and Condominium Complex per se. What Mr. Stephenson has outlined for you sounds like a project that could benefit this area. But I question the ecological wisdom of the plan as it stands. The thought of a beachfront condominium may appeal to the romantic in us all, but this plan isn't environmentally wise."

As she proceeded to explain the core results of her tests, she was oblivious to all else but her work. The most powerful tool she had was genuine concern. "In terms of storm surge alone, the Hansen proposal is risky," she argued, pointing to the carefully calculated figures now projected on a slide screen. "Once every six or seven years you folks get a storm strong enough to do significant damage to structures built so close to the beach. If the entire complex were to be moved back an additional two hundred feet, the risk would be lessened."

Again she explained her theory in detail, using statistics where applicable. By the time she finished and opened the floor to questions, she felt that her arguments had been well received. She answered the questions posed with the same patience and care, the same genuine concern for the environment.

"Great presentation," Howard said when she returned to her seat.

She smiled modestly. "I only hope I've accomplished our objective. What happens now?"

"You endure brief speeches by Brad and myself. Try to stay awake."

She gave an of-course-I-will chuckle, but with her own job done, her mind wandered. While Felix introduced Bradbury Huff, she glanced at Ross. Folded comfortably into his seat, he appeared to be listening intently to his advocate, the state representative.

The years had been kind to Ross. While his dark brown hair had a touch of gray at the sideburns, it fell over his forehead with vibrance and class. There was strength in his unbearded jaw, which flexed as he listened. The crow's feet at the corners of his eyes were etched into a light tan that spoke of a life of sun and smiles. He was perfectly at ease, maddeningly confident, and devastatingly handsome.

He blinked once, turned his head, and met her gaze and, in that instant, time stopped. In the next, it reversed, speeding Chloe back over the years to the first time she'd seen him. It had been a beautiful Thanksgiving night in New Orleans, the moment as clear to her as if it had been yesterday. She had been with Crystal then. Crystal. She still missed her sister with the kind of pain that ate at a person from the inside out.

Howard covered her tight fist with his hand. "Are you all right?" He followed her line of sight. "You can talk with him later—"

"No," she interrupted, "no need." Embarrassed, she leaned toward Howard. "I'm sorry. There are . . . memories."

"There must be," he noted softly. "And from the looks of you, they're pretty awful."

It was a minute before she said, "Not all."

"You're white as a sheet. Can I get you some water or something?"

"No. I'm fine." At his quirked brow she added, "Really," before glancing at the podium. "Is Huff almost done?"

"He'd better be. I'm next. Take notes for me, will you? I have a tendency to forget what I say from one minute to the next."

"Baloney."

"Hmmm, I could use some of that, too. Supper was very early. It's nearly ten."

At least he'd had supper. She hadn't eaten a thing. "How much longer do you think this will last?" She still had to make the return trip to Little Compton that night.

Howard checked his watch. "I have no idea. But I have to be out of here by ten-thirty to make it to Manchester for the eleven o'clock news. They're doing a live interview. I hope good old Brad speeds it up."

He got his wish within minutes. As Chloe sat back, the long-winded state representative transferred the podium to "my illustrious colleague in the New Hampshire state government," and Howard took the reins.

Chloe did take notes. It was the one way she could keep her thoughts in the present and her eyes away from Ross. Once upon a time, he had played a cataclysmic role in her life. So much had happened since that night.

When Howard finished delivering a poignant plea for the preservation of the coast, the crowd came alive with questions and comments that had less to do with scientific matters, than practical ones. They wanted to know things like how increased tax revenues would be used to benefit local residents, and who would pay for the added police and fire coverage that would be necessary, given the proportions of the Rye Beach proposal.

It was closer to ten-forty before Howard was allowed to leave the microphone. To Chloe, with a frantic look at the time, he said, "Thanks again, Chloe. Think you can cover for me here a few minutes longer?"

"Sure thing, if I can answer their questions. My field is geology, not politics."

"Don't underestimate yourself. Why not change your mind and spend the night? There are a number of nice inns close by. It'll be a long drive back to Rhode Island alone."

She was touched by his worry, but confident. "I'll be fine. Driving relaxes me. I have plenty of unwinding to do." A movement in the corner of her eye reminded her of the source of her tension. She ignored the tall figure who approached for all she was worth. "Go on now, Senator. You'll be late."

Howard's expression was wry. "I already am. Take care." He shot a glance at Ross. "Let me know what happens."

Chloe found no humor in his double meaning, particularly with Ross suddenly at her side. "I think they'd like to ask us a few more questions," he said and she suddenly wished Howard had stayed, if only to serve as a buffer. She was on her own now.

With a forced smile, she stood. "Fine," was all she was able to murmur as she walked to the podium.

Luck was with her. The questions from the audience came quickly, reimmersing her into the world of coastal geology. She parried the onslaught with ease, rising to meet the challenge in spite of an unease in the pit of her stomach. It was only when a question was directed at Ross that she let herself look at him again. The breadth of his shoulders was more marked now that his jacket was open and pulled back by the hand in his trousers' pocket. His other hand rested on the podium, fingers long and straight, tanned, relaxed.

Several questions later, a gruff-looking local came forward. "I have a question for Ms. MacDaniel," he said in a forceful voice. It brought her mind back, along with a certain wariness. "Yes?"

He stared straight at her. "I want to know what makes you qualified to be a consultant. You look awful young and awful pretty." His words took on a faint sneer. "What's with you and Wolschinski? Are you a regular on his payroll?"

A murmur of dismay passed through the audience. It was small solace for the shock Chloe felt. In the past she'd had to defend her qualifications on occasion, but never in the wake of such a crude insinuation.

Poise and professionalism were called for, and she mustered them up. But when she opened her mouth to speak, Ross beat her to the mike.

"I believe," he said in a hard voice, "that your question has no relevance—"

"Excuse me for interrupting, Mr. Stephenson." She leaned toward the mike, looking at Ross for the first time entirely in the context of the present. "I would like to respond to the gentleman." Her expression brooked no argument. She was determined. Ross straightened and backed off, seeming bemused.

She looked back at the man in the audience. "First things first, Mr.—"

"—Younger," he supplied, dropping the r at the end of his name in true New England form.

"—Mr. Younger. I have a bachelor of science in geology from Williams College in Williamstown, Massachusetts, and a master's in geology from

Boston College. I spent three years working for ConAm Petroleum, performing geological studies on oil deposits in the Gulf of Mexico. I was then able to co-found Earth Science Education, Inc., the consulting firm that was contacted by Senator Wolschinski to study the pros and cons of the Rye Beach Resort and Condominium Complex." Holding the man's gaze steadily, she pushed on. "I have control over neither my age nor my looks. And I never worked for Senator Wolschinski prior to the day he retained my services for this project." She tipped up her chin a hair. "Have you any other questions?"

Again a collective murmur went through the crowd. Just as the man shrugged and stepped back, Chloe saw the hand on the podium lift. Ross pressed his chin with his thumb, looking satisfied, respectful.

He wasn't the only one she had impressed. A different voice rose from the audience. "The taxpayers' money has been well spent for a change. Thank you, Ms. MacDaniel!"

Chloe directed a full smile across the ocean of heads as she leaned toward the microphone a final time. "It's been my honor. If my effort here has helped to preserve the natural bounty of your state, then we've all benefited. Thank you."

It was the perfect time to make a gracious, if not sweeping exit. With Ross still standing aside in deference to the crowd applauding its appreciation of her, she should have quit while she was ahead. Her mistake was in looking back at him.

His smile was devastating. Chloe felt her chest tighten, as she was caught in the throes of memory again. She was suddenly immobilized, suspended in a matrix of desire and guilt that canceled out the years that had come between, until there was only yesterday, Ross, Crystal, and the toss of a coin.

When a last-minute surge brought members of the audience to the stage, a shaken Chloe returned to the present. She had to concentrate again, listening to questions, offering answers. She stood at one side of the stage with her followers, Ross stood at the other side with his. She gained strength with each new question, so that when the last of the locals left, she felt more herself—felt more herself, that is, until she realized that she and Ross were alone.

He showed no sign of sharing either her awkwardness or her apprehension. Rather, he smiled at her, looking older and wiser perhaps, but no less alive. The air between them hummed, just as it had eleven years before.

Looking at him, Chloe grappled with a world of inner demons, but the past was better left alone. She was determined to make this reunion as brief as possible.

"How are you, Chloe?" he asked, crossing the stage to where she stood.

He was that much taller than she was. She had to tip up her head. "Fine. And you?"

"Not bad. You're looking well." He gave her a warm once-over. "Very different." Humor tugged at the corners of his lips.

"So are you." Even in spite of an inner trembling, she could appreciate the humor. "When I last saw you, you were distinctly antiestablishment. This is a switch."

His stance was a casual one, the hand in his pocket not only emphasizing the solid wall of his chest but pulling the fabric of his trousers across his thigh in a way that showed the strength of seemingly endless legs.

"Not entirely. It's just that now I save my jeans for free-time wear and my boots for cold weather."

So he, too, remembered what he had worn that night. "And the peasant shirt?" she asked softly.

He laughed. "The peasant shirt was replaced for a while by a dashiki, but I'm afraid the modern me is addicted to ordinary sports shirts and sweaters."

"Conventional," she murmured with a faltering smile, teasing him as much as she dared. It was hard to remain indifferent to this man. She felt the strain.

"Sadly so," he agreed without any sadness. "But look at you. You've done a turnaround. Last time I saw you, your hair was curled, you wore makeup, higher heels, and more daring clothes. You also talked New Orleans. Where'd the accent go?"

Chloe drew in a long breath. "It faded. I've lived up north for too long. Time does different things to each of us, I guess."

"It's for the better. You look beautiful. Unhappy, but beautiful."

His candor made her balk. Seeing him was painful enough. Talking more with him could be a total trauma.

She glanced at the auditorium clock. "My Lord, it's nearly twelve. I have to run." Straightening the shoulder strap of her pocketbook and hugging the large folder to her breast, she went to the stage steps. Ross followed. Under the guise of worry at the lateness of the hour, she quickened her step. He kept stride easily.

"You're not driving back tonight, are you?"

"I am."

"All the way to . . . ?"

"Little Compton."

"That has to be a good two- to three-hour drive. Wouldn't you do better to get an early start in the morning?"

"Can't do. I have an early appointment in the morning." Her voice sounded breathy. It was the rush, she told herself.

For long moments, Ross said nothing. They reached the front door. He held it; she passed through. In silence they crossed the lawn that separated the high school from the parking lot.

"I admire you, Chloe," he said, sounding sincere. "Your work is interesting. You obviously enjoy it."

"I do," she agreed. Relieved to be at her car, she fished in her purse for her keys. The sooner she was back at that work, back in the security of her seafront home, the sooner she could turn the past off again. Slipping in behind the wheel, she rolled her window down to let in the cool night air. With escape imminent, she grew bolder, looking up at Ross as he leaned over with his fingers curved on the lowered window. How handsome he was, she mused. She had been powerfully attracted to him then; she still was. "It was nice seeing you, Ross."

"You won't change your mind and stay over? I'm at the Wayward Sailor, an inn just down the road. I'm sure they have another vacancy, since the height of the season is past. We could grab a snack somewhere and talk."

Chloe would have liked nothing better. She knew nothing about the Ross Stephenson who was a successful businessman. Instinct told her that time spent with him would be interesting. It would also be downright dangerous, even devastating.

She sighed. "That would be nice, but I have to get back. I feel wide awake for driving. I'd just as soon put the miles behind me. Besides, I have that appointment."

Ross considered that for a minute, then held up his hands. In gracious defeat, he stepped back. She put the key in the ignition, pumped the gas pedal, turned the key. There was a click, but nothing happened. She repeated the sequence. It always worked. Granted, her small blue compact had seen better days, but it had always started for her—until, she realized as she turned the key a third time, this afternoon. She had heard the same click then, had run back into the house and brought Lee out to help. They had figured the engine was flooded, had waited and won. The car had started. But Murphy's Law said that it wasn't going to start now.

"Trouble?" Ross bent in at the window again.

"Battery, I think."

He opened the door. "Let me try."

She slid out. With an ease that belied his awesome length, he folded himself behind the wheel. The front seat was already back to allow for the length of Chloe's own long legs, and even then he gave a good-natured grimace. She had to smile. Getting in was apparently the easy part. Maneuvering now that he was there was the challenge.

But he managed. When he tried the ignition, though, he had no better luck than Chloe. He listened to that impotent click once, twice, three times. Then he hoisted himself out of the car and looked under the hood.

"You're right," he said, straightening. "It's the battery." He slammed the hood shut and brushed his palms against one another. "It looks like you'll have to stay. I don't see how you'll get someone to come out at this hour."

She reached for her bag. "I have triple-A."

"Chloe." He sighed softly. "This isn't a bustling metropolis. By the time—"

"Do you have jumper cables?"

"No." He patted his pockets. "Not anywhere close by."

"In your car?"

"It's a rental."

Her gaze fell to the pavement. She could rant and rave all she wanted, but it seemed she had little choice. "I suppose Lee could change that early appointment for me," she murmured quietly, then looked up. "And you think your inn would have a room?"

His gaze was steady. "I'm sure it would."

Not one to belabor a no-win situation, Chloe sighed. "Lead on, Ross. Lead on."

2

Ross led her to a late-model rental car roomy enough for both pairs of long legs to stretch comfortably. Vibes were something else. Chloe sensed that no space would be large enough for the ones that circuited back and forth during the short drive to the inn.

"You flew in just for tonight's meeting?" she asked, seeking to ease the silence. It was awkward, given the intimacy they had once shared.

"That's right," he answered, paying close attention to roads that were now dark and deserted.

"From?"

"New York."

"Do you live there?"

"Occasionally."

It was an odd answer. When he failed to elaborate, Chloe tried again. "Have you had to come here often?"

"More often than I'd anticipated. This project has created something of a stir." If the glance he shot her was accusatory, she accepted it as fair game and took no offense. She believed in her cause.

"From what Felix Hart implied, you move around a lot," she said.

"I always did."

It was a direct reference to the past. Then, he had been in the Peace Corps on leave for Thanksgiving, the world traveler coming stateside for a visit. There had been an air of excitement about him.

He still had it. His profile was strong, lean, preoccupied in ways that suggested big business in far places. She looked away, focusing on the view outside her window, trying to ignore a silence that she could feel and taste. She was relieved when the Wayward Sailor came into view.

Ross turned to her as soon as the car stopped. His features had softened. His tone was solicitous. "Why don't you wait here? I'll make the arrangements and find out where we can get a bite to eat. You are hungry, aren't you?"

She smiled awkwardly. "I haven't had anything since lunch."

"No wonder you're pale." He touched her cheek. "Stay put. I'll be right back."

She sat quietly, trying to think of anything but Ross. Just when she was on the verge of declaring defeat, he loped back down the steps of the charmingly ancient house. "Any luck?" she asked when he reached the car.

"There's good news and bad news." He was leaning down to talk through the window again.

"Give me the good news first," Chloe said. She needed that, needed it bad.

He grinned. "The good news is that you have the penthouse."

She looked up the inn's façade to the very top, the third floor. Assuming the attic was clean and had a bed, it would do. "The penthouse is fine." She scrunched up her face. "What's the bad news?"

He opened the door with a flourish. "The bad news is that no one serves food at this hour. The night manager here says we can raid his refrigerator, though." He paused, staring down at her for a minute before offering his hand to help her out. "The service won't be fancy. We'll be on our own." The warning note in his voice jarred her. He was remembering the old Chloe. That Chloe had been spoiled. She hadn't known how to cook, having had everything done for her for the entire eighteen years of her life. But her lifestyle had changed drastically since then.

She rose from the car. "That's fine. I think we can manage." Oh, yes, she could certainly manage to put together a meal. She was actually a fine cook now. But it occurred to her that she and Ross would be alone. She wasn't so sure about managing that.

A frown creased her brow as she entered the inn with Ross by her side. He left his overnight case at the front desk with the night manager, who cheerfully directed them into the kitchen, a decidedly old room into which every modern convenience had been crammed. Chloe made herself at home. Only after she had placed a crock of steaming beef stew, put together from leftovers, and a half-loaf of what appeared to be home-baked bread on the table did she realize that she had done all the work. But it had kept her mind occupied. Ross had been in and out of the room as she worked, finally settling down on a tall stool by a butcher-block counter to watch.

His presence didn't upset her now as much as it had earlier. She had gotten over the shock, she guessed. Still, she felt vaguely shy when they were actually ready to eat.

"Uh, is there anything else you want?" She skimmed the simple place settings, the two large bowls filled with stew. "A drink?"

He made no move to help himself. For old times' sake, so the liberated woman told herself, she indulged him.

"Milk would be fine."

He waited while she searched for glasses and filled two. She sat down opposite him. Once several mouthfuls of the thick stew had warmed her stomach, she put her spoon down. Something stuck in her craw.

"I'm not unhappy," she stated, so softly and apparently unexpectedly that Ross looked perplexed. "You thought I looked unhappy. I'm not."

He went back to eating, but slowly, thoughtfully. "No, I suppose you're not, not right now," he finally said. "But earlier, there was a look in your eyes. It comes and goes. There it is again."

The sound of his voice had been enough to spark memories. With a barely perceptible shake of her head, she chased them off again. "I do love what I'm doing," she said.

"Tell me about it. How did you get started?"

"You heard the bare outline tonight."

"The bare outline. Now I'd like to hear more." His pause was pregnant with unspoken thoughts. "Why geology?"

She shrugged. "Why not?"

He didn't pull any punches. "Because it's one of the last fields that someone raised in the style of conspicuous consumption would choose."

"Maybe that's why I chose it."

"Ah." He smiled. "You were rebelling."

"Not entirely."

"Escaping?"

She looked away. "You're perceptive. But only half right."

"Go on."

Chloe tucked a long strand of dark hair behind her ear. "It was actually a simultaneous discovery—escape and excitement. At that period of my life, I needed something that was a total change from everything I'd known before. I spent some time in Newport with friends and fell in love with the ocean there."

"You found solace?" he asked gently.

She admitted it with a small tilt of her head. "I spent a lot of time on the beach and happened to befriend an old man who felt very strongly about environmental considerations. He affected me deeply." The memory of Hector Wallaby brought a sad smile to her lips.

"He's dead?"

"Yes. I miss him. He never knew it, but in spirit at least, he was the founding father of ESE, Inc."

"Were you in college during the time you knew him?"

Chloe sat straighter. "Uh, no. I . . . my freshman year was postponed."

"So you started college late and have still done all this?"

The compliment gave her a boost. She smiled. "Once I decided to go into geology I was in a rush."

Ross smiled back. Firm lips framed the whitest of teeth, mesmerizing her for the split second until he said, "You worked for ConAm Petroleum?"

"Yes. Do you know the company?"

He shook his head. "Only by reputation." He looked at her sideways, skeptical now. "I'd have thought that if environmental concerns were your focus, the oil companies would be your archenemies."

She blushed. He made nothing easy, that was for sure. But if he wanted to be honest, she could be honest right back. "I needed the money," she said and braced herself for the response that was sure to come.

And she wasn't let down. Ross's eyes widened, then narrowed. "You needed the money?" He frowned. "Did I miss something here? I was given to think James MacDaniel was—is—one of the wealthiest men in New Orleans."

"He is."

"Then, why . . . ?"

"Among other things," she began in self-defense, "it was a matter of pride. I wanted to start my own consulting firm and didn't want to ask my father for money." Ross should know how much she had changed. He should know that she was her own woman now.

But his take on the situation was different from hers. "So you sold out to the powers that be for the amount of time it took you to gather the resources to mount a systematic campaign against those same powers?"

Chloe reacted quickly and vehemently. "That's not true. Not true at all. The work I did for the oil companies involved identifying the most likely spots for oil deposits. Wherever possible, environmental considerations were put first. And you're a fine one to talk about selling out. I had the impression, when I saw you last, that you were against everything the establishment had to offer."

Ross leaned back in his chair. "You drew your own conclusions, Chloe. Appearances can be misleading." His tone was low, his voice and eyes steady.

Chloe was stunned. She stood up and cried, "It was all a charade, then? The clothes, the beard, even the Peace Corps?" She turned away, disillusioned and heartsick. Head bowed, she grappled with the idea of an attraction based on a lie.

Ross materialized before her. "Did it matter so much?" he asked softly.

When she neither answered nor looked up, he put a finger under her chin and forced it up. Her eyes were dry, but she knew they held pain. She couldn't hide that, couldn't even try.

"Did it?" he asked.

Chloe felt a well of emotion, emotion that had lain dormant for years. Ross was so close that the warmth of his body was an intoxicant. She used the power of that to speak. "Yes. It mattered more than you can imagine."

"But why? The physical attraction between us had nothing to do with outer trappings. As I recall, we shed our clothes pretty fast." Chloe tried to pull away, he held her chin. "Don't run from it. There was something between us that you can't deny. Are you telling me you made love to an image?" His tone was suddenly cooler. "Was it an experiment for you? Was I a tool in your rebellion?" His fingers tightened on her jaw. Reflexively, she held his wrist.

"No. That wasn't it at all." She was hurt that he would suggest it. "All you seem to think about is the physical act. Yes, there was a physical attraction. With and without clothes. But for me, at least, there was more involved. There had to be." Her voice rose. "I was a virgin, for God's sake."

Ross must have felt her hurt, because he relaxed his grip. He moved his fingers back to her ear, pushing them through the long strands of her hair with infinite gentleness.

"I know that," he whispered. His eyes held the same tenderness they had on that night, when he had first introduced her to the art of love. Then, the world had been hers on a string. It certainly wasn't now, still her heart pounded in her chest the very same way. Now, as then, she was being held by the most appealing man she had ever known. He was a leader, a freethinker. He was boldly gentle, gently bold. He had confidence without arrogance, success without acclaim. He was a man who didn't mince words. She felt an instinctive respect for him.

Much of this same appeal had beckoned to her on that night. Other details might be forgotten, but not Ross and the force that bound them. It was an unfathomable force, but frightfully powerful. Eleven years ago, it had driven the fact of her innocence from her mind. Now it obliterated all remembrance of what had happened so soon after that night to irrevocably change Chloe's life and outlook.

As Ross's large hands framed her face, she felt a special warmth steal through her, awakening senses from hibernation like the coming of spring. Her cheeks flushed with the heat. Her lips parted. She was entranced all over again.

He moved closer, his face lowering. When she closed her eyes it was to savor the feather touch of his mouth on hers. It seemed she had waited forever to know its sweetness again. And guilt? Guilt was light-years away, beyond a far horizon she hoped never to reach. It had been pervasive over the years, but was out of place now. She wanted more of Ross, if only to keep the past safely blotted from her mind.

Opening her eyes, she found Ross's hot above her. His breath was unsteady, but he waited. She sensed he was giving her a chance to turn and run, but that was the last thing she wanted to do.

She met his kiss with an eagerness she hadn't known for eleven years. All the power of her femininity that had been stored up and denied now burst forth. Ross's lips were firm and knowing in response to her passion, dominating then submitting, teasing then yielding. They explored the ripe curve of her mouth with a thoroughness surpassed only when his tongue entered the act. And Chloe opened herself more with each darting flicker, with each exchange of breath.

She had come alive and was aflame. At some point her arms found his neck and coiled beyond, drawing her slender body firmly against his longer, harder one. His hands played over her back, caressing every inch from hip to neck with the devastating touch of those long fingers. And she was caught in the web they spun, neither able nor willing to move away.

Everything about Ross was utterly male, from the musky scent of his skin to the trim tapering of the hair at the top of his collar, to the lean line of his torso and the corded steel of his thighs. It was as though Chloe was innocent again, as though this was that first ecstatic night relived. She was intoxicated.

When he groaned and crushed her to him, she understood the feeling. It was a statement of a shared primal need. Ross held something for her that no other man had begun to offer. She was driven by instinct closer, closer to him.

At some point, soft bells of warning sounded. She didn't know if it was when his hand slipped from her cheek to her throat, or when his fingers began to knead her breast, or when his palm turned to her nipple. She only knew of a tug between some relic of the past that clamored for recognition, and the quickly coiling knot of need deep inside.

She fought that past by nurturing the need. Hands locked at the back of his neck, she closed her eyes, let her head fall back, and sought the mindlessness of sensual pleasure. Her lips parted; her breathing was short. But she needed more. Against her better judgment, against those tiny warning bells, she grew bolder. Bowing her head, bracing it against his chin, she was curved now, offering him an entrance he hadn't had before.

Small explosions of delight flared through her when he slid his hand into her dress. Surrounded, her breast was warm, full, and straining against his hand. His thumb and forefinger met at a nipple, driving her higher. Did reason exist? At that instant she knew of only one road to satisfaction.

"Come upstairs with me," Ross said in a voice thick with need. "Let me love you. It's been so long, princess."

Princess. It struck her that he had done the same thing she had—formed an image and held it through the years. In his mind she was still one step removed from royalty. But not in hers.

She strained away from his hands. "Please stop, I can't do this." Aroused still and upset with herself, she trembled.

"Can't?" he challenged hoarsely.

"Won't," she amended as she clutched at threads of composure. Eleven years ago she hadn't refused him. Her virginity had never had a chance. But things were different now. She was different.

"Why not, Chloe?"

She heard hurt, but it didn't make her relent. "I wish I could explain."

"Why can't you? I've seen that pained look in your eyes. At those moments—at this moment—you do look unhappy. Is it something about me? Something about what happened eleven years ago?"

For all of those eleven long years, Chloe had hidden a world of inner feelings from everyone around her. They were locked in tight. He could prod all he wanted, but they weren't getting out.

He spoke more gently. "Here. Sit down. I'll make us some coffee. You can talk."

"I don't want to talk. Some things are best left dead and buried." She shuddered at her own choice of words.

"Sit." He nudged her into the chair she had left, and she sat, if only because her legs were unsteady. He proceeded to clear the table, rinse everything, and perk a small pot of coffee. She watched almost incidentally, her thoughts far off in a world of what-ifs. What if Crystal had won that toss of the coin? What if Crystal had set out to seduce Ross and been seduced herself? What if Crystal had died anyway? Would Chloe feel the same guilt now?

"How do you take it?" Ross asked, placing a steaming mug before her.

"Black. Thank you."

After lacing his own with milk and sugar, he returned to his seat.

Chloe tried to control her thoughts by speaking first. "You've come a long way in the business world since I saw you last, Ross. How did you manage it?"

He smiled. "You mean, how did I manage the transformation from 'far out' to 'far in'? The fact is, I never was all that 'far out.' I went my own way for a while. I avoided money. I grew a beard because there wasn't modern plumbing where I was in Africa, and I didn't want to have to shave at dawn by the riverside. I wore jeans because they were comfortable, same with loose shirts. I'd grown up in a world of rigid discipline. I wanted my freedom."

"'Rigid discipline'?" She realized again how little she knew of Ross.

He eyed her with something akin to amusement. "Y'know, considering you slept with the man the first time you met him . . ."

"That's not fair," she argued. "When we were together, I couldn't think straight."

"History repeats itself," he drawled, referring to what had happened moments earlier with a mischievous grin.

Chloe didn't like being ribbed. "You didn't know any more about me that night." But rather than turning the tables, she was more deeply incriminated.

"Neither of us did much talking, did we?" Ross asked, clearly enjoying himself.

She shook her head. The only talking they'd done had been in soft moans and caresses. The attraction between them had been overpowering. "I want you to know that I don't do that as a rule. I mean, I don't make a habit of—"

"—jumping into bed with every guy that comes along? I know that, Chloe." He smiled gently. "I told you that we had something special. Do you think I sleep with every pretty woman I meet?"

"Of course not. I just wanted you to know not to expect something I can't give."

"Won't give," he corrected a second time.

"The end result is the same. You understand, don't you?"

"No, I hear you. I'm listening." He was sober. "But I don't understand. You haven't given me a good reason to understand yet. Most women with your looks would have reached the point, at age twenty-nine, where they could recognize something deeper."

Chloe felt stymied. "What do my looks have to do with anything?"

The amber gaze that touched her curves gave the answer even before he spoke. "You're beautiful, Chloe. Beautiful women have options. You've never married?"

"No."

"You must date often."

"I have friends."

"Male friends?"

"Some."

"Serious male friends?"

When she shrugged, he looked at the ceiling. "What I'm trying to find out is whether you're going with someone, living with someone, or engaged to someone."

For an instant, Chloe imagined he was a frustrated suitor. She smiled at the thought. "No, Ross. I date here and there, but there's no one special. I live alone."

When he expelled a breath, she suspected it was for effect. "Thank you," he added facetiously, then sobered. "Do you go home much?"

Chloe flinched. "No." That was another topic better left alone. "What about you? What was that 'rigid discipline' you suffered through?"

"My father was heart-and-soul Army. A career man. Our house was run like a barracks. It was almost a treat when I was sent to military school."

"Oh, my. It's no wonder you freaked out."

Ross laughed. "Freaked out? That's one from the old days."

Chloe smiled. "Sorry. It just slipped out. I can't remember the last time I said that."

"Maybe way back in the time of you and me?" He stared at her, then gazed pensively at the table. When he raised a hand and rubbed the muscles at the back of his neck, Chloe followed the movement. She half-wished she could do it for him, but dangerous was a mild word for that type of thing. Once, danger had been a challenge. Now she wanted no part of it.

Ross's confession broke into her thoughts. "I may have been pretty antiestablishment, at that. There was a certain amount of rebellion in me against routine and schedules and expectations. I guess I wasn't much different from the average flower child, except that I knew I'd be returning to the fold before long. I saw that period for what it was—a time in my life when I could stretch my legs."

Chloe chuckled. Her smoky gaze fell to the floor, where a pair of well-shod feet, ankles crossed, extended well beyond her side of the table. "An awesome task." She quirked a brow. "So how did you become a successful businessman? You obviously didn't go into partnership with your dad. But you've come a long way in eleven years. President of the Hansen Corporation." She shook her head in amazement.

"I had a mentor, like you did," he explained. "I worked for him through business school, then after. The business did well. I gradually acquired stock. When Sherman died two years ago he left me shares enough to make me the majority holder."

"Was the Rye Beach Complex your idea?"

"Actually, no. It was the baby of one of the other vice presidents. Sherman seemed to feel it had merit."

"And you don't?" Considering the force of his presentation that evening, she was startled.

"I do, with reservations."

"Why did you come up tonight then, rather than the VP who feels more strongly about it?"

Ross shrugged. "He's no longer with the corporation." He didn't look sorry. It struck Chloe that he might have fired the man, himself. She sensed his power. A free spirit, he had called himself. Now he ruled a prominent corporation. With an iron hand? Maybe. But he would use subtle methods to reach his goals.

"What do you plan to do about it?" she asked carefully.

"About what?"

"The complex. You mentioned some doubts. Tonight's meeting must have raised others. Will you change your proposal?"

"No."

"No? Building the complex as planned now would be environmentally dumb."

"'Dumb'?" he mocked with a grin.

She felt put down with that one echoed word. Exasperated, she threw her hands in the air. "I gave all the reasons in that auditorium. I won't repeat them now. You're being bullheaded. Do you go about all your building projects this way?"

"What do you know about my building projects?" he asked with a trace of lingering amusement.

"Nothing. I had only heard of the Hansen Corporation before tonight. But if it's like most other businesses, it puts the dollar bill before every other consideration."

"Not always." His voice carried a warning now, but she sat straighter and barreled on.

"Then you acknowledge that profit is your raison d'être?"

To her chagrin, Ross laughed. "I would never be where I am today if I didn't have an eye out for profit!"

She felt oddly betrayed. "That's really pathetic," she said, recalling the tall, handsomely bearded man in jeans, boots, and a simple peasant shirt. "I'd have thought that, with what you stood for at one time, you might have minimized crass capitalism. You have sold out, which just goes to show how terribly wrong one person can be in the judging of another, or how naïve."

Ross had risen. His eyes were too dark to distinguish anger from hurt. "You don't know what you're talking about. You didn't know me then, and you certainly don't know me now. When I returned from Africa that last time with my grungy denims, my dashiki, and my beard"—his eyes narrowed—"it took me all of a week to shuck them. And do you know why?"

He went on only when she shook her head. "Because I saw that there was more narrow-mindedness, more prejudice, coming from the mouths of the hippie generation than anywhere else. Because of my appearance, I was assumed to be one of them, until they discovered that I didn't always think the way they did, that I had a mind of my own. The true sign of a liberal, Chloe, is accepting people for their differences, respecting their right to be different. Those others, the ones who prided themselves on being nonconformists, declared all-out war on the establishment. And what happened?"

Without waiting for her response he went on, his voice low but relentless, his gaze intense. He put his hands on the table. "When was the last time you saw a flower child? Hmm? They've vanished. Disbanded. Lost the war." The pause he took was for a deep breath. "Well, I haven't lost. I'm working from within to change things. Did that ever occur to you, Chloe? You've been so quick to label me first one way, then the other. Did it ever occur to you that your impression wasn't even skin deep, that there's a me under it all?"

It was a while before Chloe was able to speak. She certainly didn't know Ross. This speech presented a new side of him. And he was right.

"I'm sorry," she said. "It was wrong of me to do that. I'm not always that way." She tried a smile in apology. To her relief, it seemed to work. His features relaxed.

"Only with me, eh?" He inhaled deeply and stood tall, holding his breath for a minute while his head fell back, then releasing it as his eyes met hers.

She felt suitably contrite and suddenly drained. "You have a knack for bringing out my extremes. I guess I'm just tired. It's late." A glance at the bold face of Ross's watch told her exactly how late. "Oh, Lord! It's two in the morning!" She caught her breath, looked at the ceiling, and whispered, "Do you think we've woken anyone up?"

Ross's chiding was gentle. "No need to whisper now. If our yelling didn't wake 'em, nothing will." He took the two empty coffee cups and brought them to the sink.

Chloe wiped off the table. "If it hadn't been for that battery, I'd have been back home in bed by now."

"Instead," he teased, "we've had a chance to get reacquainted. Um, acquainted."

Chloe stopped wiping and straightened. Getting acquainted was one thing, but where did they go from there? The physical attraction that had been rekindled with a vengeance earlier, weighed heavily on her now.

"Uh-uh, Chloe." He came up behind her. "Just relax." She looked back, wondering how he knew. "I can feel it in the air—that whatever-it-is that disturbs you." He took the cloth from her and tossed it into the sink. "I won't pounce. I'll just walk you to your room."

That was exactly what he did. He halted on the threshold. "The manager said he'd leave plenty of towels. I wish I could offer you something else. You seem to be without those . . . things that most women can't live without."

She smiled. "I don't need anything."

"A shirt? Would you like a fresh shirt of mine in place of a . . . a . . ."

"Negligee?" Her smile widened. "No, thanks, Ross. If the sheets are clean, they'll be covering enough. But I have to get an early start in the morning."

He nodded. "I called the garage while you were making our dinner. They'll be at your car no later than eight. Is that too early?"

"Lord, no! I have to call Lee, my partner, anyway. There's a small matter of an appointment at nine."

"Will she fill in for you?"

"No. He has work of his own to do." She grinned at Ross's startled look. "He'll cancel and explain for me. I'll reschedule when I get back."

Ross nodded, but he was gnawing on his lower lip. There was obviously more that he wanted to say, but Chloe wasn't inviting him in. That would be dangerous. Very dangerous. But when he turned and headed down the stairs to his own room, she felt disappointed. Part of her wondered if flirting with danger could end on a happy note this time.

The night manager hadn't only left extra towels, but he'd also left a package of goodies tailor-made for the stranded motorist. There was a toothbrush, toothpaste, a comb, soap, and, luxury of luxuries, an envelope of bubble-bath powder.

Chloe smiled. She'd had her share of tension today; now she would release it. The devil could take the hour; she would take a long, hot bath! Several deft flicks of her wrist sent a full stream of hot water into the long porcelain tub, which stood, in keeping with the vintage aura of the inn itself, on four clawed feet. Feeling scandalous, she sprinkled the entire contents of the envelope beneath the steaming flow.

Moments later she was immersed to her neck in bubbles. Draping her hair over the lip of the tub, she closed her eyes and gave in to pleasure. Was it true what they said about the subconscious urge to return to the womb? Was this all-enveloping warmth, this light floating what it had been like?

The womb, however, was not where she wished most to be at that moment. Rather, she thought of the arms that had held her earlier, the lips that had kissed her, the strong body that had supported her. Buoyed by a sense of euphoria, she allowed herself to think back on the full story of that night eleven years ago.

It had been the holiday recess. She and Crystal had returned from their first semester at the university to spend Thanksgiving with the family. The boys were gathered: Allan from Denver, Chris from Chicago, Tim from St. Louis—from their respective subdivisions of the MacDaniel domain. They had spent a typically revel-filled Thanksgiving Day, complete with gargantuan offerings of turkey, stuffing, salads and vegetables and fruit molds, pies and cakes and other goodies, not to mention the company of aunts and uncles and cousins galore. Later that night, she and Crystal had dropped in at Sandra's house, where a party had been in progress.

Sandra had been their best friend through carefree high school years. They hadn't seen her since September when she had left to go to college in New York, where her older brother lived.

Ross was that brother's friend. From the moment Chloe set foot into the Brownings' living room her eye was drawn to him. He had seemed to represent all the things she had never known—nonconformity, independence, singularity. Even in a crowd, he stood out. Sandra had said he was in the Peace Corps, stationed in Africa. He was tall and breathtakingly attractive in a wholly new and exciting way for Chloe.

"Gorgeous, isn't he?" Crystal had whispered in the ear of her twin.

"I'll say. What do you think he's doing here?"

"That's a dumb question. He's visiting the Brownings like we are."

They stood with their heads together, both pairs of eyes glued to Ross. Chloe asked, "Do you think he has a girl?"

"A guy like that? Girls, plural. He's oozing virility—or hadn't you noticed?"

"I noticed," Chloe drawled. "Think he'll notice us?"

"Why not? We're rich and beautiful and sexy—"

"—and young."

Crystal bristled. "What's that got to do with anything?"

"If he's Sammy's friend, Crystal, he's ten years older than we are. You don't really think he'd be interested, do you?"

"God, Chloe, you are a stick-in-the-mud. Of course he'll be interested. Men like freshness. And we are rich and beauti—"

"I know, I know," Chloe interrupted the litany, feeling a sudden surprising disdain for her sister's arrogance. So often the arrogance was shared. As the babies of the family—and twins, at that—they'd been reared like royalty. For the first time, however, Chloe wondered whether men like this stranger were attracted to royalty. Was being rich and beautiful and sexy all that mattered? Something told her that this divine-looking man would seek more, something in his gaze as he slowly turned it their way.

"Wow," Crystal whispered. "I'm going after him."

"Oh, no. It's my turn," Chloe whispered back with matching determination. "You got Roger. This one's mine."

"He won't want a stick-in-the-mud. You think we're too young for him."

"I've changed my mind. Besides, he's looking at me, not you."

Crystal snorted. "Arbitrary choice. We look exactly alike."

"All of a sudden we look exactly alike?" Chloe choked. "What about that 'added bit of spice' you claim to have? What about your last-born 'glow of vulnerability'?"

Crystal crinkled her nose. "He can't see all that at this distance."

But Chloe was vehement. "I have a feeling about him."

"You always have feelings about people. I'm the doer. Remember?"

"Not this time."

"Chloe . . ." Crystal warned in a singsong murmur.

"Crystal . . ." Chloe warned right back. "We'll toss a coin. Heads, I win."

Crystal's eyes narrowed. "I'll do the tossing. You always seem to win."

It was true. While Crystal, with her heightened impishness and propensity for instigating trouble, was often at the fore in their mischief-making, Chloe invariably won the toss of the coin. And with good reason. As the more levelheaded of the two, she was expected to be the one to produce the coin. It came from a secret fold in her wallet and served no other purpose than this. It would never have passed for currency. It had two heads. But Crystal never knew that, not even when she did the tossing herself.

And so, with the keenest of amber eyes pulling her forward, Chloe had approached the mysterious man of the love generation. Initial silence had given way to the exchange of smiles, then names. There was brief small talk, amid a riot of steamy looks. The party had paled. Forgetting their friends, they had wandered onto the patio, then taken refuge by the pool. Later they had moved on to the sloping lawn of Sandra's parents' estate.

Chloe shifted slowly in the tub. The heat of the water had dissipated, but was replaced by the heat of her body as she remembered. It had been warm that night. The crescent moon had been brilliant, repeated in the white smile that split Ross's dark beard when he looked down at her.

"You're a vision, Chloe," he whispered, sharing her fascination. "Are you real?"

"I'm real," she whispered back and was suddenly, uncharacteristically tongue-tied.

But further words were unnecessary. The guest house where Ross was staying was on a far corner of the estate. He took her there, pausing along the way to kiss her, to assure her with a protective embrace that he wouldn't hurt her, and he hadn't. He had been a masterful lover, so very gentle undressing her, so very subtle baring his potentially frightening body, so very patient as he coaxed her to heights of desire, then tender when he took her virginity. When tenderness gave way to driving passion, she rose with him, reveling in an ecstasy she had never known before.

Ross's lovemaking had been a magical experience. She would always cherish it.

She stirred in the tub, suspended between the world of memories and the present. In a final indulgence, she submerged her hand and touched the skin Ross had touched, traced the curves he had traced. Thoughts of him were fresh and near. She sighed in delight.

Then her back slipped on the porcelain. With a jerk, she sat up, but not before her hair got wet. Hissing her annoyance, she reached for a towel to wrap around her head, then soaped herself quickly and climbed out. A lovely trip into the past had ended in frustration. Satisfaction would not be forthcoming. Nor would there be a respite from the guilt she still felt.

For the guilt was only in part related to the act of loving Ross. Its other part was Crystal. Crystal—her twin. Crystal—her alter ego. Crystal—who had never known that same joy, but should have, should have at least once before her death such a short time later.

3

The long ponytail bobbed against her neck as Chloe jogged on the beach. Indian summer had come to Rhode Island, bringing bright sun and a heat that was unusual for mid-October. She wasn't about to complain, though. All too soon her daily run would require a sweat suit, hat, and gloves. Now she delighted in the freedom of shorts and tank top, which allowed her arms and legs to breathe. The sweat that dotted her brow trickled across her temple and down along her hairline. It glistened on her skin, adding glow.

It had been two weeks since she had seen Ross Stephenson, two weeks since his presence had stunned her. He had a way of doing that, she mused, as she dodged a piece of driftwood that had washed up on the beach. The slap of her sneakers on the wet sand evened out.

Eleven years before, Ross had scored a coup, conquering her mind and body within hours. Their encounter two weeks ago had been under vastly different circumstances, but it was nearly as devastating.

The physical attraction between them hadn't diminished. If anything, it was more awesome than before, if her recollection of that kiss in the Wayward Sailor's kitchen was correct. He had to have known how he would affect her, which made his disappearance the next morning all the more unforgivable.

Chloe hadn't known what to expect—whether Ross would wake her or meet her downstairs for breakfast. She had assumed that, at the very least, he would drive her back to her car. But a maid had awakened her at seven, putting a pot of fresh coffee and a plate of sweet rolls on the small stand by her bed before scurrying back out, and when Chloe reached the front desk, she learned that Ross had already checked out.

She was immediately disappointed, then annoyed with herself. It was better this way. She was too vulnerable, if the previous night's kiss meant anything. Ross made her feel beautiful things, things she didn't deserve.

She was alive. That was enough. She reasoned that it was far better that he should be gone from her life.

When the day manager had handed her Ross's note, though, she was livid. "Chloe," he had scrawled in a bold hand, "Had to leave to catch the early plane. Your car is taken care of. Someone from the inn will take you there." It was signed, "Love, Ross." and was punctuated with a period as a statement of fact.

He had no business doing that, had no business using the word love so blithely. But that was the least of it. It seemed that he had paid her tab at the inn and the cost of a new battery and its installation.

She ran on down the beach, struggling to forget about Ross, to push him from mind, to focus on work. But he remained, along with her wounded pride. She had stewed all the way from Rye to Little Compton that morning. On arriving home, she had gotten the address of the Hansen Corporation and sent a check out in the mail that same day, with a note that was much less personal than his.

"Enclosed is a check to cover the expenses I incurred last night and this morning. Chloe MacDaniel." She hadn't asked him to take care of her. She didn't need him to take care of her. She didn't want to feel beholden to him in any way, shape, or form, because one thing was clear. She had picked herself up after Crystal's death and built a new life. She wasn't letting anything threaten it.

With firm resolve she made a gentle semicircle and jogged more slowly back toward where she had left her towel on the rocks at the sea side of her home.

As she approached, though, it wasn't the house that caught her eye but the tall figure that moved away from it and began to walk to the beach. She stopped short.

He was dressed in casual navy slacks and a plaid shirt that was unbuttoned at the neck and rolled to the elbows. His dark hair tumbled in disarray across his brow. Even from a distance he looked threatening in a divine kind of way.

He must have been watching for her, must have stood by the living room window until she had come into sight. If Lee hadn't been there to answer the door, he might have left. Now she was caught—and annoyed.

Tipping up a defiant chin, she began walking. Ross made no move to meet her halfway, just watched and waited, but his stance suggested an annoyance of his own, along with a touch of the imperious. Despite his casual clothes, he looked formal.

She came to a halt before him, nodded, and offered a polite "Ross" in greeting, before shifting beyond him to retrieve her towel.

"What in the hell did you do it for, Chloe?" He was annoyed, all right.

"Do what?" She straightened slowly.

His eyes bore into her. "Send that check. You didn't lose a minute, did you? You must have had it in the mail that same afternoon."

"Shouldn't I have?"

"No. There was no need."

"I thought there was. You had no cause to pick up the check, either for the inn or the battery. I'm not helpless. I can take care of myself."

A muscle worked in his jaw. "Then it was a matter of principle?"

"Principle? I wasn't thinking about principle. I simply saw it as my responsibility. It was kind of you to offer to pay, but I feel more comfortable this way. I wanted to take care of it myself."

"Ah. The independent woman. So that's how you intend to live the rest of your life?" he challenged, and drawled, "All by yourself?"

Chloe was startled by the turn of the conversation. "This is crazy," she said. "You show up here, out of the blue, without so much as a civil hello, and start criticizing me? I don't have to defend my lifestyle to you or anyone else!" She turned away, then turned right back, confused. "Why are you here, Ross? Did you come all the way from Park Avenue to call me out for repaying your loan? Little Compton is on the way to nowhere. We're at the tip of a peninsula. So don't tell me you were just passing through."

"No." His features had begun to relax, though his eyes remained clear and direct. "I wanted to see you."

Chloe could deal with the angry Ross more easily than she could with the gentler one. Uncomfortable now, she bent for her towel and straightened holding it tight. "You could have called if you wanted to discuss the Rye Beach Complex. Nothing much will happen until the referendum in November. Unless, of course, you alter your proposal." Satisfied with her minor dig, she began to mop her face and neck.

Ross ignored the barb. "I'm not here on business. I came to see you."

"That's a mistake," she whispered, hearing pain, feeling pain.

He replied as softly. "Then again we differ in opinion." He sighed. "Look, can we walk? Your house seemed pretty crowded. I'd like to talk."

All too aware of a tingling inside, she shook her head, then tore her gaze from his and looked out to sea. "It's not a good idea."

"Just talk?"

"Fine, if it has to do with the complex. Anything else . . ."

"What are you afraid of?" he asked. "I see the same fear in you now that I saw two weeks ago. What is it?"

She shot him a chiding look that said *You're imagining it, I'm not afraid of a thing.*

"Then what can be the harm in talking? What can be so awful about walking along the beach with me for a few minutes?" He tossed his dark head back toward the house. "You have a whole crew in there just waiting to come if you scream."

"I won't scream." She spoke softly, blushed lightly. "It's not my style."

He studied her for what seemed an eternity. "Maybe that's your problem," he finally decided. "You're too composed. Maybe you need a good yell and scream to let it all out."

"Let what all out?"

He took her arm. "Come on. Let's take a walk." He pulled her gently into step beside him, and she went along. After all, what harm could come from a walk on the beach?

One fast glance at Ross supplied an answer. The magnetism was there in all its force, coming from him, tugging at her. If only they had never met before, if only they didn't have a past, there might have been hope.

"What if," he echoed her thoughts with uncanny precision, "we had never met before? Would you feel differently?"

"Maybe." She clutched the ends of the towel that circled her neck. "Would you?" some inner voice made her ask.

"No." There was no hesitancy in his response. "I saw a woman two weeks ago who interested me. I would be here regardless. It's just . . ."

As Chloe waited for his voice to pick up again, their paths crisscrossed her earlier footprints. Ross easily measured his pace to hers. "It's just what?" she prodded.

He stopped walking. She went a step farther, then turned to face him. He frowned, seeming deliberative. "It's just that after what happened eleven years ago, I feel even more justified . . ."

Her voice rose, as it often did when she was distressed. "Are you saying you feel guilty so long after the fact? Is that why you've come? To ease some long-harbored guilt? Where were you then?" she cried. "Where were you when I—"

She cut herself off. For the very first time she wondered what might have happened had Ross been with her at the time of Crystal's death. It had been late Saturday night, two days after Thanksgiving, when she and Crystal argued, Crystal raced off in her car, the accident happened. By that time Ross was on his way back to Africa. What if he had been with her through the ordeal? Would things have been different?

But he hadn't been with her. There was no changing that fact. She had survived. She had survived. Not Crystal, though.

When she closed her eyes for a moment in search of composure, Ross took her arm and said a quick, "Over there. Those rocks. You should sit down."

"I'm all right—"

"Then I want to sit down! Indulge me!" He led her to a jagged out-cropping of rocks. When they were seated on side by side boulders, he said, "Okay. Why don't you tell me about that night—and stop looking at me like I'm crazy. You know what I'm talking about. I know what I experienced that night. I'd like to hear what you did."

"Oh, Ross." She sighed wearily. "I don't want to go into this." She caught the graceful takeoff of a tern from the salt-soaked beach. "It's too beautiful here to rehash the past."

"The past had its moments of beauty, too."

Her head snapped back, but the warmth of his gaze cut off the retort that might have come. Suddenly it seemed pointless to resist his request. It was just a matter of choosing the right words. "The past did have its moments. And, yes, they were beautiful." There was a soft quality in her voice as she returned to that night.

Ross grasped the stone on either side of him. "Had you planned it to happen? When you came toward me from across that room, had you hoped that we'd end up in bed?"

"Beforehand?" She looked up in surprise. "No. I'd never done any-thing like that before. Oh, we dated plenty and went to our share of par-ties. But we had never, that is, neither of us had, ah, I mean, I had never . . ."

"I know." He rescued her from her floundering, daring to touch her cheek with the back of his fingers. Instinctively she tipped her face toward his touch, then caught herself and righted her head.

"Were you sorry you did it?" His voice was low, urgent.

"No . . . Yes . . . I don't know," she finally ended in a whisper, tugging at the towel draped about her neck. "I can't give you a simple yes or no. I've never regretted the act itself. It was beautiful."

"Then what is it about me that makes you so uncomfortable?"

The ensuing silence was rich with the sounds of the shore—the lapping of the waves, the cry of the gulls, the rustle of the breeze in the drying leaves of the wild honeysuckle. Each had the potential to soothe, yet Chloe remained tense.

"Seeing you," she finally confessed, "brings back memories of a holiday weekend that was tragic for me."

"Your sister's death."

Her eyes shot to his. "You knew?" And hadn't tried to contact her?

The dark sheen of his hair captured the golden rays of the slow-setting sun. "Yes, I knew, but not until long after I'd returned to Africa. I didn't feel then that it was my place to contact you."

"Why not?" She didn't understand that detachment. He was certainly persistent enough now.

"In the first place," he began, "it was pitiful, how long after the fact I learned of it. Sammy wrote me the news in a letter the following spring." He seemed to hesitate. More quietly, he said, "It was only then that I'd had the guts to ask him about you."

"But why?" she cried.

"Because you weren't the only one to have afterthoughts of that night! From what I could see I had seduced the virgin daughter of my host's best friend. I was twenty-seven. You were eighteen. I should have known better. But the worst of it was that I was glad I hadn't." His voice gentled. "The memory of that night helped me through many a lonely night afterward."

"Oh, Ross," Chloe whispered, feeling a great longing inside. "I wish it hadn't. It's too late to go back."

"I don't want to go back. I want to go ahead. That's why I'm here."

Anguished, she looked down. "It's no good. I can't."

"Can't or won't? We've been through this before. Well," he drew in a breath, "believe this. I may have been immature eleven years ago, running away from something that frightened me, but I won't make the same mistake twice. It was fate that brought us together up at Rye Beach, and I'll be damned if I'm going to let you get away. I've made it my business to find out every possible thing I could about you during the past two weeks. And I know what happened to Crystal."

His words hung in the air. Her eyes begged him to say no more. She bolstered the plea with her low whisper. "Then you can understand why I can't bear to think back on that time."

"It was an accident, Chloe! It wasn't your fault!"

"But she died."

"And you lived, is that it? You can't forgive yourself for that?"

She jumped to her feet. With her heart pounding a thunderous beat, she stared at him for an agonized moment before forcing her feet to move. Her steps were slow at first, then gained speed as the force of habit took over and she jogged toward safer ground.

With pitiful ease, Ross caught up. He caught her elbow, using her own momentum to bring her around. When she faced him at a full stop, he held her by both arms.

"I'm trying to be honest," he said.

"But it hurts. Can't you see that? It hurts!" She was consumed by it, a hurt that was alive and festering. He had to see it anywhere he looked.

"The only way the hurt will stop," he chided gently, "is for you to put the past behind you."

Her eyes filled with tears. "Do you think I haven't tried? Do you think I've spent the past eleven years purposely living with a ghost?"

"Maybe not, but you've done it. You haven't resolved a thing in the eleven years, if that hurt in your eyes is for real. It's your punishment, isn't it? Your punishment for living."

She shook her head and whispered, "No. That's not true!"

"Not true?" he echoed in a voice strangely mellow. "Answer me one thing, Chloe. Have you been with another man since we were together?"

"That's none of your bus—"

"It is so." He took her face in his hands, correctly anticipating her attempt to look away. His touch was gentle but firm. "I was the first. It's my brand that shaped you. How many others were there?"

"That's vulgar!" she cried.

"Maybe. Answer the question."

"I won't. Are you jealous, jealous and guilt-ridden? Well, I don't need either of those traits in the man in my life. I'm doing just fine without— without—" Her limbs trembled.

Ross drew her against him, pressing her cheek to his chest, wrapping his arms around her back. "Without love?" he asked, so softly that she might not have heard him had the word not been on the tip of her tongue.

Incapable of speech for the moment, she simply breathed in the scent that was all male, all Ross. His heart beat steadily by her ear, gradually coaxing her own to slow. His arms enveloped her and lent her strength.

"I tried." She spoke, unsteadily at first. "I dated. I still do." It was easier not having to look at him. "I even tried to go to bed with one of them." She recalled the horror of the moment. "He decided I was frigid."

A deep laugh broke from Ross's throat, a laugh that was strangely hoarse. "That's ridiculous," he crooned into the warmth of her hair, but when he tipped her face up he felt her stiffen. "Oh, no, you don't." His mouth found hers.

She fought him then. Struggling to free herself from the band of his arms, she pushed against his chest, all the while trying to evade his lips, but he was stronger than she was. The more she squirmed, the more he steadied her. His lips stroked hers, demanding the kind of response that he alone knew she had in her.

When her physical strength waned, Chloe tried passivity. The last thing she wanted was a repeat of the night in New Hampshire or, worse, that fateful night back in New Orleans. She had no right, she told herself, no right!

"Come on, Chloe," Ross growled against her lips. "Ease up."

"Don't—"

She shouldn't have said anything. The tiny parting of her lips gave him the opening he needed, and then she didn't have a chance. His tongue invaded her mouth, spreading its sweetness deep. She told herself that it was physical, that she could resist if she wanted to enough, but her body betrayed her. It swayed toward him, weak with wanting.

From an odd defense mechanism, her mind went blank. It was as though the battle between guilt and desire created a mental void. In that void there was nothing but Ross and his body, the lips that caressed her, arms that held her gently, legs that supported her. Out of that void came her response, slowly, surely, and Ross had won. Her lips moved against his, tasting, savoring. The corners of his mouth, his firm lips, his tongue— one small nibble led to another until she returned his kiss with matching passion.

"Oh, Ross," she breathed raggedly when his lips left hers to trail fire along the sensitive cord of her neck.

"That's it, princess."

"No." That word. That past.

His breath warmed her ear. "You'll always be my princess, Chloe." He nibbled at her lobe. "It has nothing to do with the past. Right now you're my princess." With a groan, he pressed her to him. She felt his desire as she tried to deny her own, but that same coil of need gnawed within her. She was on the verge of losing control.

"No!" Her scream echoed back through her with such force that only Ross's arms kept her standing. As she sagged against him, he eased down onto the sand, turning her to sit with her back to his chest, her knees bent and bounded by his. He said nothing, just held her, his arms wrapped around her middle.

Chloe couldn't have moved if she'd tried. Drained by emotional strain, she closed her eyes and breathed in deeply of the slow-cooling air.

When Ross spoke long moments later, she was surprised to hear humor in his voice. "Not bad for a novice."

"What?"

"That scream. For someone who says she doesn't do that kind of thing, you sure let loose!"

She let out a breath and grinned, feeling oddly calm. "I guess I did. You have a way of doing the weirdest things to me."

"I certainly hope so," he drawled.

"Ross—"

"Shh. I've heard enough from you for a while. I want you to listen."

"But—"

"Shh! I have something to say."

"You—umph!" The breath was forced from her by a squeeze to her middle. She didn't try to speak again.

"Better," he said. "Now, listen. I realize that you need time, and I'll give you that. But I'm not leaving. Not this time. I want to get to know you, and I want you to get to know me. We blew it on that score last time. But yesterday was one thing, today's another, and they're different, Chloe, they're different."

She liked the sound of that. Didn't know if she believed it. But it was fine for the moment. Same thing with sitting against one another this way, looking out over the last of the sunset's flaming rays. Ross provided support. And heat. She was acutely aware of his long legs, his strong arms, his broad chest, his warm breath. She might not have a right to do it, but she savored the peace of the moment.

So maybe today was different. Certainly they were eleven years older, maybe even worlds wiser. But Crystal had been an intrinsic part of her life. To forget her would be wrong. It was more a matter of acceptance. Could she accept the past and learn to live with it?

"Well?" Ross's baritone hummed by her ear.

"Well, what?" She had reached her saturation point and couldn't agonize anymore.

He nudged her ribs. "Don't you have anything to say for yourself?"

Her long pause was nearly as effective as the sigh that followed it. "I can speak now?"

"Speak."

"That's a beautiful sunset," she mused aloud. "It's a treat at this time of year, all warm and golden. Do you have any idea what would happen if the ozone layer were to be destroyed by the haphazard release of freon gas?"

4

"Chlo . . . eee."

Before Ross could respond, a call of concern came from far down the beach.

"It's Lee," Chloe explained as her partner loped toward where she and Ross sat. Ross made no move to hold her back when she slid from his grip and jumped to her feet.

The timing couldn't have been better. With those legs framing hers and the strength of that body a serious temptation, her diversion into environmental quandaries would have been temporary at best. Lee's appearance was a godsend.

Aware that Ross had risen beside her, Chloe kept her eyes on the approaching figure. "You met Lee at the house, didn't you?" she asked.

"No," he said with something of a grunt. "Another character let me in and directed me to you. Is this some kind of commune you live in?"

Lee's booming call spared Chloe from having to answer. "Is everything all right, Chloe?" He covered the last of the distance at a more cautious walk, making no effort to disguise his wariness of an equally wary Ross. "It's getting dark. I was beginning to worry."

Chloe absently clutched her left wrist, a habit dating back to the days when she wore a watch. Her fingers easily circled the bone. "Oh, my. I'm sorry. I lost track of the time. We were going to—" Suddenly aware that the two men were staring at each other, she interrupted the thought and said, "Lee, this is Ross Stephenson. We knew each other a long time ago. Ross heads the corporation responsible for the Rye Beach proposal." She looked at Ross. "This is Lee Haight. Lee and I co-own ESE."

For a brief instant, she pictured the two men squaring off, and there was that moment's antagonism. She was relieved when Ross extended his hand. It was met by an equally large one of Lee's.

Chloe was struck by those hands, but they were only the start. The physical similarities between the two men, each of whom had been instrumental in shaping her life, was amazing. Both were tall and lean; both had athletic builds. While Ross's dark hair had faint wisps of gray at the sideburns, Lee's highlights were more auburn, but both men were tanned and inordinately good-looking. Only their dress differentiated their approaches to life. Whereas Ross was the image of the casual male of the more traditional school, Lee was, in appearance, reminiscent of that earlier, more nonconformist phase through which the other had passed. While Ross wore slacks, Lee wore denim. While Ross wore a sports shirt, Lee wore a T-shirt emblazoned with an apt EARTHMAN. Ross wore well-kept loafers, Lee had on a pair of battered running shoes. And then there was that neatly trimmed beard of Lee's that stretched from ear to ear, much as Ross's had on the night Chloe had met him.

It had never occurred to her to compare the two men before, but on all counts the likeness was astounding.

Apparently Ross saw it, too. He grinned slowly, almost slyly. "It looks like Chloe's taste in men hasn't changed all that much, after all," he said, with such a lack of malice that Lee relaxed a little.

"I intend to take that statement at its most positive, friend. This little lady is very near and dear to me." He threw a protective arm about Chloe's shoulder, drawing her to him with his customary possessiveness. She had always liked that, and did even more so now. His presence made her feel less vulnerable. She chuckled when Lee added, "Are you friend or foe?"

"Friend, by all means," Ross replied.

"Then I take it you're not here on business," Lee concluded. "And you can't be passing through."

Chloe laughed this time. "I've been through all that with him, Lee. He knows precisely where he is."

Lee glanced her way. "Sounds ominous." He looked at Ross. "How long are you in for?"

"I was hoping to spend the weekend here," Ross answered with a calm that had the opposite effect on Chloe. Her stomach was suddenly filled with butterflies. They fluttered wildly when those amber eyes turned to her. "If Chloe is free."

Chloe didn't know whether Lee sensed her internal turmoil, but she was eternally grateful for the arm that tightened around her shoulders. "You'll have a fight on your hands," he said. "I have a prior claim on her. Your big corporation may be able to do without you for the weekend, but our small one isn't so generous." Looking down at her, he said, "There were several calls for you. Alabama called again on that toxic waste burning problem. I told them you'd have an answer for them by Monday."

Chloe nodded, sighing her uncertainty on the Alabama matter. "And the other calls?"

"Derry Township called on the lecture series at the community college. They want to know when the printed material will be ready to be copied. Jay called from Pittsburgh to say that he should be back on Sunday, and Debbie will have the statistics on the sinkhole study for you to see tomorrow."

"Whoa. She sure got that together fast." She told Ross, "Debbie is the newest member of the firm. She just got her degree. Her working knowledge of computers is much better than Lee's or mine." She frowned. "Boy, would I like to take more courses."

"Why don't you?" Ross asked.

"No time. Lee and I have worked our butts off trying to make ESE a functioning enterprise." She shot a look at her partner. "I think we're finally seeing the light at the end of the tunnel."

His grimace took her by surprise. Instead of agreement, she saw sudden doubt. "That's another point of discussion for the weekend," Lee informed her softly, squeezing her arm a final time before releasing her. "But, hey, it's getting dark. Let's carry on inside. Want to stay for dinner, Ross?"

Chloe bent to retie a shoelace that needed no retying. She didn't want Ross staying for dinner. She wanted to return to her life, and that meant having him leave and stay gone. Naturally, he had other ideas.

"That would be fine," he said with gratitude.

But Chloe sensed something in him. As the three of them walked back down the beach to her house, she saw the tension on Ross's face. His eyes met hers, and she was again grateful for Lee's presence.

Then Lee turned traitorous. With a grin, he said, "There's some great wine in the cellar, Chloe. The steaks are already on the counter. Why don't you take another one from the freezer? I'll meet you in the kitchen." And he loped off.

Before she could follow, Ross wrapped a hand around her long ponytail and held her in place.

"What was that all about?" he asked with a scowl. "You told me you lived alone."

She stared straight ahead, looking after Lee. "I do."

Ross moved closer. His head lowered to hers. "Then why is that fellow so damned at home in your house? He sounds like he's the live-in chef—between the wine and the steaks. What other services does he perform?"

She didn't like his implication. Still staring at the house, she said, "He's good enough to bring the trash to the dump once a week and put on the storm windows when winter comes and pump out the basement when it floods. In addition to which, his office is located here, as is mine, and the rest of ESE." Risking pain in her scalp, she turned her head and looked at him. "I thought you learned something about me this week. It's a simple fact that the address of ESE and my home address are the same."

He had released her hair. "I know that. I didn't bother to look up the home address of your partner, though. For all I knew he lived here with you."

"I told you I lived alone." With an impatience unusual to her, Chloe stalked onward toward the house. Ross was quickly beside her.

"So where does he live?"

"Over there." She pointed to a small house that was farther back from the beach but no more than several hundred yards from Chloe's.

"Convenient," Ross mused dryly.

Of her own accord this time, she stopped in her tracks. "It happens to be very convenient." She glared at his all-too-handsome face, which, to her chagrin, seemed suddenly amused. "He's a good friend, an able geologist, and a very trusting soul." When Ross dared to smile, she cried, "What's so funny?"

"Not funny." He laughed nonetheless. "Refreshing. The way you've repressed so many other things, it's nice to know you can be so outspoken. But then, you were quite good up there at Rye Beach."

"Quite good?" she asked smugly. "You'd better start rethinking those plans of yours or those good folks up there are going to vote down your entire project. It doesn't have as much to do with my being good as with the truth of my points."

"That was one of the things I had wanted to discuss this weekend," he said. He began walking toward the house again, bringing her along with a feather touch at the back of her waist.

She eyed him skeptically. "I thought this was a strictly personal visit."

"It is. This is a personal business matter."

"A personal business matter?" She shot a glance skyward. "Lord help me. What next?" The faint pressure of his hand on her back was ample suggestion. "Forget I asked that. A personal business matter. Okay. We can discuss it during dinner."

"I was hoping to discuss it privately. I actually was hoping to take you out to dinner."

"You should have called first."

"Would you have accepted if I had?"

"No. Lee and I have a standing dinner meeting every Friday night to review the week's happenings."

They had reached the base of the fieldstone steps that led to Chloe's back porch. Ross paused on the first step. "And those others I saw here this afternoon. Who were they?"

"Workers on our various projects."

"Partners in the firm?"

She shook her head. "We hire part-time people. They're mostly students, master's candidates from local schools like URI and Brown."

The pale blue of dusk was quickly giving way to the darker purples of evening in a star-filled sky. Only the spill of pale gold light from the kitchen window lit Ross's features now. It left his lines more clear-cut, his profile more distinct and dramatic. Chloe was intrigued.

"I admire you for your dedication," he said.

She continued to study him. "Do I hear wistfulness?"

His chuckle was suspiciously poignant. "Maybe. There are times—ach, that's a whole other thing."

When she would have pursued it, Lee's shout jarred her. "Chloe!" Her head whipped around. "Where are the matches? The pilot light is out on the broiler. I can't get it lit."

Ross leaned close and murmured, "And here I thought he was the one who always came to your rescue."

She turned to defend Lee, only to find Ross's lips a breath from hers. His eyes were glowing, his body warm though the heat of the day was gone, and her mouth was suddenly dry. "I think I'd better give him a hand. Pray we're not out of matches."

Her response was meant as humor, because she wasn't telling Ross the truth. Oh, yes, Lee was a willing handyman, able in nine cases out of ten. But they had a running gag over that tenth. Chloe was convinced, and had told Lee as much, that his occasional flub was intentional, his way of reminding her that he needed her, too. He never denied it. And Chloe always indulged him. Emotionally, he gave her so much. She liked giving a little some of that back.

Without further pause, she ran up the steps. It was only when she reached the top and started for the door that Ross caught her hand. He pressed something into it. She looked down at a book of matches.

"You smoke?"

"Actually," he said with a wry twist of his lips, "I carry matches around with me just in case a pilot light goes out."

"Do you smoke?"

"Through my eyes, when I'm angry."

"Ross, do you?"

"Smoke? No."

She sighed. "That's good. This is a nonsmoking house. If you wanted to smoke you'd have to sneak one in the john, or stay out here with the chipmunks."

"That's some choice. Good thing I don't have to make it. As it happens," he informed her, "my only vice is sex. Do we have to sneak that in the john, too?"

She might have choked if she'd been eating. But she recovered quickly, shook her head, and muttered a soft "Incorrigible . . ." as she pulled the screen open. She took refuge in the kitchen, where her loyal protector, Lee, was waiting.

And he filled that role repeatedly throughout the evening, taking over for her when she was distracted. He was an able conversationalist, a gracious host. She trembled to think what would have happened had she and Ross been alone in the house. She was too vulnerable, too susceptible where Ross was concerned. If she hadn't known it before, she learned it that evening.

It started before dinner, when she left the two men and went off to shower. She put on a pair of jeans and a western-style blouse that had breast pockets and a decoratively stitched yoke. Her intent was to be cool and at ease. The finished product, though, spoke of homespun femininity. Had it been the pale pink of the blouse, she later asked herself? Or the way the seasoned denims outlined her hips? Whatever, she caught Ross's attention. Her first step into the living room, where the men were nursing drinks while the steaks grilled, brought Ross's eyes her way for a perusal that set her pulse hammering. Where Chloe's peace of mind was concerned, it was downhill from there. She wanted to tune him out, but she couldn't.

The talk centered on business matters. Sitting quietly in a peacock chair, Chloe learned that Ross's headquarters were indeed in New York, but that there were corporate branches in the South and in the West.

She tried to imagine it. "You must live out of a suitcase a good deal of your time."

"I'm used to it. Don't forget, when I was a kid my family was shuttled around by the Army." At Lee's prodding, Ross elaborated on his background. Chloe found herself wondering if he had ever settled down, even for a short time, or if he ever would. She found herself wondering how as compelling and attractive a man had avoided the lure of a wife, a home, a family. When she was caught in the act of admiring him, Ross smiled in what she swore was a knowing way.

And so went the evening. Lee talked with Ross, and Ross talked with Lee. Chloe listened, joining in from time to time, trying to fight admiration without much success.

Why Ross? she asked herself at one point. Why not Lee? The two were as physically alike as brothers. But then, why had Ross been attracted to Chloe rather than Crystal? Or had he? Had Crystal been right? Had it been a case of his taking what was offered by whichever sister came forward?

That question nagged. *Had* her being with Ross been pure chance? A simple turn of fate? But what about that coin? There was nothing coincidental about Chloe winning the toss. And Ross—had he been looking at Chloe rather than at her identical twin sister? Had it all been by design, or had it been by pure chance?

She was distracted as the evening waned, unaware of looks of concern sent her way. When Lee said, "I'm takin' off now, Chloe," she was startled. Her head came up. Unsure, she straightened.

"I'm sorry," she apologized softly. "I'm afraid I haven't been much help. We haven't even gone over those things we should have."

"No problem." He smiled. "We'll do it tomorrow." Taking his cue from the disquieted look in her eyes, he turned to Ross. "Are you staying here tonight?"

"Yes."

"No."

They spoke at the same time. Chloe hurried on. "No, Ross. You can't stay here." She was determined. "There's one bedroom and one bed, and I need it."

"Why don't you stay with me, friend?" Lee offered—and for the second time that evening, Chloe could have disowned him. She wanted Ross to leave. Out of sight was out of mind. Lee's offer only complicated things.

Naturally, Ross accepted the invitation. "No imposition?"

"No imposition. The sofa in the living room opens into a bed. The back door will be open. Chloe will point you in the right direction." Before she could protest, Lee reached the door. "Good night, folks." He grinned, letting himself out with a flourish.

With a steadying breath, Chloe settled deeper into her high-backed chair, tucked her feet under her, forced her fingers to relax against the broad wicker arms, and looked across the room at Ross.

He spoke softly. "You really do look like a princess in that chair. Those peacock markings could as easily be a crown of gold as a swirl of wicker. Are you comfortable?" His eyes were gleaming, mocking.

"No," she answered honestly. "You know I'm not."

His grin held no apology. "That's a shame. I don't want you to be miserable through the entire weekend."

"You can't stay all weekend!"

"Why not? I have a place to sleep. That Lee's a good guy."

"Too good!" she grumbled. "I thought I could trust him."

Ross sat forward, elbows on his thighs, fingers steepled. "That's what puzzles me. I'm sure you can trust him, but I can't figure out for the life of me why."

Chloe instantly came to Lee's defense. "He's been a true friend to me."

"Why only a true friend? Why not a lover?"

"Lee doesn't want that from a woman."

"You mean, he prefers—"

"No. No, Ross. Don't twist things." Beneath his stare, her own insides twisted. "Lee was married once. He has two children. He and his wife divorced five years ago. She lives in St. Louis."

"Ah. Once burned . . . okay, I'll accept that."

"How kind," she murmured, but she was annoyed enough to see an opening and take it. "What about you? In the eleven years since I knew you when, what have you done along similar lines? Should I assume you've developed odd preferences?"

The instant she said it, she knew it was a mistake. Good humor faded fast from Ross's face. When he stood and approached her, she struggled to avoid cringing into the chair. There was a hard look to him.

"Would that make you trust me more?" he murmured. He towered above her for a minute, then bent over. His hands covered hers on the arms of the chair. His face was too near. "Sorry to disappoint you, but my preferences are still for the opposite sex." His lips moved closer. Chloe looked down to escape them, but his long body filled her view. Everywhere she moved her eyes, she saw him, one point more alarming than the next. If it wasn't the vee of his chest, with its wisps of dark hair edging alongside the tab of his collar, it was the breadth of his shoulders or the lean tapering of his middle or the casual set of his hips. Those hips told their own story. She tore her gaze away, completely convinced of his preference.

He grinned. "Any further questions?"

The slight shake of her head was enough to bring his lips into contact with her cheek, and Chloe was suddenly conflicted. Pull away. Move closer. Keep your eyes shut. Look at him. Look at him. Look at him.

She looked. His eyes held gentleness now. And the same desire she felt. So close. So far away. Kiss me. Don't.

He did. Very, very lightly. A ghost of a touch with shuddering intensity. Chloe's eyes were shut, her lips parted. To taste him once more . . .

When he kissed her again, his tenderness incited her need. She moved closer, clung to him with her own lips, drank in the tang of his mouth, so moist and strong yet soft. His tongue touched hers briefly before he raised his head.

"Definitely my preference." He spoke thickly, his breathing uneven.

Chloe was momentarily disoriented. It was a minute before reality returned. Then she was appalled. "What am I doing?" she asked, not realizing she'd spoken aloud. "What am I doing?"

"Letting yourself live," came the husky but gentle declaration.

Burying her face in her hands, she struggled to understand what had just happened. She couldn't face him, much less herself. Easier to hide behind the cascade of hair that fell forward, shielding her from the world.

Lost in silent self-reproach Chloe was unaware that he had moved away and returned to the sofa. He was waiting, listening, when she finally raised her head.

"Why are you doing this to me?" she pleaded softly. "Why can't you just leave me alone?"

He frowned. "Funny, I've asked myself the same question a dozen times in the last two weeks." He studied his knuckles, seeming to struggle. "It's like for the first time in years, I care."

"What do you mean?" she asked falteringly.

"You asked me what I've done with myself during the past years." He gave a snort of disgust. "I haven't been quite as noble as you. There have been women over the years."

She had assumed that, and felt no resentment. There was a certain solace in the knowledge that when all was said and done, he was still attracted to her. After all, he was magnificent. More than one of those women must have tried to tie him down.

"Didn't you find anyone special?" she asked quietly.

Ross was just as quiet. "Some I liked more than others. But, no, there was no one special. No one who meant enough to tempt me to change my lifestyle. I'm on the road all the time. I do own an old brownstone in Manhattan, but I doubt if I spend a total of three months a year there. Hotel rooms, friends' apartments, rented suites—that's been home for the past few years."

"It served your purpose."

"Yes." The amber eyes that held hers pierced her heart. They said much more, all of it silent, all of it mind bending. In the insanity of a fleeting instant, she wanted . . . she wanted . . . What did she want?

Ross sighed. "I am a successful businessman." It was a statement of fact, devoid of arrogance. "But that's not enough."

She followed his thoughts. "I can't help you, Ross."

"Can't?"

"Won't. If you're looking for a wife and a family, a home in the country, maybe a few dogs and horses, even sheep, you'll have to look elsewhere. I can't be anything but this."

His gaze sharpened. "Did I mention those things? Or are they what you wanted once? Haven't you ever wished for a husband who loves you, children, pets, friends, property? What do you want from life?"

"What I have right now. I don't want to look back, and I won't look ahead. I like this life. I'm content."

"Are you?" he challenged. "Don't you ever stop to wonder what it might have been like—"

"No," Chloe said with force and pushed herself out of the chair. "I didn't ask you to come here, Ross. I didn't ask you to stay. As of right now"—she pointed at the floor for emphasis—"I don't care what you do, but don't expect to change the way I see the world and my life. I've done just fine on my own for the past eleven years. I plan to do it a while longer." Her hand was shaking. She jammed it into the back pocket of her jeans. "I'm going to bed. Let yourself out." With a whirl that sent her hair flaring out behind, she strode from the room, ran up the stairs to her room, and firmly closed the door.

Trembling uncontrollably, she collapsed onto the bed and stared at the ceiling. Her ragged breathing was the only sound that broke the night's quiet—that, and the opening and closing of the front door when Ross left the house.

For what seemed like hours she agonized, locked in silent battle with a horde of private ghosts. If only she had never seen Ross again. To be free, once more, of this gnawing at mind and body.

But she had seen him again and, if he stuck to his plan, would see more of him before he left. There was only one solution, as she saw it. Indifference. What man would put up with that for long? Indifference. It would turn him off, wouldn't it? Surely then he would leave her in peace.

She awoke the next morning on an optimistic note, showered, dressed, and sailed downstairs for breakfast. It was with momentary dismay that she found her kitchen in use—until she recalled the night's resolve, tilted up her chin, and advanced.

5

"Ah," she said as she helped herself to a cup of the coffee he had brewed, "you've made yourself at home."

His grin was as bright as the morning sun that slanted across the porch beyond the screen. "It's a luxury. I'm enjoying it. It's not every day that I get to putter around a cozy kitchen, much less wait on a princess."

"Flattery will get you nowhere." She hoped, prayed it was so. By way of diversion, she eyed the stove. "Bacon, eggs, home fries? You're going to eat all that?"

"With your help."

"Ohhhh, no. After a breakfast like that I'd barely be able to keep my eyes open. I have too many things to do—"

"—for which you need energy. And, anyway," he called over his shoulder as he turned the bacon, "if you don't eat breakfasts like this, why such a full stock of goodies? Lee's refrigerator was bare."

"So that's it, huh?" she asked, eyes narrowing. "You're starved and my old buddy Lee couldn't help you out?" She chuckled. "Lee eats out. A lot."

"Here?"

"Do you see him here now?" she shot back.

"I haven't seen him today, period. He's not upstairs, is he?"

Shaking her head, she turned toward the large bay window, whose broad seat was her favorite perch. "That doesn't deserve an answer." Sipping her coffee, she spoke absently. "As for the state of my ice box, I eat in. A lot. Eggs make terrific dinner omelets, bacon a great BLT, and potatoes are most definitely to be baked, then scooped, mashed with a little Parmesan cheese and cream, restuffed, dotted with butter, and broiled until delicately browned on top."

The silence that followed her recitation was enough to get her to look back. Ross's expression was one of amused astonishment. "You must have memorized the cookbook."

"No. I just happen to like my potatoes that way, and I do it a lot."

Ross leaned back against the counter, arms folded across his chest. "Would you make them like that for me some time—maybe with a few lamb chops, some fresh broccoli, a little wine?"

He looked dangerous, newly showered and wearing jeans and a black turtleneck sweater. But Chloe had taken a vow of indifference. He's just a friend, she told herself, no different from Lee. Calmly enough, she said, "I make a meal of the potatoes. If you'd like to do up the rest, be my guest." She settled on the window seat and looked out at the beach. "It's another beautiful day."

"Uh-huh." His voice was muffled. He had turned back to his cooking. Too soon he was addressing her again. "Sleep well?"

"Not bad." Once she had fallen asleep. "How about you?"

He had turned to reach for plates from the cupboard. "About the same."

It was an odd choice of words, she mused, unless she was so transparent that he could see her thoughts. If there was smugness on his face, though, she couldn't see it. He was cooking. All she saw was his back. There was a full head of thick and vibrant dark hair, a torso whose firmness was shown off by the snug fit of his sweater, a pair of lean denim hips and long, sturdy legs, not to mention well-worn leather boots.

She took a deep, steadying breath. If he had dressed to kill on purpose, she could resist. She wasn't buying what he had to offer. She wasn't.

"All set?" Grinning, he placed two brimming plates on the table. When she gaped at hers in dismay, he added a gentle, "Don't worry. Whatever you can't finish, I will."

She pushed away from the window seat with a grimace. "You'd better get started then. I'm nearly finished." She held up her drained coffee cup. "This is all I usually have, with a slice of toast or a muffin." Still, she took a seat opposite him. She stared at the plate, decided that the eggs looked pretty good, and took a bite.

"Do the people you work with know about your past?"

Her eyes flew to his, warning, then haunted. She gave him a wan smile. "You make it sound lurid." She pushed home fries around her plate. "They know where I come from—some even know that I had a sister. Lee knows most of the story. But the lovely thing about my life here is that the people I know see me for what I am today. It's easier not having to constantly contend with the past."

Ross seemed puzzled. "Why do you assume you'd have to do that anywhere? It's been eleven years, Chloe. The world goes on. People accept change. You seem to be the only one who can't move on."

Chloe set down her fork. She took an angry breath. "I look in the mirror every morning. How can I forget? How can my family forget? How can those people we knew as kids forget, when they see Crystal in my face?" When sitting still took more strength than she had, she rose. "And why should I forget? Crystal was my sister. More than that . . ." She fell silent. Turning her back on Ross, she walked slowly to the window. The sight of the surf rolling onto the beach was calming.

"I'm really not like this," she murmured, speaking to herself and, yes, to him. "Morbidity isn't my style. I loved Crystal. She was my twin. Few people can understand what it meant to me to lose her."

"Maybe that's because you don't share your feelings very often." His voice was suddenly close behind her. The warmth of his body reached out. When he slid his arms around her waist and drew her back against him, she felt sheltered.

"I don't know exactly why I'm doing it now," she whispered. "Maybe it's because you've come out of that past to haunt me." She turned in his arms. Tipping her head up, she studied one strong feature after another. "Is that what you've done—come to haunt me?"

"No, Chloe." He smiled briefly, sadly. The rest of him was exquisitely tender. "I told you yesterday. I want to go forward, not back. I'm beginning to wonder about you, though. You may have to go back, to resolve all those things in your mind, before you can move on."

"But I've done so well up until now," she protested. Without thinking twice, she had put her hands on his chest. They were content to absorb his strength.

"You have. Maybe this was inevitable, though. Whether it was me or something else, you'd have had to face it sooner or later."

"It's not that bad."

"No?"

There was no censure in his tone, no pity in his gaze. He touched her cheek for a fleeting instant, then stepped away. With an exaggerated sigh, he looked at their forgotten breakfast.

"I'd better get this cleaned up. You have to get to work."

Chloe watched him move from table to sink, table to sink, and all she could think was that he'd had the opportunity, but he hadn't kissed her. He had done something else that felt oddly the same. But he hadn't kissed her. She was marveling at that as she headed for the door, bound for her office.

"Chloe?" She looked back. Ross was approaching with her mug in his hand. "Here's a refill. Take it with you?"

She did, and it helped—both the warming brew and the thoughtfulness behind it. And then, once she was settled in her office, she was safe, firmly rooted in the present. There were reports to read, studies to review, proposals to consider. The more she worked, the better she felt. For the first time since having done the lab work earlier that week, she studied the sediment analysis of samples taken along an increasingly unstable portion of the Cape Cod National Seashore.

"Problems?" This from Debbie Walker, who popped her head in shortly after eleven.

"Hi, Deb. Come on in." She smiled at her petite, sandy-haired associate. "It's the Cape analysis. I was just studying the results of the work I did last week. I have the grain sizes of the sand pretty much divided by sections. Boy, they really botched it."

"'They' being the people who put that parking lot so close to the cliff?"

Chloe sighed. "It's begun to erode already, and the locals want to sue. According to my calculations, they have a case."

"Will you be called in to testify?"

"I'm not sure. I have to work this report up into some kind of written form. Depending on what happens when they read it, whether or not the matter can be settled first, it may not make it to court." She sat back. "It's a shame that we seem to learn things after the fact. If only those developers had gotten a geologist to advise them at the start."

Debbie smiled. "You make a good crusader. I wish I could present my case as well as you do."

"I wish I could handle those computers as well as you do," Chloe returned. "Come on. Let's take a look at your statistics."

They spent the next half hour reviewing the work Debbie had done. Between them, they came up with a plan of attack on both the sinkhole in question and the people in a position to do something about it. Suitably buoyed, and with her work cut out for her, Debbie left. She was replaced moments later by a slightly groggy-looking Josh Anderson.

Chloe grinned. "Late night last night?"

"Don't you know it," Josh murmured. "But I have to discuss this curriculum guide with you. If the preliminaries are all right, I'd like to work out more of the details."

Chloe's arched brow spoke volumes, as did the slow perusal she gave the casually disheveled graduate student. "You're up to it?" With great effort she stifled a broader grin. Josh was a favorite of hers. Several years her junior, he was working toward his degree at Brown. This was his second year working part-time at ESE.

His proposed high-school geology curriculum was as fine as any she could have hoped ESE would produce.

Now he lowered his voice. "I'd really be up to it if I could take a swig of the coffee that smells so good in the kitchen."

"Why don't you?"

He kept his voice low. "There's a watchdog out there."

"In the kitchen?"

"In the living room. Tall guy, dark hair, dark eyes. He doesn't look happy with the traffic in here. Who is he? And what's he doing in our house?"

For the better part of the morning Chloe had pushed Ross from mind. Now, revived by the work that she loved, she was able to chuckle at Josh's reference.

"He's a friend," she answered simply.

"You're sure about that?"

"I'm sure. Go on out and get your coffee. If he starts to snarl, you can send him in here."

Josh's face took on a dubious I-hope-you-know-what-you're-doing look. Nonetheless, he drew up to his full sixty-seven inches, squared his shoulders, and made as grand an exit as was possible for someone going to face the proverbial giant. With a helpless grin, Chloe sat back in her chair, elbows on its arms, fingers comfortably laced.

So Ross had decided to spend the morning in her living room. She wondered if he was bored, maybe annoyed that she was carrying on as usual, perhaps growing impatient. Her grin turned smug.

"You wanted to see me?" His deep voice rumbled in from the door.

Her grin remained. "Who, me?"

He searched the room. "I don't see anyone else in here, for a change. They may not technically live here, but they run in and out all day, don't they?"

"It's an open office, you might say."

"I do say. Say, when will you be done?"

"Done?" she echoed innocently, then gestured toward the desktop. "Lord knows. I have two reports to look through yet. And Josh will be back. Here he is." His timing was perfect. "Josh, meet Ross." As the two shook hands, Chloe stared at the appalling discrepancy in their heights. No wonder Josh had been intimidated; not only did Ross tower over him, but their respective physiques were about as alike as night and day.

Instinctively protective of Josh, she pointed him to a chair. Then she said, "Ross, would you excuse us? We'll be a little while."

"I'll be waiting." He smiled as though he had caught onto the game and was playing. Then he turned and left.

Josh wasn't thick. "Listen, Chloe, are you sure you wouldn't rather go over this another time?"

"What?" she ribbed him gently. "And waste the effort it took for you to pull yourself out of bed? Carry on!"

* * *

It was a full hour later when Josh finally left. Chloe walked him to the door and had only enough time to note that Ross was occupied with a briefcase of his own, before Lee bounded through the living room. He delivered a wave in passing to Ross, looped an arm about Chloe's waist, and corralled her back into her office.

"It's about time you're free," he scolded good-naturedly. "You're a busy lady."

Chloe smiled. "I'm all yours now. I want to show you—"

The look on his face cut her off. "There's something we have to discuss first. I think," he said, giving care to each word, "that we have a problem."

"A problem?" She frowned. "What problem?"

Eying her warily, he said, "I had two cancellations yesterday."

"Cancellations?"

"That's right. The schools. They don't have the money to finance us for the next semester."

She sat straighter. "Are you serious?"

"Very."

"But I thought—"

"So did I."

"I just sent Josh out of here with a great proposal. You mean to say that he won't be able to apply it?"

"Not in Hingham or Westerly he won't. There are still the wealthier communities . . ." His voice trailed off, his implication clear.

"But not for long. That's it, isn't it? You think we're headed down a dead-end street?"

"Unless the powers that dole out money for education loosen up. They're thinking A, B, Cs. We're talking H, I, Js. We're strictly elective, they say. A luxury they can't afford."

Chloe's mind raced ahead. "A good third of our work is through the public schools. Oh, boy. We'd better rethink that."

"Smart girl."

"Private enterprise," she announced without hesitation.

"Come again? Business isn't our field."

Chloe laughed at the confusion on Lee's bearded face. "No. But I said it to Debbie earlier this morning and I meant it. What we need is to affiliate ourselves with corporations as resident geologists, be the geologists-on-call for several of these large development corporations. You know, like—"

"—the Hansen Corporation?"

The thought took her off-guard. "No," she said with deliberate care. "I was thinking more of firms like Cabot and Walker, or Fennimen East."

But Lee was grinning. "What's wrong with the Hansen Corporation?"

"Nothing," she said, but rethought her answer when Lee was clearly disbelieving. She lowered her voice. "What's wrong with the Hansen Corporation is that Ross Stephenson is its president."

"So?"

"Lee," she pleaded, "Ross is a friend. I would no more ask him to hire ESE than . . . than . . ." She went silent, at a loss for words. She was hoping to survive a single weekend with Ross. She couldn't begin to imagine working with him on an ongoing basis.

Lee grew serious. "What is he to you, Chloe?"

She sighed, giving up the struggle to find excuses. "We knew each other before Crystal died."

"He's the one, isn't he?" There was only kindness in Lee's voice, yet his words jolted her.

"What?" she whispered.

"He's the one—the man in your life."

"There is no man in my life. You know that."

Lee grew gentler. "Over the years, I've learned a lot about you. You've told me about your sister, that she died, that you rarely visit your family back in New Orleans. But you never talk about men. You're a beautiful person, Chloe. I know it, and he knows it." He tilted his head toward the living room. "I dare you to look me in the eye and deny that there was ever anything between the two of you."

She couldn't lie. Not to Lee. "I can't do that. But, whatever it was, it's over."

"You think so?"

"Yes." She said it firmly, and held her head the same way.

Lee studied her for a long minute, before making a show of wiping his hands together. "Well, then, I guess that settles that." He graciously redirected the conversation to safer ground. "I do agree with you that the private business sector could be a promising outlet. I'll be in Washington next week to work with the Coast Guard on the Gulf project. Let me see what nosing around I can do while I'm there."

"How much longer will the training project take?"

"With the government, that's a good question. And when it comes to oil spill cleanups, no amount of training is ever enough. I would guess the present phase will take another few months at least."

Chloe contemplated those coming few months. Unthinkingly, she glanced toward the door.

Lee headed that way. "I can take the hint, pretty lady." His hand was on the knob before she could call him back. "Anything else can wait. Have fun!" He left with a wink.

"Lee! Wait—"

But one dark head was replaced by another. "At last," Ross said and closed the office door. "Alone at last."

Chloe forced herself to sit back slowly. "I hadn't realized you would hang around all morning. I hope you weren't bored."

"Actually"—he circled her desk to plant himself on the corner nearest her—"I went over some papers of my own. I'm a good loser, for a morning." He cocked his head toward the door. "Ready to go?"

"Go? Where?"

"Oh"—he looked out the window in amusement—"I thought you could show me around town. I'm a stranger to these parts."

Judging from the confidence he exuded, it was a wonder that any parts were strange to him. Chloe couldn't ignore the thread of excitement that he had brought with him into the room. Indifference, she reminded herself. But it was a tough order.

Standing quickly, she tried to remedy the situation. "I wish I could help, but I still have—" A strong arm caught her waist. Before she could say another word, she was imprisoned between his thighs.

"All work and no play—"

"Makes a successful scientist."

"And a very dull woman."

She frowned, unwittingly taking his bait. "Do you think my work is dull?" Her disappointment was genuine. So was the devastatingly handsome smile that spread across his face. The hands that were looped loosely behind her, now brought her closer.

"Nothing about you is dull," he said, "except your determination to hold me at arms' length."

Arms' length was a lot farther than where she was now. Well within the circle of his arms, with her hands braced at the point where his jeans met his hips, she was under his spell.

Ross lowered his head and kissed her, tasting the sweetness of her mouth, and it struck her that she might well have been too successful at her own game. By denying the past, she was responding to him in the present alone. Her return kiss was gentle, sampling. She played with being free of all memory, all guilt. Her lips opened to his. She gave of herself as she hadn't done in years.

"That was nice," he whispered against her mouth, then pulled away and set her back before she could do it herself. He trailed a long thumb across her cheek to the lips he'd just left. "We'll do it again soon."

It was said so gently and carried such lightness that Chloe couldn't help but smile. A warm flush painted her cheeks a comely pink, complementing the gray of her eyes, which held a hint of apology. "You have a way of sneaking up when a girl least expects it, Ross. What am I going to do with you?"

His gaze told her first, and there was something heady about it, until he added, "You're going to love me one day. That's what you're going to do." She stiffened, but he went on. "Right now, you're going for a ride with me."

"I have errands to do," she protested.

"Like?"

"Like marketing, for starters. In one meal you've nearly wiped me out."

"So we'll go to the market. What else?"

She ad-libbed. "I need new house plants for the living room. With winter coming on—"

"Winter? It's creeping up toward seventy again today. How can you think of winter?"

"It'll be here. And anyway, the sooner the plants get used to the house, the easier it will be for them to adapt to the cooler weather."

His gaze narrowed. "I bet you talk to your plants."

"No. If I did that, they might think I was flaky. I want my plants to respect me."

She doubted Ross heard her. He was focusing on her mouth, looking entranced. Suddenly he slid the fingers of both hands through the hair on either side of her face, brought his own head down, and kissed her again. This time there was a hunger there hadn't been before, a new urgency. This time Chloe was frightened. How not to lose herself in that hunger?

"Ross," she cried, "don't, please, don't."

He released her. His voice remained husky, but his eyes held a promise. "I won't push you now. But you will love me one day. One day soon."

"You're wrong—"

"Not this time, princess." He paused to let his breathing steady. "Let's go. We'll stop for lunch first. I'm starved."

Chloe took a steadying breath of her own. "After that breakfast?"

"That breakfast," he grumbled, "was interrupted. And anyway, that was this morning. It's nearly two. Any more feeble excuses to try on me before we leave?"

Chloe looked around her office. Its familiarity gave her strength. Indifference. She could do it.

"Not a one," she said, preceding Ross from the room without another word. It was only when they reached the front door that she felt an odd sense of adventure. Eyes alight, she turned back to Ross. "I have an idea. Let's take the bike."

"I have a better idea," he countered, pulling the neck of his turtleneck away from his skin. "Let's change into cooler things. I hadn't expected it would get so warm."

Assuming that his clothes were still at Lee's house, she felt generous. "Okay. You go back and change. I'll just sit here and—hey! What are you doing?"

It was pretty obvious, actually. With a fast tug he freed his sweater from his jeans, crisscrossed his arms, and smoothly whipped the black turtleneck over his head and off. Never, ever, would Chloe forget that moment when, muscles stretched, his chest came into view.

Lightly bronzed, with a liberal hazing of hair that tapered toward his navel, it was a solid wall of hard, glorious flesh. Her mouth went dry. She could only stare.

"My bags are right here," he replied, retrieving a soft leather duffel from beside the sofa. Long arms pulled at the duffel's zipper. Deft fingers exchanged the sweater for a lighter, short-sleeved jersey. He quickly drew it over his head. Once more Chloe trembled as that body stretched, flexed, then settled back down, mercifully covered again.

Ross grinned. "There. Easy enough. Do you need to change or anything? Are you cool enough?"

Chloe didn't think she would ever be cool enough again. "Uh, I'm fine." She cleared her throat awkwardly, turning and escaping to the wide-open spaces without any further attempt at wit. And she had suggested taking the bike! They would be better off swimming. They might not get to any store, but they would have a barrel of much-needed cold water between them!

But too late. He was at her heels as she led the way to the side shed that housed her motorbike.

"You drive this yourself?" Ross asked, eyeing the small vehicle with something short of trust.

"Sure," she said, praying that he not hear her breathlessness and guess its cause. "It's great for the fresh air, uses practically no gas, and does much less by way of pollution than my car." She paused. "Unless you'd feel safer—"

"No. No. I'm game. Don't forget—of the two of us, I'm the original hippie."

Chloe drove with Ross straddling the seat behind her, and it was totally traumatic. He was near, so near. His arms were locked about her waist, his body tucked against hers. Even the October breeze whipping by did nothing to relieve the intimacy of the trip. When he spoke, it was a nibble at her ear. A nibble? Had he really done that—or was it a product of her overworked imagination?

Indifference. Uh-huh.

The road they traveled was one she covered daily. Its sides were edged with maples and oaks, grown ripe and mellow now, on the verge of bursting into autumn flame. Fields sprawled to the right, wooded pastureland to the left. Ahead undulated a path to Sakonnet Point, the very tip of the finger of land on which Little Compton sat just across the bay from Newport.

If Ross was aware of the havoc his nearness wreaked on her, he kept his smugness in check. Once, in a gesture of soft intimacy, he released her waist to gather her hair together in his hands, twist the long fall once, and tuck it inside the back of her shirt.

"The better to see the town," he murmured wickedly. He had to know that her neck tingled from the touch of those fingers, her ear from the brush of his breath, so much so that she was oblivious to much of their surroundings. When at last they reached the wharf, with its graceful fleet of pleasure craft, she was almost sorry. The intimacy had been nice. She was strangely torn.

Not so Ross. "Ah! There's a place that looks like it'll fit the bill. Can we eat there?"

The ultimate humiliation had to be being bested by a restaurant. Apparently the way to a man's heart was through his stomach after all. But then, Chloe wanted no part of Ross's heart. The restaurant could have him.

She smiled, pleased to have so neatly talked herself sane. "If you're really hungry, this is the place to be."

Ross was really hungry. He was game to sample most anything and everything, from clam fritters to little necks on the half shell to swordfish puffs, a specialty of the house.

Chloe savored his enthusiasm, taking pride in pointing out the small groups of local fishermen on the pier arduously scraping barnacles off tall-stacked lobster traps. The bright yellow of their rubber overalls was a bit of sunshine stolen from the sky, adding a spark to the otherwise sleepy air of the harbor. It was, all in all, a peaceful lunch, filled with good food, thirst-quenching beer, and conversation that stuck to the more general, less personal topic of travels, foreign ports, and favorite hideaways.

"The ocean is beautiful," Ross admitted at one point, "but I still prefer the mountains. There's nothing more lovely than that feeling of seclusion you get in a small cabin tucked into a neat cleft, with stretches and stretches of piggybacked hills to keep the world at bay."

"Then you've never been on the beach on a foggy morning," Chloe returned softly. "It's like being in a gentle white cocoon, with the solace of knowing that humanity is near, yet out of sight and sound for as long as the mist should choose."

"You like New England."

"I do."

"You'll be staying here?"

"I will."

He sighed good-naturedly. "Then we'd better get you to the market or you won't make it through the week, much less the winter."

On that comfortable note, they left the restaurant, spending leisurely moments wandering along the breakwater before returning to the bike.

"I'll drive this time," Ross said with an arched brow and a palm out for the keys. Chloe was only too glad to relinquish the responsibility. Seated comfortably behind Ross, she was more in control of her emotions.

What she hadn't counted on was the broad expanse of his back, the sense of contentment that flowed through her as the wind rushed freely through her hair, the gentle fatigue that a night of little sleep, a morning of busy work, and a full stomach had induced. Indifference had no place here. Without a care to the wisdom of the move, she wrapped her arms about his middle and laid her cheek against his back.

It was heaven, pure and simple. She didn't have a care in the world. Ross was at the helm, competent and strong. Over the wind that sailed by came the steady beat of his heart, steadying her in turn. She didn't know what it was about this particular man that affected her so deeply, nor did she care just then. It was enough to enjoy the respite from responsibility and to give herself up to his care, if only for the brief ride home.

The brief ride home, however, grew longer and longer. Peering around Ross's shoulder, Chloe saw that they were on a different road entirely.

"Do you know where we are?" she called.

"Roughly. Where's your market?"

He followed her pointing finger, turning this way, then that, until the town common came into view. Typically New England, it had a white-steepled church at its hub and a variety of rural shops and boutiques. Chloe found everything she needed at the grocery store, reluctantly took Ross's suggestion that the plants be saved for another trip, then climbed behind him onto the bike to return to the house. Not one wrong turn later she was on her own front steps.

The moment of reckoning was at hand. "Will you be returning to New York now?" she asked.

He had finished stowing the bike in its proper spot and advanced on her with a grin. Relieving her of the large brown bag she'd been carrying, he took her elbow and guided her toward the house. "Not yet."

"You're going back to Lee's?"

"Not yet."

"Then what are you going to do?"

He held the door open for her to pass, and followed her into the kitchen, where he began to unload and store the groceries as though the place were his. "I want to make a few phone calls." He glanced at his watch. "Then wash the car, catch the end of the Giants' game, shower and shave, and take you out to dinner."

His recitation was so nonchalant that Chloe would have guessed he spent every October Saturday this way, at least as far as the first part went. As for taking her out to dinner, it had certainly never happened before.

"It's unnecessary," she said.

"Which part—the calls, the car, the game, or the shower?"

"The dinner! Lunch was enough to even us up. There's no need for anything more."

A muscle worked in Ross's jaw. "It's not tit-for-tat, Chloe. I'd like to take you out to dinner."

"I appreciate the thought, but—"

"No buts. We're going out for dinner. Period."

"What if I have other plans?"

He arched a dark brow. "Do you?"

"I could just as well," she hedged, "for the way you just assume I'm free."

"Well, are you?"

It wasn't that she didn't want to go to dinner with Ross. On the contrary. She liked being with him. She just didn't want to get used to it.

"Chloe?"

"Yes," she said, sighing. "I'm free."

"Good. Say, about eight?"

"But—"

"Eight it is. And Chloe?"

She felt totally helpless. "What?"

"How about if we dress up?"

"Dress up? I haven't 'dressed up' in months. Things here are very casual. There's nowhere—"

"There is," he argued gently. "Leave that to me."

Chloe lowered her eyes and studied the floor, then slowly shook her head. "Ross, I'd really rather—"

"For old times' sake?" he dared ask. "Today we played 'far out.' Tonight, let's play 'far in.' Come on. How about it? Just this once?"

The odd note of pleading in his voice brought Chloe's head slowly up. He looked so innocent, so hopeful, that she couldn't turn him down.

"Just this once," she gave in softly, forcing the semblance of a smile to vulnerable lips.

There was no semblance of anything in Ross's smile. It was blatantly broad and open, relieved and pleased. It warmed her, reassured her, amused her. And it most definitely excited her.

That terrified her.

Before she could back out, though, he said, "It's a date. See you at eight."

He turned and made for the phone, leaving Chloe to gather the pieces of her fast-splintering resolve and struggle with makeshift repairs before evening rolled around.

6

It wasn't an easy task. Ross seemed to be everywhere she turned. He used her office to make his calls, lounging back in her chair, legs long and straight, crossed lazily at the ankles, propped on the corner of her desk. His presence filled the room so that it took a conscious effort on Chloe's part to quietly creep in and steal her own work. He followed her every move with interest, though he was at the same time maddeningly capable of carrying on his end of what was obviously a business discussion.

After retreating to the back porch to bask in the rays of the westward sun, she put her best effort into organizing the papers on her lap. But her best effort was sadly lacking. Her mind wandered. Then Ross appeared in the flesh to ask about a bucket, a sponge, and some old towels. He was right on schedule, his self-satisfied air announced. He vanished, then reappeared and deposited the car-wash gear on the sandy grass beside the very same porch on which she sat.

Would he do it here? she wondered. The smooth hum of his car's engine as he pulled the vehicle close by the side of the house was her answer. He wanted an audience, the rat.

She should have gotten up and left, but she sat right there in the large wood-slatted porch chair, watching while he put his best effort into washing, drying, and polishing his sporty brown BMW. As he stretched to soap the roof, the muscles of his shoulders bunched. When he squatted to scrub the whitewalls, the muscles of his thighs swelled. When he reached across the front windshield, his shirt separated from his jeans, giving fleeting, devastating glimpses of a flat, hard belly. And through it all was the sight of hands and forearms at work, lightly tanned, softly haired.

When Chloe had taken as much as she could, she stacked her papers into a pile, left the chair, and, without a word to explain her sudden departure, went into the house. To clean? She hated to clean! How else, though, to expend some of the nervous energy that had gathered inside?

She swept the floors and vacuumed the carpets, all at doublespeed, all with every bit of elbow grease she could muster. Tables, chairs, countertops, and shelves met similar fates beneath her dustcloth. Perspiration beaded on her upper lip. She barely noticed.

The football game offered a different torment, but one that was no less agonizing. She was polishing the aged oak banister halfway to the second floor when the familiar sound wafted up, and she sank down on the homey wool runner in defeat. The football game—what memories it brought. That sound—the excited roar of the crowd, the babble of color commentators, the endless streams of kickoffs and passes, punts and first downs, fumbles, tumbles, and pileups—brought back the days in New Orleans when the men of the family gathered for their weekly fix. Her brothers— it had been so long since she'd seen them. Were they watching this same game? And how was her father feeling? He wasn't young anymore. Should she make the effort to go back before . . . ?

"Chloe? Are you all right?"

It wasn't until Ross spoke that she realized he'd even approached. Nor had she been aware of the tears in her eyes. With a hard swallow and a feeble smile, she willed the sadness away. "I'm fine. I think I'll go for a run."

Leaving Ross where he stood, she pensively covered the last of the steps to the top landing, disappeared into her room to change into running wear, then went back down the stairs and outside. Her sneakers beat rhythmically down the beach toward the far end of the bay, much as they had done at roughly the same time the day before. Had it only been twenty-four hours since Ross had shown up? Already he seemed so at home here. Worse, at odd times it seemed natural to have him here.

The questions kept pace with her jog. Was it only that Ross was a face from her past? Was he a link to those people who had once meant so much to her? Did she crave the warmth of her family? Was Ross, by association, an extension of them?

Without answers, she paced herself for another ten minutes before turning around. When she reached the house she didn't bother to stop at the door. An easy lope carried her into the kitchen, through to the living room, and up the stairs. No sign of Ross—so much the better. Jogging in place with the last of her pre-shower energy, she piled her arms with fresh towels from a surprisingly low stack in the linen closet and went to her room for a robe. There she stopped dead in her tracks.

Where an open expanse of pale lavender quilt had been when she had left, was a landscape of male artifacts. And clothes. His clothes. He had made himself perfectly at home. This was the limit.

A fit of fury took her to the bathroom door. Better judgment stopped her on the threshold. The sink taps were running. If she barged in, what would she find? The tremble that snaked through her had nothing to do with fear. Rather, she conjured up the image of Ross shaving, a coat of white lather covering his jaw, a towel—her towel—covering his loins, and nothing, nothing else, covering or covered.

As she stood rooted there, the shower went on, the curtain clattered back on its hooks, and . . . her mind's eye saw it all. The towel fell away. With total nonchalance, he stepped into the shower.

Mercifully, he couldn't hear her low cry as she whirled back toward her bedroom, cursing both Ross and her imagination all the way. But she couldn't curb her curiosity entirely. Approaching the bed with an odd shyness, she studied his things. There was the leather duffel she had seen earlier, plus a larger, flatter suit bag, unzipped to reveal a pair of gray-blue tweed lapels. There was the smaller canvas case that had contained his shaving gear, if the travel-sized bottle of cologne left behind was any indication. There was a shirt—white, freshly laundered, lightly starched. There were a tie, clean socks, shorts—

"Oh, Lord!" she exclaimed softly. If every stitch of the clothing he intended to put on was here on her bed, exactly what did he plan to wear for the trip from the bathroom?

Anticipation constricted her throat, making breathing harder. The aftereffects of her jog had faded; this quickening was due to desire. Ross turned her on. Part of her wanted nothing more than to give herself to him. Give herself? Hah! She would take as well, take as she had been too naïve to do eleven years before. She felt suddenly greedy, possessed with a need to satisfy the gnawing inside.

"You're back!"

Chloe whirled around.

Undaunted by her alarm, he grinned. "I'd hoped to be out of your way." He gestured in token apology toward her bed. "Guess I misjudged the time." He shot a look at the hall. "I helped myself to your supplies. That okay?"

That okay? The towel was draped around his hips with as much panache—and as little ceremony—as she had earlier imagined. It hung low on his stomach and left little to the imagination. She dragged her eyes upward, following a narrow line of hair past his navel to his waist and slowly higher.

"Chloe," Ross began in husky chiding, "do you have any idea what it does to a man when a woman looks at him that way?"

It took every ounce of her willpower to keep from lowering her gaze in curiosity. "I'm sorry—"

"Oh, don't be sorry." He came closer. Though he didn't touch her, his body was no more than a breath away.

And she felt it, felt the need. She put a hand to his chest to ward it off, but it was a sorry miscalculation. Her fingers found a mat of soft, dark hair that sprang, warm and still moist, from the freshness of lightly bronzed skin.

The pounding of her pulse frightened her so that she tore her hand from his chest and thrust it behind her back. She felt a huge measure of guilt. If he did also, it was hidden behind desire. His amber eyes smoldered, heating her all the more. The need, ahhhh, the need. The ache to be held and loved . . .

Ever so slowly, Ross lowered his head until his lips shadowed hers. She felt them, wanted them. Her own parted in silent invitation. She closed her eyes to savor the sensation. But he never kissed her. Rather, there was a soft exchange of breath, a whisper of lips against one another, sweet, sweet torment.

Chloe felt ready to burst, willing to beg. But that was a sure road to self-disgust. So she finally did what she had meant to do all along. She pressed against his chest, pushing him gently but firmly away.

As he slowly straightened to what was, even barefoot, an awesome height, he cleared his throat. "You'd better wait downstairs," he said in a voice that was thick and taut. "I'll finish up quickly."

She took his suggestion. By the time she reached the bottommost step, sanity had fully returned. Swearing softly, she traipsed through the kitchen and stood on the back porch looking out on the beach. But the tide within her was high. No amount of cooling breeze could stem it.

He had to leave. It was as simple as that. Indifference was a pipe dream. He stirred her too much.

Having him around today was a taste of what it might be like to have him around all the time. She wanted to say she had hated it, but she couldn't. There had been something nice about waking to find a man in her kitchen cooking her breakfast, something nice about knowing that he was patiently waiting for her to finish work, something nice about going marketing with him, even about finding him in her shower. It had been nice. But would any man fit the bill?

With a sigh, she shook her head. It had to be Ross. Always Ross.

"It's all yours, princess!" he called.

Chloe looked up in surprise to find the horizon pink-orange in advance of sunset. Back over her shoulder, Ross stood at the kitchen door, silhouetted by the light inside.

"Be right there," she called, looking at the sunset again, gathering composure. When she felt in control, she returned to the house. She caught a trace of cologne when she moved past him, but moved steadily on until she was safe in her room.

Promptly at eight she descended the stairs, wearing a pale blue sheath of lightweight wool appropriate to the fast-cooling night air. Its lines were simple; it was nipped in at the waist and wrists, lightly flared at the sleeves and skirt, and deeply slashed into a vee at the throat.

She worried about that low vee. The dress was simple, but provocative. She had bought it the year before for one of those blundered attempts at a date, and would have avoided it for that reason. Unfortunately, it was the only dressy dress in her wardrobe that was of recent vintage.

In other respects she felt confident. Her hair was brushed to a fine sheen, swept back behind either ear, and held in place with buds of pale blue silk. The single pearl at each ear matched the strand around her throat. And her eyes were luminescent. From her makeup, perhaps? Whatever, she felt like a porcelain princess descending the stairs.

Ross was clearly pleased. "You look lovely," he said, gently taking her arm.

She felt suddenly shy. "Where are we going?"

"Farmington Court."

She caught her breath. "In Newport? How did you ever get reservations?"

"Oh, I managed," he said with a coy grin.

Chloe's excitement was genuine. "They've only had the dining room open a few months."

"You haven't eaten there yet, then? I was hoping I'd be the first to take you."

"You are," she said and tried to get a handle on her breathiness. "I usually eat in, remember? No, I haven't eaten at the Court, but I've wanted to. I heard that the dining room is gorgeous and the food incredible." She arched a brow. "You are hungry, aren't you?"

Ross smiled. "Since we're dining in style, I'll try not to paw through the pâté." He tossed his head toward the door. "Let's go."

The drive to the farm took them in a large U, from one fingertip of land, back to the mainland, then out to the other fingertip. Their conversation was light, in contrast to the heavy darkness that had fallen. Even the moon had disappeared behind gathering clouds.

Chloe was vitally aware of Ross. His strapping presence filled the car and her senses, adding to her excitement.

Farmington Court was on the outskirts of Newport. Without any help from Chloe, Ross found the place with ease.

"How did you find out about the Court?" she asked when the farm appeared on a gentle rise ahead. "Not many people know about the dining room here. Not many outsiders, that is. It's a well-kept secret."

His smile reflected the bright lights of the house. "Maybe it's supposed to be a secret, but it's slowly creeping out anyway. I had a recommendation from a friend in New York who's been here." He paused, then confessed, "I'm not a total stranger to Newport. Little Compton, yes. Newport, no. I was here last summer."

"You were?" she asked cautiously.

He nodded. "I spent several days here sailing with friends."

"I didn't know you sailed."

"There's plenty you don't know about me." With a flick of his wrist, he turned the car into a space in the graveled lot. He slid from behind the wheel, rounded the car, and helped her out.

She learned something else about him when they passed through the door of the sprawling seaside estate. Not only did he greet the maître d' by name, but he spoke in fluent French. Along with her Southern accent, Chloe had long since lost what little French she picked up as a child in New Orleans. She remained silent, enjoying the smooth, romantic sound.

Following several moments of low conversation during which both men seemed equally at ease, the maître d' showed Ross and Chloe to the smallest of the three rooms that had been converted for public dining. It was exquisitely decorated in Colonial style, with a smattering of the English, a dab of the French, and a triumphant dose of pure Americana. This particular room held only three tables, each set for two. Theirs was in a far corner, lit softly by a candle. It was an intimate setting, one Chloe would have wished to avoid had she been thinking clearly.

But she wasn't. At some point Ross had ceased to be a part of the past. There was only the candlelit present. She looked over the flickering flame and met his gaze.

"Do you like it?" he asked, endearingly eager.

She smiled. "I do."

"I asked the maître d' to bring a bottle of Chassagne de Montrachet."

If his fluency in French amazed her, his knowledge of fine wines was no less astonishing. Fine wines were something she did know something about, a legacy of her father's acclaimed cellar. Unable to resist, she grinned. "So that's how the Army sedates its brats. Fine wine. And here I felt so sorry for you. I'm sure the Chassagne de Montrachet will be superb."

Ross laughed. "The Army had nothing to do with it. I developed a taste for wine after I left the Peace Corps. I have several treasured bottles at home—a Mouton-Rothschild, a Château Lafite-Rothschild. My favorite is a 1959 Côteaux du Layon from the Loire Valley."

"Whoa. Very impressive. What other goodies do you have up your sleeve?"

His right hand flew to his left cuff, one long finger making a pretense of searching. The search was forgotten when the maître d' reappeared, wine in hand, to present the bottle to Ross.

While he studied the wine, Chloe studied him. It was a luxury that the drive through the night hadn't offered. Now she drank in his good looks with as much reverence as he gave to his wine.

He looked wonderful. His suit was the gray-blue tweed she had seen on the bed. Same with his white shirt and crimson-on-navy tie. She blushed as she recalled the other items she'd seen, then pushed those aside and focused on the chiseled features before her. They were strong, yet relaxed, and exuded confidence. The darkness of his hair and the sun-touched hue of his skin contrasted with his shirt at neck and wrists, adding a crispness to his appearance that was enhanced by the fine cut of the obviously hand-tailored fabric. He was the epitome of the man of the world—suave, assured, experienced, and content. To all outward appearances he held the world in his palm.

Was he vulnerable in any way?

"Why the frown, princess?" He leaned forward to exclude the maître d', who worked at uncorking the wine.

"I'm not frowning." But she was. She felt it. "I was wondering . . ." When the maître d' poured a sip of wine into Ross's glass and waited, Chloe held the thought.

Ross lifted the long-stemmed goblet, inhaled the scent, took the pale liquid into his mouth, patiently let his taste buds warm it, finally swallowed. "Excellent," he complimented the very pleased maître d'. Without further fanfare the goblets, first Chloe's, then Ross's, were filled.

"What were you wondering?" Ross asked the instant they were alone again.

"Whether you're happy. Are you content with your life?"

"For the most part. There are still things I want." The directness of his gaze should have tipped her off.

But she was too curious to see. The softness of her voice spread to her lips, now moist with wine. "What things?"

"You hit on them yesterday, actually. I want a wife and children."

"But you've waited this long."

"Not by choice."

"Then why?"

His crooked grin did stranger things inside her than even the wine, with its gentle warming touch. "I'm not totally different from that man back in New Orleans. I'm an idealist at heart. I always will be. I have a certain image of what love should be like. If I can't have it that way, I'd rather not have it at all."

Chloe looked down. What was love? What would she have wanted from it had she allowed it into her life? She watched Ross's fingers, curling absently around his goblet's stem. At that moment, love would have meant reaching out to touch them, to thread hers through them.

Burying her hand in her lap, she said, "Tell me about that image, Ross. In its most ideal form, what should love be like?"

He stared at her, his eyes a pensive gold. He seemed to weigh and balance, to sift through both sides of a private debate as the quiet sounds of the restaurant drifted by.

Chloe waited, sipping wine, buoyed by it. Her thoughts wandered, but not in debate. There was nothing to debate. Ross Stephenson was even more appealing than he had been in her memory all those years. He was a man for today, to be sipped and savored like the wine he poured into her now empty glass.

When he spoke, she was grateful for the wine's mellowing shield. "When was the last time you were home?"

"Home?"

"New Orleans. Do you go back there often?"

"No." New Orleans was the past. She wanted the present. "What does that have to do with anything?"

"Love. You asked me about it. I'm asking you the same. You loved your family once. Do you still?"

"Yes."

"But you never see them. Don't you miss them?"

Even in spite of the wine, she grew defensive. "I do."

"How often do you call home?" he asked gently.

"Every so often."

"And the last time you flew down?"

She hedged. "It was a while ago."

When he leaned forward to pursue his point, she sensed that he really and truly cared. "Why, Chloe? What does love mean to you that you can ignore those same people who worry themselves sick about you? That can't be what love is about."

"We're talking about different kinds of love. One kind you're born into, the other you choose."

"The end result is the same. Once a man and a woman make that commitment and marry, they face the same kinds of trials that your family faced. You've run away—"

"Don't." She clamped a hand on his arm. "Please don't, Ross. I don't want to talk about this."

His voice gentled. "You have to talk about it sometime. There are so many things you've refused to face, about yourself, about your family—"

"Not tonight," she insisted softly. She let her eyes plead, only because her voice kept its dignity. "I want to enjoy myself tonight. Please?"

Ross stared first at her, then at the tablecloth, then at the far wall. When his gaze finally returned she saw a glint of humor. "When you look at me like that, I'd do anything!"

"Anything?" She clutched at that.

"Anything."

"Then tell me about the Picasso exhibit. You saw it when it was in New York, didn't you? Was it as spectacular as the reviews claimed?"

"Every bit."

She waited for him to say more, but he simply stared at her.

"Go on, Ross. Tell me about it."

His gaze narrowed. "I'm not giving up, Chloe. We'll get back to that other conversation sooner or later. For now I'll humor you."

"I'm waiting," she sang brightly, making light of his threat. "The exhibit?"

The evening passed more quickly than she could have dreamed. Not only did they discuss Picasso, but they delved into politics, Wall Street, and the National Football League as well. For Chloe, the Châteaubriand Bouquetière with Béarnaise Sauce was incidental, as was the mellow red wine that flowed with the appearance of the beef. Her attention was on Ross and Ross alone.

When was it that she had vowed indifference? That morning? What a fool she had been to think she could remain indifferent to Ross for long. She knew her eyes were sparkling and her cheeks flushed, and she couldn't seem to stop smiling. Indifferent? Fat chance. Even aside from the physical, she found him to be the most interesting, well-informed, articulate man she had ever known. Though they didn't agree on everything, he respected Chloe's right to her own opinion. It made conversation free and relaxed, neither one fearful of offending the other.

The blend of Ross and the wine put Chloe at ease. When he suggested that they take dessert cheese home to eat with fruit overlooking the ocean, she was all for it. Unfortunately, it was downright chilly when they emerged from Farmington Court, and it began to drizzle during the drive home.

"So much for a gentle evening breeze," Ross grumbled as he hustled Chloe up the front steps to her door between increasingly large drops of rain. "The living room will have to do."

"That'll be fine. I'm in the mood for Debussy anyway, and it would have competed with the surf."

He smiled at her. *"La Mer?"*

"I had another of his works in mind." Once inside, she went straight to the shelves below the stereo unit, where she kept a small but cherished collection of works of the masters. With pride she pulled one CD from the lot.

Ross's brow shot up. *"L'Après-midi d'un faune?"* Again his accent was flawless. "I haven't listened to that in years!"

"I always called it *Afternoon of a Faun.* I like the way you say it, though. It sounds so much more romantic."

"It is a romantic piece."

Ignoring the note of caution that sounded from somewhere in the back of her mind, she took out the CD. The entire evening had been romantic, so why not this? If she was enjoying herself, why stop?

Ross squatted to study her collection. His expression was all male and distinctly wicked when he winked back over his shoulder. "You have Ravel. Should I put that on?"

She had seen that video, too. "Debussy will be fine," she said without batting an eyelash.

Richly pictorial chords filled the room. Chloe sank into a corner of the sofa, put her head back, and closed her eyes. She was aware of movement within the room, but concentrated on the music floating softly through the air about her. She was dreaming, wakened only by the warm lips that kissed her bare throat once. Her eyes flew open.

"Come sit with me and have some cheese." He took her hand and coaxed her to the floor beside a plate of cheese and fruit. She slipped off her high-heeled sandals.

They sat in front of the sofa and chairs, on the thick cream-colored area rug that covered the hardwood floor. Chloe was the keeper of the edibles, slicing fruit and cheese, stacking a piece of one on the other to offer Ross. He lounged casually on an elbow, legs stretched and crossed as he kept their wineglasses filled.

"Are you trying to get me drunk?" she teased.

"What fun would you be drunk?" He paused. "Are you sure you don't want to listen to Ravel?"

"Don't you like Debussy?" she asked innocently. Ross simply topped off her wineglass.

In the hours that followed they talked more. Chloe asked Ross about his childhood and discovered that he had both a sister and a brother, that he had studied the violin during one of his mother's culture binges, and that he had been expelled from school for a day after tossing a water bomb from a second-story building and soaking kids in the playground.

"A water bomb? Ross, how could you? That's the type of thing the girls always hated!"

"That's why I did it."

"Come on," she chided, her eyes half closed, "a ladies' man like you?"

"Sure. I was eight at the time. It satisfied my need for machismo."

Chloe laughed at the idea of an eight-year-old Ross striving for machismo. He certainly didn't need to strive now.

"You have three brothers, don't you?" Ross picked the perfect time to turn the conversation. She was in a more relaxed, more open mood than earlier. It didn't occur to her not to answer.

"Uh-huh. Allan, Chris, and Tim. They've gone into Daddy's business." She frowned. "I haven't seen them in a while."

"Will you be going down for Thanksgiving next month?"

November was the last time of year she ever went to visit. "No. I think Tim will be in New York then. I may meet him there. I'm not sure. I haven't heard from him in a while."

"Do you call them?"

This time, she did smell the trap. "Oh, no, you don't, Ross Stephenson. I'm not so tipsy that I can't see what you're doing. It won't work."

"You won't tell me about you?" he asked with such honest disappointment that she almost gave in. Almost, but not quite. There was too much she didn't want to face tonight. This was a night for the present. She shook her head in silent insistence.

"Then sit closer." Before she could protest he had shifted so that she leaned against him as he leaned against the sofa. "There." His voice was pleasantly husky. "Comfortable?"

"Ummm." She was extremely so. In fact, she couldn't think of a place where she would have been more comfortable. Ross's chest was broad under her cheek, his arms were gentle around her, his heartbeat a pacifying tattoo through her.

Time became an expendable entity; there was no need to move. They sat quietly in one another's arms, lulled by the music that continued to play. Debussy had long since given way to Grieg and Tchaikovsky.

Given the wine, the song, and the man, Chloe was mellow. So she had no problem when Ross said, "You and Crystal were identical, weren't you?"

"Technically, but there were differences we could see."

His breath rustled the hair at her temple. "Were you inseparable as kids?"

"Pretty much. Since the guys were a lot older than we were, there were only the two of us around the house."

"You had a built-in playmate."

"Uh-huh. It was fun. She was the more adventurous. I was the more conservative."

"But you were the one who approached me that night, not Crystal. I always wondered why."

Chloe tipped her head back to look at him. "We argued about who you were looking at. I thought it was me. Crystal said you wouldn't see the difference." She paused. "Who were you looking at, Ross? Me, or Crystal?"

His lips curved gently, tickling her nose for an instant. "You both looked the same."

"We did not. Come on, which one was it?" Her teasing was gentle, but she needed to know.

Ross raised his eyes. "Ah, let me think. There was one with dark hair curled to the left, and one with dark hair curled to—"

She pinched his ribs. "I'm serious! Or were you just interested in any pretty girl?"

He sobered then. "I wanted you, Chloe. I saw the difference. Your sister was just as lovely, but you had something more. I can't quite explain it."

He didn't have to. Knowing that he had chosen her was enough to ease part of that guilt she had felt over the years.

He tightened his arms. "Okay, princess. Now you tell me. Why were you the one who came forward?"

"I wanted you more."

When he sucked in a breath Chloe's hand slid lower on his abdomen. On dangerous ground, she raised it to the point where his tie lay in a loose knot, where the top two buttons of his shirt were released. His chest beckoned. She touched it and found it wonderfully warm.

Ross's voice grew thicker. "You argued?"

"Not exactly."

"If Crystal was the more impulsive of the two, I can't believe she gave up without a fight."

"I wouldn't call it a fight."

"Then what? What settled it?"

Chloe was suddenly unsure. What they had done sounded crass. But she had come this far. "We, uh, we tossed a coin."

"Excuse me?"

"We tossed a coin."

"To see which one of you would get me?" At her nod he burst into a laugh. "Chloe MacDaniel! I'm appalled! You mean to tell me that you let the toss of a coin decide whether you or your sister would seduce me? That's awful!"

She leaned closer, whispered, "It wasn't a fair toss." Tempted headily by the male tang of his skin, she kissed his chest.

"Excuse me?"

She cleared her throat. "I knew I would win."

Ross held her back, staring in bemusement. "Explain, please."

"Crystal and I used to play tricks on one another. We each had our strong points. She always beat me when it came to motivating herself. She was the first to get behind the wheel of the car, the first to choose the prettiest dress in the boutique, the first to snag the telephone caller. I prided myself on being the clever one."

"And this coin toss?"

Chloe begged forgiveness with her eyes. "It was my coin. I called heads."

Understanding slowly dawned on Ross's face. His grin was appreciative. "And the coin had two heads?"

"It did."

Whatever he might have thought of her for having cheated, he was undoubtedly pleased that "winning" him had meant so much to her. "That deserves a kiss," he said and lowered his head.

7

Chloe met his lips without hesitation. She had waited for this all evening. They had been building toward it from the second she had agreed to dress up and go out to dinner with him. "Just this once," she had told him then. Now the words echoed through her. Just this once she would relax in Ross's arms. Just this once she would taste his love. Just this once she would be free of the past.

She'd had too much wine. No doubt about that. Would she want this if her head were clear? Maybe yes, maybe no, but it made no difference. Right here, right now, she was where she wanted to be.

Ross appeared equally content, if the leisure of his kiss meant anything. He tasted her again and again, seeming to find something new each time. She sure did. Once it was the sweetness of wine on his lips, another time the firmness of his mouth, another the heat. His kiss was a heady brew, warm, moist, and intoxicating.

Seeking more, she spread her hands over his chest and discovered a textured surface beneath the smoothness of his shirt. He was a man of many layers to be explored, one by one. She was the explorer, on an ocean of desire, clinging to him as to a raft on a rising sea of sensation.

His tongue sought and caressed, sucking hers deeper, sparking greater response, and she gave it unconditionally, opening to him in delight. Soft sighs were breathed and swallowed, one mouth to the other.

The urgency built. Just when she needed it, he deepened the kiss. His lips controlled hers now, as did the hands that framed her face.

His voice was thick against her mouth. "Do you have any idea what you do to me?"

Her answer was a breathy, "I know what you do to me. It happens every time."

"Does it? It's been a long time since you were with a man."

"By choice. By choice." Tipping her head back on his shoulder, she studied his strong jaw, straight nose, amber eyes. "It was never a trial for me before. I've never really wanted another man."

"Is it a trial now?" he whispered, momentarily cautious. "What do you want, Chloe? Do you know?"

She answered by dipping her head and putting her lips to his throat. Intoxicated by its musky scent, she freed the knot of his tie and released the front buttons of his shirt. Her sigh warmed him when her hands slid over his flesh, but his moan prevented her from going on.

He pushed his hands into her hair. "Look at me!" His eyes were hot with desire. "Do you know what I want, Chloe? I want to feel you. I want to know every inch of your body. Half measures never worked for me with you. I need to be inside you. Can you accept that?" His gaze flickered over her flushed features. "Will you hate yourself tomorrow?"

The question took her by surprise. She didn't want to think about tomorrow. Her eyes filled with the tears of a deep, emotional yearning. "I don't know what I'll feel tomorrow, but I know what I want now. I know what I need."

"Why now?" It was another surprise question. "Eleven years ago it was rebellion."

"Not rebellion."

"Then why?" he asked more gently.

She took a deep breath. The scent of his skin gave her strength. "Yes, you were different. The other men we'd known had been handpicked. Our brothers were as fussy as our parents. But there was more for me. You were new. Refreshing."

"A challenge?"

"Maybe."

"Do I challenge you now?"

"Yes, but that's only part of it." Need loosened her tongue. "The pull is there, just like it was eleven years ago. Don't make me try to explain it, because I can't. Lord only knows I didn't want to feel anything for you! You were the one who showed up uninvited, remember?"

He smiled dryly. "So you've told me."

"You bring back memories. Maybe what I need is to wipe out those memories with new ones."

His smile turned wry. "You are using me."

When Chloe pushed herself up, his hands fell away. She was on her own, as she had been all those years. And she knew what she wanted.

"Yes, I'm using you! I'm using you to show me that I can feel and live. I'm using you to help me put the past to rest. You're right. I have to do that. But don't you see," she ended on a note of pleading, "that you're the only one who can help me?"

For long moments, silence was as thick in the air as the lingering heat of passion. Finally Ross lifted a hand to her cheek. "I want to believe it, Chloe. Want it bad."

"Then make love to me. You show me what love should be like."

With a low animal sound, he reached out and pulled her under him, kissing her fiercely, erasing everything but the here and now. Chloe put herself into his hands. Trusting him fully, she lost all inhibition and returned his kiss with everything she had.

His lips moved on her neck, inching down into the dip of her dress. "I've been wanting to do this all night," he whispered moments before his mouth found the bottommost point. He kissed her there, wet, open-mouthed, then rose again. His mouth was ready when he cupped her breasts and lifted them there.

Chloe sighed softly. She squeezed her eyes shut, buried her fingers in his hair, and held him closer.

With excruciating slowness he drew back her bodice, freeing her breast bit by bit. Her insides quivered when her nipple was bared. His breath was hot, the air cool. Arching closer, she watched his tongue touch the pebbled tip, circle it, touch it again.

"Ross!" she gasped, straining beneath him, needing more.

"Love is torment, Chloe. It's wanting and wanting and wanting until you would do anything to get. Be patient."

She tried, but it was a torment, indeed, to watch him pull his shirt from his pants and release every single last button. She bit her lip to keep from reaching out to touch him. He could have been sculpted in clay by a master, he was that beautiful, more beautiful even because he was real. He was human, manly, alive.

Her patience was pushed even further when he drew her up, reached behind to slide her zipper to her waist, then pulled her dress down, easing her arms from their sleeves. Bare to the waist, she needed his touch, but his eyes caressed her first. Her breasts swelled, begging to be cupped and held.

"They're not the same," she whispered falteringly. "I was much younger then."

A sound came from deep in his throat. It gave credence to his words. "Maybe younger then, but better now." His eyes said it was true. With trembling hands, he palmed her breasts with such soft, gentle motion that she nearly cried out again.

Patience slipped slowly away. When she thought she'd seen the last of it, Ross drew her to him, crushing her breasts against his chest in a move that stole her breath.

He made another deep sound, this one very male, very satisfied. His hands moved over her back, covering every inch of its smooth surface, and Chloe followed his lead. Eyes closed, she savored the feel of him, letting her palms play on his back, then drawing away to glory in his chest. His nipples were as flat and hard as hers were raised and swollen. His neck was as strong as hers was slender. His skin was as tanned as hers was creamy. Their bodies were so different, but the light in his eyes matched that in hers. She saw desire there. It was hot and heavy.

Chloe could barely breathe, much less speak. She was as aroused as she had ever been, and more with each touch of his fingers or tongue. The beat of her heart skipped rapidly on, driving heated blood through her veins. She was free. She was alive. She wanted to belong to Ross then more than anything in the world.

Sensing her urgency, he pulled her up. As she stood, her dress slid past her hips to form a pale blue circle on the floor. Aware of the admiration in his eyes, she stepped out of it wearing nothing but a pair of small silk panties.

When he held out his arms, she went to him and wrapped hers tightly around his neck. Her breasts were crushed against his hairy chest. She burned from within.

"Chloe . . . Chloe . . . Chloe . . ." he chanted softly, reminiscent of that soft September breeze in New Hampshire. But she couldn't think back, not with his fingers skimming her hips, then moving up her sides and around. He was exquisitely tender. She felt cherished, desired, and loved, if only for the night.

"Hurry." She arched against him, her body aflame with need. "Hurry."

Setting her back, he unbuckled his belt and undid his pants. His eyes devoured her hungrily as he pushed everything off, then knelt to remove her panties.

She was trembling with excitement when he dragged a cushion from the sofa to the floor. He lowered himself and held out a hand, and for a minute she couldn't move, couldn't take her eyes from his body. It was perfect in every way, thoroughly masculine and fully aroused. Eleven years ago she had been too shy to study him, but she wasn't now. He seemed to stretch forever, one long limb connected to another by firm sinew. Had she been an artist she would have drawn him. But she was only a woman.

"Chloe?"

She took his hand and stretched out against him with a soft moan. He felt wonderful against her. When she began to touch him, he sucked in a breath.

"Oh, God," he whispered gruffly, "oh, God, that's it." His chest rose and fell, lungs labored. "Feel it, princess?"

There were two kinds of feeling, the physical and the emotional. Chloe experienced both. High on the fullness, she moved freely over his body. Her fingers found delight with every touch, her heart satisfaction. She reached his most electric parts as he reached for her.

"Now," she begged, desperate and demanding.

"Kiss me first," he murmured thickly. When she turned up her face, he moved over her, slipping between her open thighs.

She cried into his mouth when he thrust forward. Anything she might have remembered of the past was gone then, paling in the light of the present. Her body exploded and flamed, burning hotter with each thrust of his hips, with each progressively deeper penetration. She rose and rose, straining higher, higher, until her body burst into spasms of something akin to heaven.

She cried out again when she heard Ross's cry. She felt the tightness of his muscles, the pumping of his hips, then, joy, a grand pulsing inside her. He held her as tightly as she held him, and there was joy in that, too.

For what seemed a glorious forever, they lay that way. Finally, his body damp, he slid out to lie beside her. The night air was broken by ragged breathing, both his and hers.

Chloe lay stunned. Then, suddenly and inexplicably, she was overcome. Pressing her cheek against Ross's drumming heart, she began to cry.

In a frightened voice, he asked, "What, princess?"

"Just hold me. Hold me tight."

He gathered her to him as though she were the most precious thing in the world, and held her while she cried. She couldn't explain why she did it, and he didn't ask. He simply held her, stroked her back, whispered sweet nothings of comfort and support against the top of her head.

Gradually her eyes dried and her pulse grew steadier. "I'm sorry. I don't know what came over me."

"How do you feel now?"

"Better." She took a last jagged breath and rubbed her cheek against his chest. "Satisfied." She thought about that and finally tipped up her head. "I actually feel great. That was the most beautiful—" Her words died when her throat constricted again.

Ross turned them so that they lay on their sides, facing one another. He traced the slim lines of her cheek and jaw, then ran the tips of his fingers down her neck to her collarbone.

Chloe felt a stirring inside. She must have looked startled, because he laughed.

"Didn't think you could feel it again so soon?" When he slid a leg between hers, she moved against it, but he didn't tease her. He was suddenly serious. "It was beautiful, princess. Even more so than before. I've lived all these years wondering whether I had imagined it. I tried for it over and over. And here, in one shot, you've done it again, and more."

"Not me. Us." She touched him lower.

He gasped. "You're gonna do it again," he said and kissed her.

This time was slower, more leisurely. Ross was the connoisseur, showing Chloe how to tease and withhold, playing the martyr when she did. She took delight in learning the nuances of holding, caressing, leading him to the brink, staying there, and, incredibly, the force of the passion was even greater. This time, when it was done, there were no tears. Eyes closed, she nestled against him, replete and happy. She didn't have a care in the world.

Oblivious to the steady rain that beat down on the roof of the house, they slept. Their twined bodies offered warmth, the soft rug offered comfort. It was nearly four in the morning when Ross gently woke her.

"Let's go upstairs," he whispered, kissing her ear.

Groggy and disoriented, she reached for him. "What is it?"

He was on his knees, gathering her into his arms. "Nothing. I just want to take you to bed."

"You're not leaving?" Her arms tightened around his neck, but he chuckled.

"I want to take you in bed—"

"Are you . . . again?"

"Shhh. I want to be able to remember what your bed feels like, for all those long lonely nights ahead," he drawled. He crossed the living room and took the stairs with her in his arms and a minimum of effort. "I want you to be haunted the same way," he added, less humorous now. "You'll lie in your bed and remember the feel of me until you're ready to burst."

Fully awakened, Chloe was warm all over. Her breast was snug to his chest, her hip nestled against his naked belly. It was still night. Under cover of darkness, she could do anything. Her lips turned recklessly to his shoulder, her tongue moistening a spot, her teeth leaving a mark.

"Heeeey! Watch that!" He put her down, letting her slide slowly over the length of him. His hand stayed at the small of her back, pressing her against a full erection. To Chloe's amazement, she was just as aroused.

Their lips met, open now and sure. There was no limit to this pleasure, only the need for more and more.

"The bed," she croaked in haste, tearing herself away to pull back the quilt. She fell onto the sheets with him, and there was a fury to this union, a blend of yearning, fear, and unbridled greed. Morning was coming. They couldn't get enough of each other. When they finally climaxed and collapsed, their bodies were slick and exhausted. Again they slept.

* * *

When Chloe opened her eyes next, it was to the gray light of a soggy morning and, more brightly, to Ross. His dark hair was disheveled. He was staring down at her.

Breaking into a smile, he said, "I wanted to see if it would work."

"See if what would work?"

"If I could wake you up by willing it. I've been sending brain waves."

"Brain waves didn't wake me." She yawned. "I'd have woken anyway."

He stretched and grimaced. "I feel well used."

"That's one way to put it," she said, but she was thinking ahead. How not to? Morning was here.

She rolled away, but he rolled her right back and held her in place with an arm on either side. "Don't. After last night you can't turn away."

"Can't?"

"Won't. Let's talk," he said gently and sat up. His eyes wandered to her hair, which was spread on the pillow, then the sheets, which bunched at her navel. He looked at everything in between as though it were priceless. At last, in a deep voice, he said, "I love you, Chloe."

She reached to cover his mouth, not ready for that, but he caught her hand and pinned it to the pillow. Leaning down, he gave her a long, silencing kiss. When his mouth left hers again, he said, "I love you and want to marry you."

She shook her head.

"I do," he insisted.

Her heart ached. She wasn't ready, wasn't ready at all. "Last night we made love. Saying 'I love you' is something else entirely."

Ross didn't budge. "Argue as much as you want, but you won't change this. I love you. I wish I could say that I loved you eleven years ago—it would all sound romantic. I wanted you then. I knew that there was something in you—deep in you—that intrigued me. But I didn't get to know you. A few hours is too short a time."

"It's hardly been much more than that now," she protested.

"It's been more than two weeks."

"It's been less than two days."

"Tell me you didn't think of me."

She recalled those long hours after New Hampshire. "I can't. I thought of you. But in order to love a person you have to spend time with that person."

"You're clutching at straws. I love you. If you were honest with yourself, you'd tell me that you love me, too."

That was what she feared most. There was no place in her life for that kind of love. "You don't know what I feel."

"I know what I felt last night. You couldn't have faked your reactions. Sorry, Chloe, but you responded out of love. That's all there is to it."

"No. Not all." She needed time. She knew what she had to say. "I responded to you out of need. Call it lust or physical desire, but don't call it love."

"You're afraid," he announced.

There was a deathly silence. The air pulsed between them.

"You're afraid to let go of the past," he went on. "It's so much a part of you that you're terrified to live without it."

"That's not true," she cried.

"Then why don't you try? You did it for a night—why not for a week? A month? A year?" He softened. "I'm not asking you to renounce your past, just to accept it and move on." He paused, suddenly a shade unsure. "You did enjoy last night, didn't you?"

"Oh, yes," she breathed so quickly that her words stopped dead for lack of a follow-up.

His smile filled the gap. It was a full, warm curve of the firm lips that had given her such pleasure through the night. His gaze dropped to her breasts, then her bare middle. When he bent to kiss her navel, she clutched his hair. But to push him away? Or to hold him there? Lord, she didn't know.

After a night of beauty, the morning was dreary and dark. After a night of clear-cut emotions, the new day's emotions were muddy and dense. She needed time, needed space. Turning her face into the pillow, she let her hands slowly slide from his hair.

"I want you to work for me, Chloe."

Her eyes shot back to his. "Work for you? How can I do that? I have my own business."

He brushed a tendril of hair from her cheek. "I mean, I want to retain your firm."

She was startled. She hadn't considered this twist. "For what?"

"To cater our board meetings," he drawled facetiously. "Come on, you know what you do. I'd like to hire ESE as a geological consultant, starting with a set of revised plans for the Rye Beach Complex."

Business, then? Suddenly self-conscious, Chloe drew the sheet to her armpits and sat up. She forced a feeble smile. "So it's bribery now? You'd try to hook my business, then slowly reel me in?"

"If necessary." His grin came and went. "I've toyed with the idea all week. It was what I wanted to discuss when I arrived Friday. What do you think? Will you do it?"

"No."

"Why not? It's a good business move."

"Actually," she thought aloud, "you're right. It is a good business move. I'll do it, but only if Lee handles the work."

"I don't want Lee."

She had never doubted it. "That's why I can't do this. Can you imagine us trying to work together? After last night? I'm not sure how much work we'd get done."

He sighed. "At least you don't deny that."

"I never did. I just don't know how much more there is to it than that." But she lied. Making love with Ross was as close, as deep, as merged as she had ever been with another person, and that included Crystal, which was saying a lot. She would always be attracted to Ross, would always feel that special connection.

Sadly, she slipped out of bed and stood at the window. She felt as lonely, as dismal as the day. Was the pain of separating from Ross worth the joy of being with him? Was the pain her punishment for self-indulgence?

She heard his footsteps behind her and sighed when he circled her waist and drew her back against him. For another minute, no more, she would savor it. Another minute, that was all.

"I have to leave this morning," he said softly.

"This morning?"

"I have a date in New York."

"A date." That stopped her. "Business or pleasure?"

"Pleasure."

She turned. "You just told me you loved me."

"I love her, too."

The mischief in his eyes tipped her off. "Your mom."

"Smart girl," he said with a smile.

Chloe was inordinately pleased. "I didn't realize she lived in New York."

"She doesn't. She's visiting."

"And you left her for the weekend?"

"With pleasure." And he showed no sign of guilt. "My mother has never been the easiest woman to get along with. And the fact that I loaned her my place pleased her more than my company would have. But I promised to take her to an opening at an art gallery she sponsors." He cleared his throat. "She's on another of her infamous culture kicks."

Chloe couldn't help but grin. "Like the violin lessons?"

"Like the violin lessons."

Their eyes shared amusement, but it faded fast. In its place was raw desire, back with a vengeance.

"Ahhh, Chloe," Ross murmured and caught her lips.

She tried to turn away. "It's too late." She turned back again, needy. She kissed him, then breathed, "We have to stop. Really, we do."

But she wanted him too much for that. He backed her to the bed and followed her down, and she met him willingly. When he was gone, there would be soul-searching aplenty. But not now. Not yet.

8

Her soul-searching began the instant the brown BMW pulled from her drive and disappeared from sight.

"I'll be in touch, princess," he had said when he kissed her good-bye.

"You shouldn't, Ross," she had said, though her throat was tight with emotion. "It's better this way."

He hadn't said anything more, had simply turned on his heel and walked off.

The sense of loss she had felt then should have eased as the day wore on, but it didn't. It grew sharper, forcing her to a deeper level of soul-searching. On this level she felt great guilt. Twice, now, she had been with Ross. Had it not been for the first time, Crystal might still be alive.

The pain of her memory of that time was so great that she rarely went there. Now she did. She and Crystal had double-dated that rainy Saturday night and had returned home on a sour note, largely from Chloe's distraction. When Crystal confronted her, Chloe told her about Ross. She hadn't meant to gloat, only to share the excitement.

But Crystal was furious. Hurt, jealousy, anger—Chloe had never been able to sort through her twin's rage. Crystal had run from the house, taken her small sports car, and sped away. Within an hour the police were at the door to report that the small car had skidded on the wet road and slammed into a tree. Crystal had died instantly.

Chloe twitched. Her forehead was bathed in sweat. Throwing an arm over her eyes, she sank more deeply into the sofa. For years she had lived with the guilt of causing Crystal's death.

But there was new guilt now. Ross had fallen in love with her and she had allowed it to happen. Since she couldn't marry him, he would be hurt, which was the last thing she wanted. He deserved the best, the finest. He deserved a wife and children and all those things she might have wanted herself, had life been different. Causing him pain increased her own pain ten-fold. Because, when all was said and done, she loved him, too.

That was the deepest layer unearthed in her soul-search. She did love Ross, but it had no future. There would always be yesterday and the ghosts she lived with. Ross had stolen her heart, but only a part. The rest had either died with Crystal, or died a little more each time she saw the grief on her parents' faces. Ross deserved a wholehearted woman. She wanted that for him.

After developing a throbbing migraine, Chloe was in bed by eight, and there was pain beyond her head. Ross's scent clung to her sheets, the remembered feel of his body seared her skin. She burned inside, with no outlet.

In time she fell asleep. After two nights without, it was deep and mercifully uninterrupted. She woke up only when Lee hollered from the foot of the stairs, "Chloe? Rise and shine!"

She yawned, stretched, remembered and felt pain, then relief. Lee often woke her with a yell. This wouldn't be the last time. Life would go on without Ross. Yes, it would.

Climbing from bed, she showered, dressed, neatened the room and joined Lee for breakfast.

"Good weekend, kid?" he asked around a mouthful of toast.

"Not bad."

"So what happened?"

"Nothing."

"He didn't sleep at my place Saturday night, Chloe."

She helped herself to coffee. "How do you know he stayed over Saturday night? How do you know he didn't go back to New York?"

"His car was here Sunday morning."

She couldn't begrudge him the gentle teasing. He was a dear friend. "You're getting snoopy in your old age."

"I live right next door. How could I miss it?"

"You could have looked the other way."

"And pass up the pleasure of seeing you blush? You don't do it very often, you know."

With determined steadiness she sipped her coffee. "I'm not doing it now. What you see is the freshness of morning—"

"—made fresher by a stimulating weekend."

"Stimulating," she said with a grunt. "That's one word for it."

"He's a good man, Chloe. I liked him."

"He liked you, too. The two of you aren't all that different."

"Maybe because we care about you."

Chloe smiled. "You're sweet." She changed the subject. "When do you leave for Washington?"

"Hold on, pretty lady. I'm still curious. You and that guy had a thing going once. Is it on again?"

Quietly, she said, "I never talked about 'a thing' with Ross. I said I knew him and that whatever might have been between us was over. Don't read something into it that isn't there."

"You make a nice pair."

"It's not your affair."

Lee backed off. "You're right. It's not. If I had any sense I'd marry you myself."

Chloe was suddenly cross. "I wouldn't say yes to you, either!"

"So he did ask you." Her partner smiled. "Fast worker, that one."

Unable to come up with a suitably indignant retort, she stood up with her mug and made to flee to her office.

"What about breakfast?" Lee's voice trailed after her.

"I'm not hungry!"

"You shouldn't work on an empty stomach."

Ross had said the same thing Saturday.

"I'll live!" she shouted over her shoulder and closed the office door.

The telephone jangled, a merciful reminder of the workday ahead. It was Alabama. Had she made a decision on handling the study for the citizens' group in Mobile? No. She hadn't even thought about it once during the weekend. It would mean a week on location taking samples of Gulf water and testing the ocean floor composition. It was a potentially fascinating project, since the toxic waste burning plan was so new.

"Yes, Ms. Farwell. I'll take the job. What's the exact status of the waste burning now?"

A gentle voice responded with concern. "The tanker will be leaving Mobile two weeks from tomorrow loaded with oil contaminated with PCBs. Those PCBs are cancer-causing. The company that owns the freighter claims that by the time the oil is completely burned, any toxic acid emitted in the smoke will have been neutralized by the seawater. We doubt that."

Chloe made notes as the woman talked. "Where do they plan to do the burning?"

The woman knew her facts and offered them up, along with a detailed list of the equipment Chloe would need. She also advised Chloe on making arrangements with the local university for the use of their lab.

Hanging up the phone, Chloe was pleased. With the use of a lab, she would be able to spend evenings analyzing the samples she collected. Four or five days out, and the job would be done.

The project was exciting. More than that, the escape from Little Compton was just what she needed. It would give her a head start at putting Ross out of her mind.

Her pencil moved over the paper, making further notes on the Alabama project. She would fly down in three weeks, by which time the tanker would have reached its proposed burn site and started to work. Three weeks would take her into the second week in November. After a week in Mobile, Thanksgiving would be at hand.

Thanksgiving. She felt a soft, distant shudder. Should she go home? Alabama was in the vicinity of Louisiana. Mobile was a hop, skip, and jump from New Orleans. She hadn't seen her parents in a long time. She missed them a lot. Same with her brothers. One of them might be there, too.

But there would be memories of another Thanksgiving, not only in Chloe's mind but in those of her parents and brothers. Could she face those? In eleven years she had never made it home for Thanksgiving. They must have guessed why. No doubt they were relieved. Looking at Chloe was seeing Crystal, too. She hated to impose that on a family Thanksgiving.

The phone rang again. "Chloe? Howard Wolschinski here. I just got a call from Stephenson. He's ready to talk." He paused. Chloe didn't know what to say. "Are you still there?" he asked.

"I'm here, Howard." She sighed, resigned. She should have known. "That's good news," she said with forced enthusiasm. "Has he given on all of our points?"

"He hasn't given on anything yet. But he says that he hears what you're saying and is willing to have you work with his people to revise the plans."

"That's fine. My studies and findings are all clearly outlined in the report I did for you. I'll have one of my assistants give him a call."

"He wants you."

"Did he say that?"

"Loud and clear. His exact words were, 'If it were anyone else, I'd have doubts. But Chloe MacDaniel has a spirit that can convince the men of the Hansen Corporation that they'd be dumb not to follow her advice.' I wrote it right down, Chloe. Thought you'd be pleased."

"Oh, yeah," she murmured under her breath. The snake. He'd stolen her own words.

"What was that?" Howard asked.

"Ah, nothing, Howard. Just a thought." She cleared her throat. "Are you sure he won't settle for another member of the firm?"

"I doubt it. You'll work with him, won't you, Chloe. I told him you would."

"Howard, how can you do this to me? Why can't you convince him that another member of the firm—even Lee, my partner—will do just as well?"

"I suppose I could try if I wanted to."

"But you don't."

"No."

"You just lost my vote."

Howard laughed roundly. "Thank goodness you don't live up here. You'd have the whole district against me. Seriously, though, we have to get moving on this. The referendum is scheduled for early November. Ross wants to meet with you A-S-A-P so that his team can get to work on some changes."

"A-S-A-P. When is that?"

"Yesterday."

I met with him yesterday, she thought. "I can't make it before Wednesday, Howard." It was just another job, she told herself. Just another job.

"Wednesday will be fine."

"Should I meet them up at the site?" One place would be as bad as the next. But if there were others around, the temptation would be less.

Howard dashed her hopes. "He wants you in New York. That's where the drawing boards are. He'll make arrangements for your transportation and housing. I have to get back to him later to tell him when. Wednesday, you say?"

She gave a low but very audible drawn-out sigh. "It's as good a day as any."

"That's my girl! I'll call you with the details. Okay?"

"You're the boss."

She should have felt victorious, hanging up the phone. If Ross caved in, there would be no need for a referendum and the Rye Beach Complex would be built on an environmentally sound plan. How much better could things be?

Tossing her hair over her shoulder, she grabbed her now empty mug and stomped through the living room into the kitchen, where she poured more coffee and reached for the sticky bun Lee had left. That was when she spotted the open door to his office.

"Lee!" She burst in, rousing her partner from the depths of a thick folder. "Lee, you're just the person I need." So much for gentlemen's agreements. Despite what she'd told Howard, if Lee would fill in for her, she would send him to New York. She could play just as dirty as Ross.

"Umm?"

"I need you to fill in for me in New York on Wednesday. Can you make it?"

He was shaking his head before she'd even finished. "I'll be in Washington. Why? A problem?"

"No. Nothing much." She mumbled the last and turned away.

"Chloe. Get back here. You'd never rush in asking me to fill in for you for nothing much." A look came over his face. "Oh." He cleared his throat. "So he called you, too."

She frowned. "Howard called you?"

"Ross called me. I think his offer is good."

"Offer? Ross? What are you talking about?"

It was Lee's turn to frown. "I'm talking about the phone call I received from Ross Stephenson no more than a half hour ago. He wants to retain our services. What are you talking about?"

A furious Chloe leaned on Lee's desk. "I already refused him! I'm talking about the phone call from Howard Wolschinski saying that Ross is ready to revise the Rye Beach proposal."

"That's great!"

"It's not! He wants me to work with him and that's the last thing I want to do!"

Lee was suddenly very gentle and very serious. He pointed her into a chair and rounded the desk to make sure that she sat. Perching nearby, he said, "Okay, pretty lady. Tell me about it."

She felt utterly helpless. "Ross is willing to make the changes, but he refuses to go by my report. He wants me to work with his people, in person, in New York."

"I gather," he said, stroking his beard, "that you aren't bothered by New York, per se."

"You gather correctly."

"Chloe, what's wrong?" he asked softly. "The man seems intelligent and honest. You shouldn't have any problem. You can be in and out of the city in no time."

At wit's end, she said, "He thinks he's in love with me, that's the problem. If it were only a matter of business, I wouldn't worry. But Ross says he wants to marry me."

"So what's the problem?"

"I can't marry him." She pleaded for his understanding. "And I'm not sure I can take his constant pressure."

"Are you afraid you might give in?" He erased the question with a wave. "Backtrack. Why can't you marry him? You're free."

"Not quite."

"You're not making sense, pretty lady. From what I can see, there's nothing in the world to keep you from marrying Ross."

"What if I don't love him?" she blurted out.

"If you don't love him, then you're right to hold out. And if you don't love him, you'll have no trouble putting him off. He'll get tired after a while." Lee was watching her face very, very closely. "That's not the real problem, is it? You do love him."

She blew out a breath, turning it into a sigh, and looked at the ceiling. "I suppose. But I can't marry him. Being with him can only be painful for both of us."

"If he believed that, he wouldn't be asking to work with you."

She grunted. "So why did he call you?"

"He wants to retain us as consultants. Did you actually say that you refused him?"

"Yes. He brought it up yesterday morning before he left."

"But it's what we need, Chloe. You mentioned trying to get corporate work when we talked on Saturday. The timing couldn't be better."

She eyed him sharply. "Did you say something to him while he was here? Did you tell him we were looking for new business?" She didn't want Ross's pity, or his charity.

"I did not! For one thing, I didn't have a minute alone with the man from the time I left here Friday night. You monopolized him."

She snorted and looked away. "He's as sneaky as they come."

"That's no way to talk about the man who loves you."

"Lee, puleeze."

He held up a hand. "Okay. I won't tease. This isn't teasing stuff. He'll pay a monthly retainer as an advance on services rendered. If we work more, we bill him for the overage. If we work less, we keep the retainer. It couldn't be better."

That didn't surprise Chloe. Ross might be a rat, a snake, and a fox, but he wasn't a thief.

"The work is right up our alley," Lee was saying. "The Hansen Corporation is involved in dozens of different projects at any given time. There'd be variety and involvement in important issues—"

"You're right, Lee," she cut in. "I can't argue. The logic of this is perfect. By all means, accept his proposal, as long as you work with him." She said the last with a touch of venom. She was being pushed into a corner, and was striking out at the only person in sight.

"He'd be hiring the firm, Chloe. I might be working on one project, you might be called for the next."

"I don't think I can do that on a continuing basis. It'd be too painful. You can work for him. I won't."

"But your area of expertise is different from mine."

"My mind is made up."

Surprisingly, there was little tension in the silence that followed. Chloe wanted to think that her outburst had cleared the air. At least, she'd been honest. Lee knew how she felt.

"You know, Chloe," he said, sitting straighter. "You were right the other day when we talked. I don't know everything about you—all those little secrets you keep bottled up inside. I didn't even know so many existed until this business with Ross." He grew beseechful. "But you have to work out whatever it is that's bothering you. Hell, you should be with him, Chloe. He loves you, you love him. Do you have any idea how many marriages are based on much less?" Lee had been married. He knew this first-hand.

"But a man like Ross deserves more than I can give him."

Lee tossed a hand in the air. "That's a bunch of crap, and you know it. If you want him, you can work out the kinks that hang you up." He rose and went to the window, stared out, turned back. "Damn it, Chloe, you have so much going for you. Are you going to sit back and let some great mystery from the past ruin your future? I thought you were a doer! You wouldn't be where you are today if you didn't believe in working for what you believe in."

Chloe couldn't say a thing. Lee had never talked to her this way before. If another man had said what he had, she would have ignored him. But she couldn't ignore Lee. She respected his opinion too much.

The horrified look on his face said that he hadn't planned the outburst. He softened. "Hey, I'm sorry. I came across a little too strong." He paused. "But I meant what I said. Either you can let it continue to get you down or you can fight it." He thrust the long fingers of one hand through his hair. "Ach, I don't even know what it is. But I believe that you can overcome whatever. I don't know what you were before, Chloe, but you're a strong woman now. Don't let a good thing escape."

She smiled sadly. "You don't understand."

"No. I don't." He sighed. "What say we drop it for a while?" At her nod, he added a final thought. "But promise me that if you want to talk, you'll come to me? I have broad shoulders."

She stood and gave him a hug. "Thanks, Lee. I appreciate that." Stepping back, she looked up at him. Funny, he was warm and strong and in his way as good-looking as Ross, but she felt no desire, no great inner spark.

Lee held out a hand. "Friends?"

She met his hand. "Friends."

"And we'll accept the offer from Stephenson?"

She yanked her hand back. "No. Yes. I don't know." She strode toward the door. "Do what you want!"

* * *

How to go from high to low in seconds, she mused, as she returned to her office and settled in at the desk. Ross was forcing her hand, totally determined. What was it he had said about love being wanting and wanting until one would do nearly anything?

She did have options. She could stand firm and refuse to have anything to do with Ross, send someone to New York in her place for the Rye Beach negotiations, systematically shuttle retainer work to another member of the firm.

Another option was more dangerous. She could go to New York and do his work, remaining neutral. Did she have a chance in hell of doing that?

Lee's words returned with frightening clarity. Did she love Ross enough to fight herself—and her past—for him? Could she go back to New Orleans and face the ghosts, finally put them to rest?

She hit emotional overload with that last thought. Too much had happened too fast. She couldn't think about it anymore. There was work to be done—if she was to be en route to New York by Wednesday.

With a long steadying breath, she sorted through the papers before her. There were people to call, meetings to set up, reports to plan out before she left, and the rush was for the best. Her mind would be filled. Worrying was useless. Only time would give her the answers she needed.

Unfortunately, Ross wasn't as patient, but he received a different Chloe on the phone that afternoon, a more subdued one. She recognized his voice immediately, had been half expecting to hear it. Its sound sent a ripple through her, but it died quickly. She was exhausted.

"How are you?" he asked.

"I'm fine."

"It's good to hear your voice. I miss you."

"You've been gone barely twenty-four hours."

"You've been counting, have you?"

She hadn't. Well, maybe she had. But she wasn't about to admit it. "I'm counting now. I have five different reports to go through this afternoon, not to mention phone calls, proposals, and what-have-you. It seems I have a rush job in New York. Some snotty executive thinks his work is the only thing that counts."

"I can see you got up on the wrong side of the bed. Bad morning?"

"Busy."

"Anything interesting?"

"Uh-huh."

He sighed. "Ah. We're pulling teeth again."

"No. There's just nothing I feel like discussing." With you, she might have added. He had intruded on her life far too much.

"You sound down." He sounded concerned. "Is something wrong?"

"I'll be fine." But she wondered. Much as she fought it, the sound of Ross's voice affected her.

"What is it, Chloe? Please tell me. Something's bothering you. I can hear it in your voice. Your spirit's gone." He paused. When she said nothing, he said, "I'm driving up."

"No! I'm okay. Really. I'm tired. That's all."

"You have no idea what I feel when I hear that pain in your voice."

"Then why did you do it?" she blurted out.

The silence was long and heavy. Then he sighed. "You've, ah, figured out my messages?"

"You could say that. What I'd like to know is why you had to go behind my back to box me in. Why didn't you call me directly?"

"I mentioned it to you last weekend. You refused. I may be many things, but I'm not a glutton for punishment. That's your specialty." Chloe gasped, but he went on. "I had no intention of calling you this morning to rehash what I said yesterday. There seemed to be more effective ways of convincing you—"

"—forcing me . . ."

". . . convincing you to work with me. It makes good sense. You're the one familiar with the Rye Beach proposal and its problems. To bring in someone else would be a waste of time. As for the other—"

"The other is Lee's affair," she cut in. "He's handling any account with the Hansen Corporation. If you want to work with him, be my guest. I can vouch for his credentials and his skill, but I won't be involved."

"Then why are you upset?" he asked a little too calmly. "If Lee will be doing the dealing, it won't affect you."

"Fat chance," she murmured not quite softly enough.

"Ah, ah, princess. Let's have none of that. If you're into soft murmurings, use them to talk about love."

"Ross."

"I love you."

"So you've said." She tried to sound indifferent, but her tone was more of a plea.

"I mean it. That's why I'm doing all this."

"What?" she cried in a facetious show of emotion. "Don't you value my brilliance, my experience, or my expertise in the field?"

"Depends on what field you're referring to," he drawled. "In the field of passion—"

"That wasn't the one I was talking about, and you know it. Why do you twist my words, Ross? Do you like upsetting me?"

He was suddenly sober. "No. I'm trying to goad you into facing your feelings. I love you, Chloe. I want to have you near me, so I manipulated your cooperation. You may not be ready to admit that you need me as much as I need you, but I have no pride. I need you, and I'm not giving you up. Not yet, at any rate."

Chloe listened sadly. He sounded honest and sincere. Maybe he did need her. But what about her needs? "You're rushing me, Ross. I don't know whether I'm coming or going. Please, give me time?"

"You have till Wednesday. I've made arrangements for you to take the nine-fifty train from Providence."

"The train? I'd rather drive. It's more convenient."

"I don't want you driving into the city. Leave your car in Providence. Your ticket will be held there for you and I'll be at the station waiting."

"Ross—"

"It's settled."

Her lips turned down. "That's what I like about you. You're so democratic."

He said a gentle "I love you, too," before hanging up.

9

Ross was indeed waiting at the station when her train pulled in. She had barely stepped onto the platform when he was beside her. He took her bag and her arm in one smooth move. "Have a good trip?" he asked, glancing down as he guided her along.

"It was fine." And she had to admit that there was something fine about being met like this, something that went beyond mere convenience. New York was New York, always a little intimidating. Ross's protectiveness felt good, though she wasn't about to tell him that. "Where are we going?" she asked when he hustled her to a cab, then gave the driver the same Park Avenue address to which she had sent her check.

"I thought you'd like to see Hansen's corporate headquarters. The team working on the Rye Beach Complex won't be meeting until tomorrow, but you might feel more comfortable seeing the layout before you get bogged down in work. I have things to take care of while we're there."

Indeed, he seemed all business. There was no welcome kiss, no hug, not even in the privacy of the cab, and she wasn't complaining. She had felt a jolt seeing him back at the train, and felt tingles even now. She needed all the time she could get to regain full control.

The Hansen Corporation was every bit as impressive as she had known it would be. Ross Stephenson wasn't one to do things halfway. As she toured offices that consumed three full floors, no one she saw was idle.

Her guide was one of the vice presidents, a soft-spoken man whom she instantly liked. Ross himself had disappeared with a soft apology shortly after they arrived. She saw nothing of him until late afternoon, when he materialized in the drafting room, where she was admiring the architect's plans for a museum and theater complex in Des Moines.

"What do you think?"

Delight lit her face. "It's wonderful, Ross. You have a brilliant architect. From the looks of the plans, this museum will be a drawing card for all of Iowa."

His smile held satisfaction. "That's what we're hoping. Any suggestions?"

She grinned. "You mean, will I now go on and pick the thing to bits on the geological score?"

"Something like that."

"I have no way of knowing about this particular project. Looking at the designs, I can mention potential sources of worry—drain pipes, for instance—but unless I know something about the land there, I can't offer constructive criticism."

When Ross put his lips by her ear, she realized that it was the nearest he'd come since she arrived. The warmth of his skin by her cheek sent a tingle through her. "Thank God for that," he said in a stage whisper, though they were alone in the room. He straightened. "The day's pretty much over. Let's get going."

Chloe gathered her things. It had been an unexpectedly pleasant and interesting afternoon. If each of her days here were like it, she might survive after all.

But something hung heavy in a half-hidden corner of her mind. It had New Orleans written all over it. After New York, there would be Rhode Island, then Alabama. Should she do New Orleans after that? Would it solve anything? Would it change her feelings for Ross?

No doubt, she did love him. Walking down a long corridor with him now, she felt like a princess. He ruled the place, but he was gentle and caring. He loved her. Was she worthy of that?

They were silent during the cab ride to Ross's brownstone. "You'll be staying here," he told her calmly, breaking what was almost a truce.

"Ohhhh, no," she balked, but followed him out of the cab. "I'll go to a hotel. The city is full of them. You can go inside and make a call to book the room that should have been booked on Monday."

Ross led her up the front stairs to the tall oak door, turned the key in the lock, and let them in. Once inside the gracious hall, he took her coat. "There are three floors here. I sleep on the second. You can have the third all to yourself. I'm not suggesting that you sleep with me, only that you stay here. It'll be more convenient."

Chloe recalled what he had said on the phone about needing her near him. Separate bedrooms? On separate floors?

Remembering Rye Beach and feeling suddenly lighter, she said, "Okay. I'll take the penthouse." She had taken the penthouse in Rye Beach, too. They shared that past, and a grin of remembrance now.

"Come," he said warmly. "I'll show you around."

From first to second to third floor they went, examining furniture, art-work, and memorabilia from his travels. No room in the house would have won a designer's award, yet every room had a warmth that reached out to Chloe and made her feel at home.

Ross, too, made her feel at home. He put no pressure on her, so she put none on herself. They ate at a nearby restaurant, then returned for a quiet evening of reading. When Chloe excused herself shortly after eleven, he bid her good night with a noticeable lack of lechery.

"You'll find an extra blanket in the closet. If you want more towels check the cupboard in the bathroom." He looked up from his papers, but didn't rise.

"I'll be fine." She smiled. "Good night."

"Good night. Sleep well."

One glance back as she left the room told her that he had returned to his papers. She took the stairs slowly, one flight to the next. This was a side of Ross she had never seen. In the past their relationship had been shaped by physical attraction. Now Ross seemed either immune, or holding his interest in check.

Whichever, she was grateful. Living with him, working with him could have been a nightmare. As it was, she was aware of the fact that he would be sleeping one short flight away. More than once that night she held her breath, hearing a sound, wondering if he was making the climb.

Her bedroom door remained closed, and when she fell asleep, she slept well.

It was good. Thursday and Friday were packed with work, long hours spent huddled with the masterminds of the Rye Beach Complex. They were amenable to her suggestions, often mildly questioning, sometimes strongly doubting, but always ready to listen. Ross was absent during most of the work, dropping in to check on the progress, but otherwise yielding to the men beneath him.

Chloe asked him about it Friday evening. "I thought you'd be more comfortable if I kept my distance at the office," he said.

"But aren't you concerned about the project? For all you know the revised plans may be unacceptable to you personally."

"I doubt that," he replied, smiling comfortably. "I trust you. And I trust the men you're working with. They know what I want." He paused, eyes changing, voice lowering. "So do you."

Her throat grew tight. It was the first thing he had done that was at all suggestive. For that reason, she indulged him the lapse. And because the lapse was brief, she let him bribe her to stay in New York until Sunday with a pair of choice tickets to the Big Apple's newest hit musical.

"How did you ever get seats?" she asked in excitement, reaching for the telltale envelope. Ross only raised it much higher, out of reach.

"I have ways." He laughed. "You haven't seen it, have you?"

"You know I haven't! It only opened last week, and you've known every one of my comings and goings since then."

He smiled smugly and changed the subject, but Chloe easily acclimated herself to a Sunday return to Rhode Island. When he announced that he had work to do at the office on Saturday morning, she binged on Fifth Avenue, treating herself to a new dress, shoes, and a purse. Again, though, there was that dark tugging at the back of her mind. The outfit was for New Orleans. If she went, she wanted her parents to be proud. *If* she went.

Saturday afternoon was something else. Had she planned a few hours in the city, they couldn't have been as exciting as the ones Ross planned. From museum to park to ice cream parlor and back, it was a dream time. He was intellectually stimulating and wonderfully adventurous, even-tempered to a fault.

He appeared to be surviving abstinence with no problem but a tic in his jaw. She noticed it when they were the closest—standing side by side before a Calder mobile at the Guggenheim, walking hip to hip through the squeeze of the crowd at Rockefeller Center, sitting knee to knee at a small table in a quiet restaurant.

At least, she wanted to think the tic was from that. She wanted to think he was feeling the strain, because she certainly was. His hands-off policy made working easier, but it did nothing for the desire she felt. It grew through all of Saturday, all of Saturday evening, all of Saturday night. By the time they returned from the theater in the early hours of Sunday morning it was near to bursting.

She took his lead and put it on ice. In the living room for a nightcap, their conversation was as soft and pleasing as the entire four-day stretch had been. She felt happy. Then she went upstairs, alone, to the bedroom that had been lonely all week, and the ice melted. She dozed and woke, shifting in bed with little hope of relief from frustration. She tried to think of other things, but Ross kept her restless and aching. It was dawn when she finally crept from bed and went to the window.

The city was rising. The deep purples and blues of night were beginning to fade to lighter hues. The tallest of the skyscrapers to the east wore the first pink traces of the sun on its uppermost windows. It was lovely and peaceful. Only the dull ache inside her marred it.

"I couldn't sleep," came a voice at the door. She turned to find Ross standing there. Standing tall, his features hidden in the shadows, he wore a robe that wrapped at the waist and hung to his knees. The unruly rumpling of his hair gave truth to his words. "How 'bout you?"

Her throat was tight. "The same."

She watched him slowly approach. Each step brought him closer to the window, until his features were clear in it. Though his eyes reflected her own torment, he touched her cheek with a tenderness that made her want to weep. She couldn't pull away. She was desperate for his love.

If there were germs of reason floating around, they vanished with his first kiss. What remained was a hunger that had been days in building. Chloe gave herself up to it without a thought.

Ross touched her everywhere, caressing her through the thin lavender gown, and she touched him right back. But his robe was thick, and she grew impatient. The robe was easily opened and his body bared. She touched him then, bringing low sounds from his throat, and the feeling of power was heady. He began to shake under her stroking. His penis grew thick and engorged.

Moments later, her gown fell to the ground with his robe. His mouth ate at hers, as he lifted her and carried her to the bed. The weight of his body pinned her to the sheets, but there was no pain in it for Chloe. She welcomed his force, wanting even more.

"Yes!" she cried, clutching at his hips to pull him closer.

But Ross tensed at the sound of her voice. He was breathing hard, pressing his forehead to the pillow by her ear. She felt him rock hard and large against her, but he didn't enter.

"I swore I wouldn't do this," he whispered hoarsely, "swore I'd keep my hands off you. I've tried. God knows, I've tried!"

When he raised himself to look at her, his expression shocked her into awareness. "Don't go!" she cried.

"I have to. For this one release, I'd be buying a huge packet of pain."

"No!" Her fingers tightened on his shoulders until her knuckles turned white. She was close to panic. "Please, Ross. I've never asked you for anything else. But please . . . now . . . I can't bear it!"

The impetus was hers, lips and arms and hips all working against him until he surrendered with a moan. Falling to the bed and rolling to his back, he drew her over him, and she loved him that way. She couldn't say the words he wanted to hear, but her body could show him what she felt.

It did that, and quite well. By the time the sun's golden rays breached the windowsill and glistened on their sweat, they were totally spent.

Rasping breaths broke the air, but otherwise, all was quiet. Something was wrong. Chloe felt it the instant her pulse began to slow. There was no talk. No closeness. The satisfaction that usually kept them warm and entwined faded fast.

Ross rose from the bed, retrieved his robe, and left the room. Alone again, Chloe curled into a tight ball with the covers pulled to her ears.

Apparently, it was time to put up or shut up. Ross couldn't live with half-measures—but then, had she really thought he would? Her body might love him to bits, but if she couldn't love the rest with her head and her heart, there was no hope.

She heard the front door slam shortly after he left her room. She didn't know where he went, and he was back in time to take her to the train station, but even the short ride there was awkward. It wasn't until she was about to board the train that he said more than a full sentence, and then his voice was quiet.

"I'd like to follow through with the liaison between Hansen and ESE, but I think Lee should handle the account. You're right. It'll be too difficult any other way, at least for now."

Chloe wanted to argue, but no words came out.

His eyes held defeat when he looked at her a final time. "I'll be here, Chloe. When you're free, let me know."

On the Saturday after Thanksgiving, Chloe boarded a plane. It taxied and took off, then climbed into the sky and headed north. New Orleans fell behind. New York was ahead. She was going back to Ross.

She tried to sleep, but was too excited. She ate dinner, she read a magazine, she looked out the window and smiled. Where a haunted woman had been just a few days before, was one with a newborn peace.

She had come a very long way in a very short time, but it hadn't been easy. There were dozens of doubts and second thoughts dogging her through Mobile, and added days spent wavering there, then fear and unsureness when she arrived at her parents' home in New Orleans on Thanksgiving morning.

Now, as the plane began its descent, she shook her head in amazement. So many years lost over a misunderstanding. But it was cleared up now. It was better. She would call Ross the minute she landed. He would be totally surprised.

But she was the one in for the surprise. Ross was at the airport to meet her, standing tall and dark and vibrant. In a moment of déjà vu, their eyes met over the crowd. Chloe stopped in awe, knowing that her next steps would be as momentous as the ones she had taken eleven years ago. But she was a woman now and finally free to love. Breathing deeply, she ran forward.

Ross met her halfway and crushed her in his arms, holding her tightly enough, long enough to say what he felt without words.

Chloe owed him the words, though. When she drew back to look up at him, her throat was constricted by the same emotion that brought tears to her eyes. A mouthed "I love you" was the best she could do. It was enough.

His face lightened. His eyes glowed. "Let's go home," he said, and, arm in arm, they did just that.

A short time later, they were in Ross's living room, sitting on the sofa, facing one another. He held her hand tightly, while she tried to put into words everything she had learned in New Orleans.

"It was a tragic comedy of errors," she began. "I had blamed myself for going with you and upsetting Crystal, even for tossing that coin, and I felt so guilty when she died that I withdrew into myself. When my parents couldn't get through to me, they sent me to stay with friends in Newport in the hope that the change of scenery would do me good. I thought that they just didn't want me around to remind them of what had happened, so I stayed away. One misunderstanding after another."

"But it's over?" he asked, so obviously needing reassurance that she lifted a hand to his cheek and kissed him.

"Yes," she breathed. "It's over. I was really worried about my mother for a while there. When she learned what I'd thought all these years, she was beside herself with grief. We spent that whole first night talking, just the two of us." She grew pensive. "I'd never had her all to myself before. There were always the three of us. But Mom was great, even as upset as she was. She explained so many things to me. It helped."

She looked again at Ross. His eyes were warm with understanding, urging her on.

"She talked about having twins, about watching them grow, about knowing their similarities and their differences. She pointed out that if the tables had been turned, and Crystal had had the affair, I'd have reacted differently. In other words," she sighed, sad but hopeful, "Crystal's reaction was part of her personality, just as the guilt I've lived with all these years is part of mine."

"Is?" Ross asked softly.

"Was," she corrected herself, looking directly at him. He couldn't miss the pleading in her gaze. "I'd like to put it behind me now. Will you help?"

Her pulse tripped for a minute until Ross's wide smile sent it racing on. "That's why I'm here."

She frowned. "Why are you here? I mean, how did you know to be at the airport?"

"Your parents."

"You talked with them?"

"Yesterday." He looked pleased with himself. "You were overdue in Little Compton. Lee called me, we plotted your course, and put two and two together. When I realized you'd gone home I knew why. It was all I could do not to join you there. But it was something you had to do, wasn't it?"

She nodded. "I told them about you."

"Lucky you did. It made the explanations simpler." He paused, vaguely playful, vaguely curious. "What, uh, exactly, did you tell them?"

"That you loved me, that I loved you, that you'd asked me to marry you. But I also told them that I had to work things out there with them, to finally accept Crystal's death, if I ever hoped to be as much of a woman as you deserve."

At the last, all playfulness drained from Ross's face, leaving a vulnerability that was the flip side of his usual strength. His hand trembled slightly when it cupped her face. "Have I told you how much I love you?" he whispered, kissing her eyes, nose, and mouth in turn.

"You'll have forever to tell me," she whispered back.

"Then you'll marry me?"

"Uh-huh."

"Ahhhhh." With the long sigh, he hugged her again. His breath was warm against her ear.

"Tired?"

His neck smelled of him. She shook her head against it. "Nope."

"You're sure?" He tightened an arm around her waist. "It was a long flight."

"I'm not tired." She grinned. "I don't think I'll sleep for hours."

Ross rose from the sofa and held out a hand. Chloe put hers in it and let him draw her up and into his arms.

"I love you, Ross. You know that, don't you?"

"I have for a long time. I'm only glad you can finally say it. You're free, aren't you, princess?"

She sighed, then smiled and said with a touch, just a touch of New Orleans, "I do believe I am."

He laughed out loud and rolled his eyes. Keeping an arm around her to hold her close, he walked her to the stairs and up.

Lilac Awakening

In memory of my father,
who gave me an eye for detail.

1

Nightfall was nature's last resort in a bid to blot out her own splendor. For much of the afternoon across the upper Vermont countryside, ominous dark clouds had hung over the forested peaks, swarming, breaking, and regrouping in a macabre arabesque. Rather than stifling beauty, they enhanced it with a muted gray softness, sifted over the deep greens of the hillside. The power of the land was an awesome one, embodied in the proud posture of the pines on the hill, the free flow of the river winding through the valley, the gaiety of the orange Indian paintbrush swaying with meadow grass in the breeze. Darkness was only a thin veil over this primal beauty. Seeing through it, Anne Boulton felt blessed, and doubly grateful that she had left the city.

The summer had been an oppressive one in New York. Heat and humidity had rivaled each other, stubbornly clinging to highs that beaded foreheads and furniture with sweat, and made everyone and everything sticky. As the skyscrapered congestion closed in on her, so had well-intending friends and family, coaxing her out to lunch, when she wanted a tall cola and a salad at home, dragging her to the theater, when she craved a quiet evening alone, spiriting her away for a weekend of busy companionship, when she fancied a good book and healing solitude. In the end she wanted Jeff, but Jeff was gone.

Now, cocooned by darkness, she curled in a large upholstered chair. The wood fire in the hearth offered the only light, its orange and gold flames flickering hypnotically before her dark eyes. This was her first evening here. If the isolation, the peace were a harbinger, she had made the right decision in renting the house for the week. Time was precious, but it abounded here. She planned to read, to take walks, even to work. Mostly, though, she planned to think.

Late September in Vermont was the perfect time for soul-searching. With promises of misty mornings and golden afternoons, newly ripening apples and sweet corn, deer and squirrels and crisp mountain air, it was a perfect antidote for her malaise. The small house on its high perch was everything the rental agent had promised. No matter that her small car had nearly come apart jolting over bumps and ruts in the steadily climbing dirt road, the house was charming. It sat peacefully in the arms of giant maples and towering firs, its brown weathered shingles and silver slate roof blending with the earthen road and the gray of the sky. Low shrubbery, aged a fall green, bordered the house. Taller lilac bushes, their fragrant blossoms long gone but imagined, straddled the ebony front door.

Inside, the cottage was as compact as its surroundings were generous, with an open-hearthed living room at the front, a kitchen, bedroom, and bath at the rear. A narrow stairway on the far side led to a dormered attic. Decorated functionally and comfortably, the whole was a far cry from her elegant New York apartment, but the difference pleased her. This was a neutral spot, a place of few luxuries and no memories, a place where she could face life for the pleasure of the day.

And this had been a tiring one. Its morning had been filled with last-minute errands—to the bank for money, to the library and the bookstore for the week's entertainment, to the university for a delivery and a pickup, to the market for food. Its afternoon had been one of steady driving, then storing groceries and unpacking bags.

The fireplace had beckoned. Anne was bone-weary, had been lacking in stamina for weeks. As the wing-backed chair held her slim form, the dancing flames lulled her into recollection of a dinner with her parents the weekend before.

"I don't understand," her mother had tried to reason with her, "why you have to take off all by yourself. We've tried so hard to do what's best. Have we failed?"

Anxious to ease her mother's worry, Anne had forced a smile. "No, you didn't fail. I just want to get out of the city for a while. You know, get a little of that fresh-air-and-color-on-my-cheeks type of thing?"

"Well, you could certainly use that," came her father's deep voice. Tall and distinguished-looking, Anthony Faulke's sturdy frame belied his near-sixty years. Anne took the darkness of her hair and eyes from him, though her willowed shapeliness was her mother's. "But we'd have liked to have you join us on the shore in several weeks. Won't you reconsider and wait until then?"

Anne shook her head. Not a hair moved. It was in a somber knot at the nape of her neck. "Now's the time. I've already made the arrangements and paid for the place."

Her mother tried again. "But you've never enjoyed traveling alone. Wouldn't it be better to have someone with you? If I didn't have the charity luncheon on Wednesday, I'd go with you myself. You need company, Anne."

Anne hated worrying her parents. They had suffered nearly as much as she had, having to stand by and watch helplessly as their elder daughter's life fell apart. When they looked at her, Anne knew what they saw. She saw it in the mirror each morning, the pallor in an oval face framed by pitch-black hair.

Still, she said, "I really have no choice, have I, Mother? I've been more fortunate than others, always having someone to be with. When it wasn't you and Dad, it was Peggy, then my roommates at college, then Jeff." Her voice caught on his name. She had long-since cried herself out, but that little break in her breath remained.

Marjorie Faulke grasped at straws. "Call Peggy. She won't be starting classes for another few weeks. She'll make the trip with you."

But Anne shook her head. "No, Mom. Peggy's terrific. For a sister, I couldn't ask for finer. But she has her own life, her own friends. It's not her job to baby-sit me. And I'd really prefer to be alone." Her voice hardened. "I'd better get used to it, don't you think?" Oh, yes, there was anger. Its only cure was through the courts, but it would be months more before things were resolved there.

A silence had hung over the intimate round table, its elegant place settings and fine food forgotten. This had become a pattern, this family gathering turned wake, but it had to be broken. Anne had to start to live again. The trip to Vermont was a first step.

As the full blaze in the fireplace settled to a more sedate crackle, the patter of raindrops broke through Anne's reverie. Stretching her legs, she stood, smoothed out her jeans, and padded barefoot to the front window. The darkness was dense. Staring out through rain-spattered panes, she was grateful that she had shut the car windows and locked the door. The idea of going outside to do it now didn't appeal to her. As she stood, hands by her sides, eyes straight ahead, she could see nothing but the black of night and her own grim reflection.

She didn't need friends to tell her that she looked gaunt and spectral. Her cheeks were pale, hollowed by a weight loss that had cut into gentle curves all over her body. Her mouth was more often drawn thin and straight now, rather than curved in a smile. Dark eyes that had once danced with happiness, now spoke of loneliness, and her hair didn't swing. It fit her mood, which was restrained. Even now she had it tied back with a thin strip of black velvet whose ends were lost in the ribbing of her black turtleneck sweater.

This, too—this ghostly appearance—would have to change if she planned to start a new life.

She had been paralyzed for weeks after the previous January's debacle. The thought of a future without Jeff was still alien. They had been married for seven years, though it had seemed forever. Anne was a sophomore in college, a language major, when she had met him during a summer of study in France. He was one of the few Americans she had seen during her three-month stay with a family in a small village west of Limoges. His means of transportation had been a bicycle, his means of communication a brilliant smile, until he discovered she spoke English. From then on they were inseparable. He revised his touring plans to accommodate her, and when they returned to the States at the end of August, friendship became courtship. He was also from New York, his family home an hour's drive from her own. By January she had transferred to his midwestern university; they were married the following summer. Only two years apart in age, they grew up together, passing through the college years of flux and idealism with hours of carefree camaraderie and first love. Both had come from hard-working, upwardly mobile families that helped them financially until they were on their own feet. But money hadn't mattered, even when Jeff became a successful investment consultant. What mattered had always been Jeff and Anne, Anne and Jeff. Then, abruptly, it was Anne, alone.

When the stupor finally began to wear off, she took stock of her assets. She had a home—a spacious, well-furnished, stylishly decorated condo. She had money enough to live in it comfortably, with leftover to invest. She had friends. She had family. She had her own car, one not as sporty as Jeff's Audi, but small, reliable, and gas efficient. And she had her work.

Fluent in French and Spanish, Anne worked as a freelance interpreter through most of her marriage. At first they had needed the money, later not so, but she enjoyed her work, and with nothing to keep her at home, it filled the hours when Jeff was at the office. When they planned a trip, she took on less work. When Jeff had a business trip, she took on more and was busy until he returned.

More than once during those long, morbid months, she had wondered what would have been if she had been with him on that last, fateful trip. They might have been together still.

But they weren't. She was alone.

Gradually she took on more work, branching off into textbook translation for local universities. As opposed to interpreting, where she had to be personally on the spot at a given time on a given day, there was more flexibility in translation. Once the material had been picked up, she could tackle the job on her own schedule, in the comfort and privacy of her apartment.

The work was plentiful. She could pick and choose. Between her availability, her competence, and her promptness, she was in demand.

On occasion, she met overeager professors, even some young and attractive ones who were aware of her situation. She remained courteous and professionally efficient, but she refused to date them. It disturbed her, even angered her, that men thought she would want to date so soon.

Memories of Jeff were too near, too vivid, too dear. Those memories would eventually settle in, she knew, and she might date then. For now, though, she'd had enough of love and pain.

This trip was good in that sense, too. It gave her excuses to avoid dating. Between getting ready to leave with a million errands to do, being physically out of state for the week, and eventually returning to a huge pile of work, she was safe. She didn't have to worry about men in the backwoods of Vermont. She was hoping she wouldn't see anyone in the week she was here.

Pretty reclusive for a former socializer, she mused without a hint of remorse.

From the hearth, the sudden crumbling of an ash-split log startled her. She whirled from the window, eyes wide in alarm. When she realized what the sound was, she took a breath and uncurled fingers from fists. After months of being bitten to the quick, her nails had grown into nicely tapered tips. And there was her wedding band, wide and gold, gleaming with deceptive brightness, on the third finger of her left hand.

When the fire spoke again, cackling for a feeding, she knelt before the warm stone. Taking a piece of dried birch from the large wood basket, she laid it over the broken embers. The log heated, then burst into flame. It was an omen, she vowed, as she picked up her book from the floor by her chair. Slipping large tortoiseshell glasses over the bridge of her nose, she settled back between the chair's wide wings. They were a comfort, these wings, serving to keep her sights on the fire before her, rather than on the darkness behind.

Her ticket to freedom lay in her lap. Ever an avid reader, Anne had escaped into books in recent months, when all else failed to calm her. As a friend, a book had advantages over the human variety. It was there whenever she needed it, it vanished as easily, and it never asked questions, expected witty replies, made awkward suggestions, or otherwise overcompensated for its own inability to right the wrongs of the world. She had packed a friend-a-day supply for this trip. That was all the company she needed.

The hardcover in her hand was a biography. She opened it now, and was suddenly caught up in the same world she was trying to flee. On the inside cover of the volume was an inscription that she hadn't noticed earlier. It brought back a storm of memories.

"To my favorite sister-in-law. Have a marvelous vacation and be sure to spend a week with us when you get back. MaryEllen."

From the first, Jeff's family had adored her. They had always insisted that they would hold Jeff personally to blame if the marriage ended. In that spirit, they had stayed so close to Anne's side that she had to finally beg them for space. They had eased off, but with reluctance.

Anne's parents had persisted, urging her to give up the apartment and move back home, but she refused. She knew that as crammed with reminders of Jeff as the apartment was, it was better than the Westchester home where she had grown up. To return there would be an admission of failure—failure to make the kind of happy life her parents had.

A ghost of a smile lifted the corners of her lips. Her childhood had been happy indeed, even those awkward adolescent years when she was an ugly duckling, by modest accounts. Oh, her parents denied it, but the mirror didn't lie, and, anyway, the ugly duckling became a swan well before the Senior Prom. By that time she was quiet and graceful, thriving academically, socially, and emotionally. Nothing in her rosy first twenty-seven years had even remotely begun to prepare her for the heartbreak at the start of her twenty-eighth.

Brought back to the present by a pang of hunger, she closed the untouched book and went to the kitchen. She flipped on a single light, mixed tuna into a salad, put a pot of coffee on to perk, and toasted rye bread. With the sandwich plate in one hand and a coffee mug in the other, she retraced her steps, flipping the light off with a nudge of the elbow.

Her hunger surprised her. Unusual for her, she finished the sandwich. Revived, she sat back in the chair, the mug warming her hands as the fire warmed her feet, and it suddenly struck her that she was beginning to feel. It had been months since she had smelled coffee brewing or felt the barefoot plushness of a carpet. But the coffee did smell good. Same with the burning logs and the pines outside, and her feet did feel, albeit smooth-sanded oak planks rather than the thick carpeting of home.

Pushing the glasses up on her nose, she stared at the biography, but it wasn't a biography kind of night. Jumping up, she returned to her room for a replacement. Mystery or romance—the choice was easy. A romance might appeal to her later in the week, when she was feeling stronger. She took the mystery and set off.

The addition of several logs brightened the blaze in the hearth. Edging her chair closer, she read from its light, and the book drew her in. Within a chapter, she was the heroine. She was only marginally aware that the rain was coming harder, beating with increased force against rooftop, windowpane, and clapboard. It was a fitting backdrop for the story of a young woman stranded in the deep woods in a cabin not unlike her own. Anne felt a quick qualm at the comparison, debated switching to the romance after all, but was inexorably drawn back to the tightly written piece. Burrowing deeper into the chair, she gave herself up to the plot.

She read for two hours, pausing only for more coffee. The gold watch on her wrist read eleven, but she was wide awake, stimulated by caffeine, her new surroundings, and the riveting edge of the story. As Chapter Four became Five and then Six, the mystery deepened. Accidents were neither accident nor coincidence. Someone was after the heroine. No, something was after her, or so it appeared from the bizarre markings left by footprints, paw prints, or whatever in the winter snow. Terror slowly mounted. The woman was trapped, hunted, doomed. As Chapter Seven ended and Eight began, she hatched her escape plan against seemingly insurmountable odds. Then, complicating an already desperate situation, came the blizzard. Gale force winds, blinding snows, chilling temperatures conspired to keep her at the mercy of the wild beast that stalked her.

With a thud, Anne put the book facedown onto her lap, heart pounding in vicarious fright. *Mystery, my foot,* she mused with regret, *this book is sheer horror!* It wouldn't have been so bad if she'd picked it up last night or last week in New York. Here, though, she was alone, isolated from the familiar, a good three miles from a shred of civilization.

Spooked, it took her a minute to realize that what she'd assumed to be the thundering of her pulse was the thunder outside. Lightning followed quickly, brightening the dark side of the room for a shocking instant, its blue-white gleam icy in comparison to the warm orange glow of the fire.

Hastily she added several more logs, desperately needing to put the book down, desperately needing to read on, knowing that she wouldn't be able to sleep until the last page had been turned and the mystery solved. She raised the book again to another deafening clap of thunder. It vibrated through the house along with tongued bolts of lightening.

Anne's nerves prickled then, because, in the thunder's wake came another noise. This one was more human and threatening. A car was approaching, coming nearer, loud enough to be heard above the storm. It reached her front door and stopped.

Huddled in the chair, she held her breath. It was twelve thirty-five, well past normal calling hours even in the city. Perhaps one of the villagers wanted to warn her about the storm. Perhaps someone was lost. Perhaps . . . perhaps . . .

A furious pounding came at the door. Had it been a gentle knock, Anne might have dared answer it. But this knock was angry, clearly no neighbor expressing concern. At least the door was locked, though she wished fervently for the dead bolt she had in New York.

"Open up! It's wet out here!" The voice was deep, gruff, and angry. "Open the damn door!"

Anne didn't budge. This was her cottage for the week, and she had the papers to prove it. She didn't have to open the door.

But the banging went on, hard knuckles on wood. "Come on, whoever you are, open the door! I'm getting soaked and I can't reach my key."

His key? Was this a common visiting place? Had the realtor forgotten to tell her something?

Feeling vaguely guilty at being warm and dry while someone was out there wet and cold, she approached the door. "Who is it?" she yelled, resting her forehead against the smooth oak.

"It's Mitch, dammit. Open up!" An impatient hand jiggled the doorknob from the outside.

"I don't know any Mitch," she shouted over the storm. "What do you want?"

What came back was a menacing growl. "I want to get dry. For God's sake, open up. I do have a key, but if I have to put these bags down to get it, I'll be madder'n hell when I get in there!"

Assuming she could believe him, he had a point. If he did have a key and would eventually open the door whether she liked it or not, she could save him the effort and spare herself his anger. Cautious, she reached for the knob. She opened the door a few inches, leaving her weight against the wood in case she didn't like what she saw.

Without warning, a heavier weight thrust it full open, throwing her back into the room. Startled by the unexpected force and cursing herself for her naïveté, Anne lost her balance and tripped, falling backward onto her bottom with a thud. From that vantage point she watched, wide-eyed, as a huge man entered, savagely dripping water. He tossed in several large bags before slamming the door shut and leaning against it.

The fire had begun to die, leaving only the faintest glow to light his face, but it was enough to show a tight jaw, sneering lips, and eyes that impaled her.

"You bitch! What took you so long? Why didn't you open the door? Can't you see what the weather is like? And who sent you anyway? Was it Joe?" Narrowed eyes gave her an insolent once-over. "No, it must have been Lennie. He goes in for the plain, scrawny type."

Anne was dumbstruck by the sudden turn of events.

"What?" he went on. "No denials? No coy protestations?" He unbuttoned his heavy wool jacket, shrugged it off, and tossed it onto an empty chair. Even without its bulk, with only snug denims and a dark turtleneck, he was imposing.

To her horror, he advanced until he towered directly over her. "Well? Don't you have anything to say? Or are you just going to lie there, all helpless and inviting?"

Anne found her tongue. "You shouldn't be here. Get out!"

A coarse laugh filtered through the sounds of the storm. "Ah, having second thoughts, are you? Reneging on your little deal so fast?"

Anne slid backward on the floor. "I think there's been a misunderstanding."

"Right in one! I don't know who you are, but I don't want you or any other woman up here. So"—he lowered his voice but failed to relax his jaw—"I'd suggest you pick up your little carcass and get out."

Anne was incredulous. "I will not." Her eyes didn't leave his for a second, though she inched farther away.

Suddenly he was crouched before her, steel-muscled shins imprisoning hers and making movement impossible. "What did you say?"

Willing a strength she didn't feel, Anne held his gaze. "I said that I wouldn't leave. I'm here for the week. If anyone is leaving, it's you. Now!" She practically shrieked the last. Between frustration and fear, she was losing composure.

But her order had the opposite effect. The man moved forward, resting his weight on his right hand, on the hard floor inches from her hip. "So this is a new kind of game," he taunted.

"I don't know what you're talking about," she said, but her voice fell to a whisper when his face came closer. "This is no game."

Lit by the pale orange cast of the fire, his lips were firm and grinning wryly. His eyes narrowed again, homing in now on her mouth, which quivered. She couldn't move. Terror rose up from the pit of her stomach.

"No game?" he echoed as she struggled to pull herself free of his leghold. With the grace of an athlete and the power of a lion, he stretched fully over her, flattening her onto the cold floor.

Panic hit then. "Let go! Get off me!" Futilely she pushed against him, but his body weight was awesome, stealing her breath. Gasping for air, she continued to push as his mouth lowered. "No!" she cried and wrenched her head to the side.

He brought it back with a firm hand. "No game, you say? We'll see about that." His lips seized hers with a steadiness that held her head flush against the oak planks. Startling in intensity, relentless in duration, his kiss had an animalism that was primitive and raw.

She fought desperately, writhing beneath him until one large hand seized both of hers and pinned them to the floor above her head. Only then did his lips finally release hers.

Fighting tears, she gasped for breath, and all the while he studied her. When he finally spoke, he was calm and cynical. "Tears? That's not part of the game plan." In an effort to raise himself, his hand tightened on hers, forcing them to bear the brunt of his weight. She cried out in pain when her wedding band dug in.

He freed her quickly then, and sat back on his haunches. She recoiled, crawling backward until she hit a wall, then jumping to her feet and racing to the hearth. She grabbed the only weapon in sight, a heavy iron poker.

"Don't come near me," she warned in a high-pitched whine.

Her threat reached its mark. He didn't move a muscle.

Silence hung heavy in the air. Even the rain had eased to a gentle pat-ter on the roof. The storm was ending. But what was she to do now? As the gravity of her predicament settled in, a fit of trembling shook her with such force that the poker waved precariously.

Appearing to sense her terror, the man rose slowly, palms open and out from his sides. "Take it easy. I won't hurt you."

"You already have." She raised the poker higher.

"Put that thing down," he ordered, but gently, all anger gone now. "You're apt to hurt yourself."

She shook her head and held the poker at the ready.

"Look." He sighed, running his fingers through the damp hair that had fallen across his forehead. "Let me turn on a light. At least then I can see what manner of woman has the upper hand on me."

She eased up on her stance. Light would help her, too.

He crossed to the nearest lamp and turned it on. It bathed the room a warm yellow. "That's better," he said and turned to face her.

Anne took a good look at her would-be assailant. He was tall and rugged, thinner than she had first suspected, though the breadth of his chest and shoulders spoke of strength. His sweater was black, his jeans faded, though darkened by rain at the hem, where they fell over sodden brown leather boots.

She had expected a dark and glowering face. What she saw were fea-tures that were strong but kind, skin that was clear and only faintly tanned, hair that was thick and blond, turning silver, in damp waves.

There was an underlying gentleness. But his lips were stern, his cheeks lean, his jaw set. And eyes that were silvery hazel stared at her without a blink.

"If you've finished," he said with a mocking twitch of his lips, "would you please put down that poker? You can see I'm not a thug,"

She lifted the weapon higher. "How about a rapist?" She wasn't being deceived by a sweet-talking, good-looking man.

A muscle flexed in his jaw. "I'm no rapist. I wouldn't have forced you into anything. Especially once I saw that wedding band. I don't fool around with married women."

Tears threatened again. How bittersweet that the symbol of a marriage that had ended should save her from the unspeakable. So she had Jeff to thank still.

"Who are you?" she asked in a quavering voice.

"You really don't know? Come on, you're holding all the cards. You can confess."

Her voice came stronger. "Who are you?"

Still he persisted. "It was Lennie, wasn't it? He's been trying to set me up with a woman for weeks now!" His frustration sounded sincere.

"Who are you?"

With a sigh of defeat, he thrust a hand in his pocket. "Mitch."

But she knew that already. "Where are you from?"

"New York."

"You just drove up from there?"

"Yes."

"Why?"

He shot her a surprised look. "Why what? Why did I just drive up, or why am I here?"

"Both." As Anne's pulse steadied, she lowered the poker.

"I just got here because I had a late meeting this afternoon and couldn't leave the city until it was done. I'm here because I need a week's rest, free of all human contact. All human contact."

"Why are you here?"

"I just told you."

"But, why here, in this house?" She was beginning to think straight. He didn't look like a thug. And he could have taken advantage of her when he was on top, but he hadn't.

He rubbed the back of his neck, much as she had when she'd first arrived. "I come here often. And I'm sure I booked the weekend with Miles."

So he did know the realtor. He deserved credit for that.

She relaxed her grip on the poker. "It looks like good old Miles made a mistake." Thinking about it, she frowned. Her eyes fell. Absently she ran a faintly shaky finger over the lip he had bruised.

In a single deft move, he had the poker out of her hands before she knew he was there. In that instant, terror returned. She had been duped.

"All right, ma'am. Now you answer my questions," he ordered.

When she tried to step back, he grabbed her shoulders and held her in place. The discrepancy of their heights appalled her. Even accounting for the fact that she had no shoes on, Mitch was nearly a foot taller.

"Who are you?" he asked with an air of command, even subtle threat.

She began to tremble again. "Anne."

"From . . . ?"

"New York."

"So"—a smile touched his mouth but went no further—"we're of the same stock."

"Hardly."

Her sharp gaze and clipped response erased his smile. "When did you arrive?"

She resented his questions. She had a rental agreement. This was her place. "I don't see that this—"

Hard fingers dug into her upper arms, stopping short of a shake. "When did you get here?"

"Early this evening."

"Why are you here? Both versions."

He had relaxed his grip on her shoulders, but she wanted out all the way. "Can I sit down? My legs are wobbly."

He held his hands out to the sides for an instant, then dropped them. The right went to his waist, the left to his pocket. "Be my guest. Sit."

She retreated to the wing-back chair and watched him add logs to the fire. He used his right hand. His left remained in his pocket. It struck her that he avoided using it.

He approached her again, tall and imposing. "Why did you come?"

She tipped her chin in defiance of his stance. "I'm here on vacation. I arranged it with Mr. Cooper and prepaid for the week."

"You have proof?"

"Of course."

"Let me see."

She scowled. "Why should I show you anything? You're the one who barged in here uninvited."

He leaned forward, resting his hand on the arm of her chair, bringing his lips infuriatingly close to her ear. "Get it," he demanded under his breath, then slowly straightened to let her pass.

Moments later she reappeared to find him studying the fire. He took the paper she offered and skimmed it.

"Looks authentic enough," he conceded. With a muttered, "That fool," he turned back to the fire.

"Where's your proof?" she challenged.

He clenched his jaw. "You'll have to take my word for it."

"No, thanks. I want proof. Or you can just take your things and leave. I didn't drive all the way up here to share a cabin with a man I don't know."

His mouth thinned to a grimace. "Looks like you're stuck with me, lady."

She was suddenly angry. "No way! I came up here to be alone, and that's what I plan to be. If there was a telephone, I'd call the local police to get you out, but there isn't one, and I don't relish the thought of driving out in this weather. So I'm asking you to leave like a gentleman."

He stared at the fire. "Who said that I was a gentleman?"

"I'll give you the benefit of the doubt. Now, do you leave, or do I . . ." Her voice trailed off. There was no alternative.

And, damn it, he knew it. Slowly, he turned toward her. "Or do you what?"

Frustrated by the situation, infuriated by his calm, she gave in to the need to shout. Loudly. "Look . . . Mitch . . . I don't know who's to blame for this fiasco, but I'd like you to leave. It's been a long day and I'm tired. There's obviously been a misunderstanding, but I have every intention of spending the week here, and I'm paying for that time right now. So, do you go?"

His expression was unchanged. "Tonight? No."

"What do you mean, no? You have no right to be here."

His voice was suddenly as loud as hers. "I have every right to be here, but that's between Miles Cooper and myself. Let's get one thing straight." His eyes darkened to a charcoal green. "I don't want you here any more than you want me here, but for tonight, at least, we're stuck with each other. We'll work something out in the morning."

"But you can't stay here tonight."

"Why not?"

"Because I'm here!"

"So?" His eyes were hazel again, calmer, strong.

A flush warmed her cheeks. "I thought I'd made it clear that I wasn't part of a conspiracy. Well, let me take it one step further." Her breathing faltered, but she let loose with what she'd been trying to tell the whole world for weeks. "I'm not interested in you, or any other man. Can you understand that?"

"I hear you. I'm not sure I believe you." Audacious eyes fell from her face to her neck to her breasts. Mockery faded when he looked at her wedding band. Frowning, he drew himself up straight. "I think I've had it. Good night." As he brushed past her, she grabbed his arm in alarm.

"Where are you going?"

"To bed." His words were blunt, his tone chilled.

"Oh, no, you're not."

He arched a brow. "Are you going to stop me?" Slowly he looked down at the white-knuckled hand on his arm.

She released him fast. "But you can't stay here!" He continued on toward his bags. Unable to think of a better course, she followed. "I said, you can't stay! There must be some place in the village."

Piling luggage under his right arm, he headed wordlessly for the stairs. Abruptly, he stopped, turning his head only enough to call over his shoulder, "I assume you're sleeping down here?"

She had no power, no power at all. "Yes, but you have to leave."

He turned to face her. His smile was polite, his eyes frosty, his voice cool. "I will in good time." Taking the stairs two at a time, an astounding feat, given his bulky burden, he disappeared into the attic, leaving her at a total loss for words.

2

Anne didn't budge. Her arms hung limp at her sides, her bare feet were flat on the floor, her eyes were glued to the attic door, which closed with a resounding bang. Even the faint sounds from within—the scrape of a chair leg, the creak of the mattress under one bag, the thud of another on the floor, the jangle of metal hangers on a wooden rod—failed to move her.

A crick in her neck finally brought her back to reality. Hands bracing her lower back, she rolled her head in a circular motion in an attempt to release tension.

Bizarre. Bizarre situation. A real-life drama in place of a fictional one, discarded now on the floor by the fire. But there wasn't a thing she could do. She could agonize over it for hours, but that fact wouldn't change.

Retreating to her bedroom, she closed the door tightly and propped a chair against the knob the way her heroine had done in Chapter Six, or thereabouts. Quickly, she slipped into a long flannel nightgown, pulled her hair from its knot, and took refuge under the bed's heavy quilts.

Despite the chair at the door, she wasn't frightened. Not really. Mitch's story irritated her, but it was believable enough. Or, rather, he was believable. There was something about him—his intelligent manner of speech, his clean appearance, his refined air—that spoke of breeding. Granted, he'd been pretty crude at the start. But even that could be explained away. He seemed neither malicious nor vengeful, only angry at the rental agent's error.

What to do? She had no choice but to sleep on the matter. Come morning, a solution would be found. It would have to be found. This was her week. She wasn't sharing it.

But sleep eluded her. She cursed the two cups of coffee that she'd had, the unfinished paperback, the creaking that came from the room above her. She finally fell into a restless sleep, only to be awoken at intervals by the creak of that bed. It was nearly dawn when she realized that she wasn't brooding about Jeff for a change. On that ironic note, and thoroughly worn out, she slept soundly.

What seemed only moments later, she was jolted awake by a thunderous noise in the kitchen. Livid, she bolted out of bed, whipped the chair from the door, and stormed toward the source of the racket.

"What, in God's name, was that noise?" she shouted, rounding the kitchen door in time to see Mitch picking up the first of a scattered mess of pots, pans, and metal utensils that covered the linoleum by the stove. He wore a navy velour robe that barely touched his knees, and was barefoot like her. And disheveled. And very, very cranky.

Shooting her a sidelong glare, he bellowed, "What kind of housekeeper are you, piling things in the cabinet like that? Did you really expect them to stay put once I opened the door? And where in the hell is the orange-juice press? My Lord, woman, get to it and clean up this mess!"

Friends who knew Anne to be easygoing, even-tempered, understanding, and accommodating would never have recognized the spitfire she suddenly became. It had been too long a day yesterday, too long a night last night, too disturbing an ordeal for months, for an ounce of poise to survive.

Dark eyes flashing, she confronted him. "You clean it up. I didn't make the mess, and I'm not your slave! It happens that I didn't touch that cabinet when I arrived. Put your blame on whomever you please, as long as it isn't on me! And what right do you have to wake me up? This is my vacation, or didn't you hear that last night?" Only a deaf man could have missed a word now. Goaded by his indignant stare, she ranted on. "This noise was enough to wake the dead. Not that I needed anything as loud as that to disturb me. Your twisting around up over my head all night was bad enough! Just because you have insomnia doesn't mean that I have to have it!"

His stare was chilling. "You wake up in a lovely mood, don't you? Very different from my usual women." He looked her over, head to toe. "That's quite an outfit, also different from my usual women."

Naturally, Anne had left her robe hanging in the closet. Whirling on her heel, hair flying out behind, she returned to her room, put on the robe, then, with a wave of weariness, sank down onto the edge of the bed, elbows on knees, face buried in her palms. Inhaling deeply, she tried to still the throbbing at her temples.

His women. His women, indeed. She wasn't his or anyone else's.

The sorrow of that thought deflated her. If Jeff could only see her now!

Ashamed, she gathered up a towel and soap in the hope that a long, hot shower would ease her tension and improve her mood, and for a short time it did. The water pressure was strong, sending steamy trails over the taut muscles of her neck and back. Rich-lathering shampoo left her hair squeaky-clean and shiny, hanging in damp clusters about her shoulders when she finally emerged, toweled herself vigorously, and returned to her room.

Half an hour later, wearing a navy sweater, jeans, and sneakers, she headed for the kitchen to make coffee. It was already hot on the stove. To her surprise the floor was free of debris, the offending cookware stacked neatly in the cupboard.

She smiled a bit smugly. So he had cleaned up himself. Take that, male chauvinist pig! And he had made himself scarce.

Helping herself to coffee, she took a seat at the table. Despite the outburst, she had actually slept until ten-thirty. Now she heard footsteps on the stairs and the slam of the bathroom door. All she had to do was to wait until he finished his shower and dressed. Then they would face their dilemma like adults.

When the shower started, she relaxed back in the chair, combing her still-damp hair with slender fingers, spreading it out over her shoulders to dry. Her gaze was drawn through the three-sided window of the breakfast nook to the backyard. She hadn't seen it the afternoon before and found instant pleasure in the rustic scene, the well-kept lawn, the scattering of maples and pines, the intermixing of apple trees with fruit hanging ripe and ready for picking. The morning mist had begun to burn off, speared here and there shafts of sunlight.

The scene was exactly what she had hoped to find, so peaceful and quiet, that she was unprepared for the roar behind her.

"You used up all the hot water! Damn it, don't you have a considerate bone in your body?"

Mitch stood in the door of the kitchen, dripping wet, wearing nothing but a towel around his hips.

For a second, she couldn't breathe. He was incredibly well built. Arms and shoulders of granite flanked a chest that was tanned, sinewed, and matted with fair hair made darker by the water. His stomach was flat and firm, his slim hips a solid start for muscled thighs and lower legs.

Swallowing convulsively, Anne forced herself to look away. "I'm sorry," she murmured. "I didn't realize there would be a shortage."

"Didn't realize?" he mocked loudly. "Well, next time, realize. I like my showers long and hot, too!"

Annoyed that he was annoyed, since this was her house for the week, she took a mouthful of coffee and then nearly choked. "My God," she cried when she finally swallowed, "this coffee is like mud! What did you put in here? Or should I ask"—her eyes narrowed—"how much of my coffee did you put into that pot? I don't see any groceries of yours around here. Make yourself right at home, thanks a lot."

His anger faded. Lips twitching, he leaned nonchalantly against the doorjamb. "Why shouldn't I make myself at home? I plan to spend the week here."

She sputtered out a furious laugh. "Oh, no, you're not." She rose quickly, forgetting every good intention to keep calm. "You'll have to find another place. I'm sure you'll have no trouble, what with your delightful personality and winning smile."

With an arrogant shift of his shoulders, he left the doorjamb and placidly headed away. "You find the substitute," he called over his shoulder. "I'll be staying here."

She trailed him. "You can't!"

At the bathroom door he turned so suddenly that she nearly bumped into him. She took a defensive step back.

He raised his right arm to rest high on the door. His left, with an angry red scar glaring from its upper half, hung by his hip. His body was a solid wall of stunning man.

"Are you going to stop me?" he drawled with an insolent silver gleam in his eye.

Anne tried to think up a sensible reply. When none came she turned on her heel and retraced her steps. She was hungry, she told herself. She needed breakfast. But she didn't do more than nibble on the scrambled eggs and toast that she made.

What to do. If she wasn't so far away from home and so badly in need of that distance, she might have simply packed up and left. But she wasn't staying out of pride. She did need the distance.

"Aren't you eating?" Again his voice startled her. This time, though, he was fully dressed. His jaw was clean-shaven and smelling of a lime aftershave. His hair was neatly combed and reached back collar of his wool plaid shirt. A wide leather belt hugged his hips, dark blue jeans his legs. Tan desert boots color-coordinated with his hair. His eyes were light green and calm.

He repeated the question. "You're not hungry?" The way he looked at her plate said that if she wasn't, he was.

With a sigh of defeat she pushed the dish across the table. "Help yourself."

With an exaggerated, "Thank you," he lowered himself into a chair and took her up on her offer. She was starting to think that he might actually have manners, when he said, "Geez, no wonder you're so thin. You've scrambled these eggs so dry they're impossible to swallow. If this is the way you always cook, it's a miracle you haven't wasted away to nothing."

Anne's jaw dropped. Jeff had never complained about anything, least of all her cooking.

Sitting straighter, she said, "If you don't like my cooking, then don't eat it! As a matter of fact, I don't like you very much, so why don't we dispense with breakfast and get to work finding a solution to this mess." Only when she stopped, did she realize she'd been shouting. There were also tears in her eyes again. Again. Jamming her knuckles against her mouth, she looked away.

More softly, Mitch asked, "How did you get into this mess, as you call it, Anne? Why aren't you with your husband?"

"That's none of your business."

"Are you divorced?"

"No."

"Are you working on the separate-vacation concept?"

"No."

"He doesn't know you're here?"

She gave a bitter laugh. "No."

"You've run away?"

Her composure cracked. "Will you leave me alone? Just go! Get out! Let me be!"

He didn't move. "Why did you leave your husband?"

"That's none of your business!"

"No? In my book, marriage is a precious thing. Some people treasure it and then lose it through no fault of their own. Others throw it away. If we're going to spend the week together, I want to know which it is. So tell me why you left him. If it was just your lousy cooking or your selfishness in the shower, he'd have left you." He paused. "Is that what happened?"

She looked him in the eye. "He didn't leave me. I didn't leave him. We loved each other. He was in an accident, and now he's dead. Dead!" Her chair scraped across the floor as she stood abruptly, reached angrily for his plate, and stormed to the sink. She slammed the food facedown in it. Then emotion overwhelmed her. Bracing shaky arms against the counter, she hung her head. Helplessly she gave in to quiet sobs.

She didn't hear him come up, but there was a genuine softness in his voice. "I'm sorry. I wouldn't have pushed if I'd known. It was thoughtless of me."

She brushed at the tears. "It doesn't matter." But it did. It had been months since she had cried, but she couldn't seem to stop. When she brushed them away, more tears came. To her horror, they came faster, until she was a sniffling bundle of misery.

Had she been thinking clearly, she would have shied from him the instant his hands touched her shoulders. But clear thought was beyond her. She needed comfort, and he offered it. Turning her, he pressed her head to his chest and held her while her whole body shook.

"Better?" he murmured when she finally quieted. He stroked her hair, smoothing loose strands from her damp cheeks as she nodded. It was only when he framed her face with his hands to inspect it that she realized she was hugging his waist.

Awkward, she blushed, stepped back, and turned to leave.

"Wait," he ordered, but gently now. "Why don't you sit down. I'll make breakfast for both of us. You can even water down the coffee if you'd like." He hesitated. In the silence, she saw a glint of humor in his eyes. "Funny. I've taken my coffee strong and black since I was sixteen. Someone told me it would put hair on my chest. I guess you don't want that, do you?"

Anne smiled sadly. "Not quite." Her voice still quivered, but her eyes were drying fast. She felt more calm now, purged.

"You sit down," he repeated, "while I cook. Then we'll decide what's to be done about this . . . mess."

Anne helped herself to a fresh cup of coffee, adding hot water from the tap, then returned to her chair. He worked in silence, cracking eggs into the heavy iron skillet, toasting a fresh batch of bread, pouring two glasses of orange juice, toting it all to the table.

She ate everything on her plate, matching him egg for egg, toast for toast, juice for juice. Then he poured her a second cup of coffee, filled the creamer with water and put that too before her.

Back in his chair, he said, "I spent a lot of time last night thinking about this. I planned to do some fishing, some hiking, some reading, and a lot of sleeping. What had you wanted to do?"

She tipped up her chin. "Read. Work. Take walks, explore the neighborhood, enjoy the solitude."

He looked out the window. Bright sun lit the yard. "Look, this may sound crazy, but I think we can both stay here. We both seem to want quiet and solitude. We can each just go our own way." He looked at her. "I know this area, and, trust me, there won't be another place to stay on such short notice."

She tucked a handful of hair behind her ear. This wasn't quite the vacation she had imagined, but he had a point. He didn't seem willing to leave. Barring her own return to New York, there wasn't any alternative.

Her thumb moved on the ceramic mug. "This isn't what I wanted."

"Me, neither. But it's the only fair thing. If I have to put up with your hot showers, you can put up with my black coffee."

"What about the beds? Every move you make rattles on the ceiling. I wanted to sleep."

"Yeah, I wanted that, too, but the bed up there is too damned small and uncomfortable. Why don't you try sleeping there?"

"Because you're there."

"Then why don't I sleep downstairs?"

"Because I'm there."

"Damn it," he sighed, "I don't want to share your bed. Why don't we just switch?"

She wasn't a fool. "After you've told me how small and uncomfortable the attic one is? No way!"

"Then don't complain about the noise." In one swift move he was up, stacking the dishes, dumping them in the sink. When he turned back to her, a silver wave had fallen across his brow. "You clean up. I cooked." He left the room so quickly that Anne's protest met thin air.

"But—it was—my food—" Slowly she faced the dishes. If this was a preview of the week, things looked grim.

But Anne was tired of grim, so she took a positive approach. Starting with a long walk through the woods, she followed the line of a low stone wall across the hilltop and down a gently graded slope until the road intersected her path. The view was spectacular from several points where the forest door opened to the village below, its tall white church steeple catching the afternoon sun.

As she followed the dirt road back to the house, the climb steepened. She stopped to rest a time or two. All was peaceful. The murmur of the breeze was a welcome switch from the grating sounds of the city, the lush ferns on the forest floor were a far cry from stone sidewalks, the chipmunk skuttling through the brush was far better than a guard dog on a leash by the curb.

Accustomed to the gray of the pigeon, she smiled at the chickadee's black cap and white bib and the red breast of the robin. She watched the play of the sun through the boughs of thick, healthy trees. The crispness of the air, sharp without chill, invigorated her.

When she finally returned to the house, Mitch was nowhere about. No car, no man, no note. Exhausted from fresh air and lack of sleep, she stretched out on her quilt and fell into a deep and restful sleep.

The tension of the past weeks took its due. When she awakened, it was dusk. After freshening up in the bathroom, she fixed a supper of soup and crackers, then settled before the fire to finish the mystery she'd started. But the story's momentum had been broken. She never quite got back into the terror of it.

When she finished the last page, she sat back to watch the flames. Their play entranced her, calmed her, lulled her into a peaceful daze, and for the very first time, and at long last, she felt removed from Jeff's death.

It had been a nightmare—first news of the plane crash, then the limbo when rescue teams set to work, hope when survivors appeared, total and utter despair when the worst became reality. But her heart felt lighter now than it had at any time since then. She didn't know if it was the change of scenery, or the start of true healing. But it felt good.

Of course, Mitch was still gone. Though it was after nine, he hadn't returned. Just as well. They were like fire and water.

She had to give him points, though. He hadn't gone on and on about what a shame it was, how young a widow she made, how tragic that Jeff had been taken from life in his prime. She'd had enough pity to last a lifetime.

So he can't be all bad, she mused, even if he does make bitter coffee.

The evening passed quietly. Anne left her chair only to feed the fire. After a time, her lids grew heavy. She fell into deep sleep from which only the sensation of movement much later disturbed her. She opened groggy eyes to find herself in Mitch's arms.

"What are you doing?" she cried and began to squirm.

He held her tighter. "Putting you to bed." They were already at the door of her room.

"Put me down. I don't need your help."

He dropped her on the bed. "Don't worry. I'm not doing you any favors. I'm thinking of me. You were sleeping in my chair."

Before she could begin to call him out, he pivoted and left, slamming the door behind him.

Sunday brought more of the same. On the plus side, the weather was grand, crisp and clear once the early-morning fog lifted. Having slept her fill, Anne was up early, putting on her own pot of coffee to assure herself a cup to her liking, before showering and dressing. The door to the attic remained closed. If Mitch was still asleep, he slept soundly. Everything overhead was silent.

After breakfast, she rewalked yesterday's route, this time extending it to the brook that babbled down the far hillside. In keeping with the nip in the air, the first of the birch leaves were starting to yellow. The sun picked them out from the rest and added a glow.

Removing her sneakers, she rolled up her jeans and, where the water was shallow, waded across flat granite boulders. It was the kind of thing she and Jeff would have done. Now she was alone, yet strangely peaceful. Enjoying herself, she leaped lightly from stone to stone.

Returning invigorated to the house, she tackled the first of the papers she had to translate, making good headway with the English-to-Spanish piece until her stomach grumbled. By then there were stirrings from the upper quarter. She worked until he was in the bathroom and dallied in the kitchen until he returned to his room. When he came downstairs, she was back at work, sitting at the small desk that stood beneath a side window of the living room.

Then the trouble began. For nearly ten minutes he looked over her shoulder while she worked as best she could. Then he made a racket with pots and pans in the kitchen. When that ended, there was whistling, loud and persistent, the same tune, over and over and over again.

Worst were interruptions of the "Hey, where is . . ." variety. First it was, "Hey, where's the salt?" Then, "Hey, where's the ketchup?" Then, "Hey, where's the large spatula?"

By this time she knew he was baiting her, so she didn't scream. Calmly, she put down her pen, set her glasses aside, and made for the kitchen to register a civil complaint.

"Are there any more—omigod, what are you doing?" She ran across the room, only to drop her outstretched arms in disgust and raise her eyes heavenward in search of patience.

"What's the trouble?" He was all innocence.

She peered once more into the half-empty jar in his hand. "Those are my macadamia nuts. I've been saving that itty-bitty jar for this vacation!"

"So I'll buy you another jar. Is money that tight?"

Anne scowled. She reached for the jar and clamped on its lid before he could take more. "It's not the money. It's the principle. I love macadamia nuts."

"I'll get you more," he repeated calmly.

She returned the jar to the cabinet. "Can I trust you to leave it alone, or do I have to put it in my room?"

He grinned and folded his arms on his chest. "I haven't had macadamias in ages. I'd forgotten how good they are. But you can trust me. At least, when it comes to the nuts."

For a split second, she thought she heard something sexual in his drawl. Then, dismissing it as a figment of her imagination, she turned and stalked off.

By Monday, a pattern emerged. Anne rose early each morning and hiked the countryside. Mitch slept late enough to ensure a replenished supply of hot water for a long shower. Meals were widely scattered and eaten alone from supplies that remained separate and distinct.

By Tuesday Anne felt well rested and relaxed. If Mitch continued to toss in his sleep, she had either gotten used to the noise or she slept soundly enough herself to blot it out.

He woke up earlier than usual that day, packed a lunch and vanished, leaving Anne with the solitude she wanted. Strange, though, between work, books, and other incidental activities, she kept thinking about him.

She was living with the guy. Well, not in that sense. Still, her friends would be stunned if they knew, her family appalled. But she was comfort-able here, physically and emotionally. This world was divorced from that of New York. Same with Mitch. So, she didn't know his last name. The anonymity here felt right.

With Wednesday morning came the awareness that her vacation was com-ing to an end. By Friday afternoon she would be heading back to the city. Thinking about it over breakfast coffee, she felt a pang of disappointment. All things considered, the vacation had been a good one. She would miss this country when she had to leave it behind.

Determined to make the most of the remaining days, she spent more time in the woods than ever, reveling in the beauty of the flora, the free-dom of the fauna, and the luxury of time itself. It was past noon when she returned to the cottage. Leaning against the trunk of an old apple tree in the backyard, bathed in its sweet scent, she tipped her head back and squinted at the sun through the fruit.

Inspiration struck then. Pulling her jacket off, she spread it on the soft grass. Then she began to pick apples, selecting only the fullest and deep-est red of the lot to add to the growing pile. When the last of the best lay on her jacket, she calculated her own agility, studying the upper branches, taking stock of her options. Casting prudence aside, she braced a rubber-soled foot against the trunk and carefully hoisted herself onto the first branch, bringing a whole new batch of fruit within reach. Balanced gin-gerly, she plucked one, then another, filling her free arm slowly.

Then she looked down and saw Mitch right at the foot of her tree. Startled, she lost her balance. Apples rained to the ground in a crimson storm. When she began to fall, she twisted sideways, grabbing back at the low branch to catch herself. Mitch caught her before she hit the ground, though not before she'd been scraped by the ragged bark and jutting off-shoots.

"Why did you creep up on me that way?" she cried the minute her feet touched ground. He released her instantly, but not before she saw him flinch in pain. With a gasp of pain herself, she sank to the grass and rubbed the knee she had bumped on the branch.

"Are you all right?" he asked.

She probed an aching elbow. "Fine. I'm fine."

"Are you always this clumsy?"

"I wasn't clumsy. You frightened me, sneaking up like that."

"Who did you think it was?" he asked dryly. "There aren't a whole lot of other people around here, or hadn't you noticed?" Frowning, he bent to gather apples that had fallen. "You should be more careful. You could break a leg that way."

"Is that the voice of experience talking?"

His jaw was tight. "You could say that." He tossed more apples onto her jacket. But he only used his right arm. The left hung idle.

"Is your arm all right?" she asked.

He glanced sharply up. "It's fine."

"You favor your right."

"It's fine. Can you walk?"

As she stood, testing the knee, he pulled her jacket around into a bundle, lifted it, and set off for the house.

She limped after him. By the time she reached the kitchen, he had put the apples beside the sink and disappeared. Grateful for the privacy, she collapsed into a chair, twisting her arm to see the scrapes on her elbow.

"Here, let me take a look at that."

Before she could resist, Mitch deposited a bottle of disinfectant and a washcloth on the table, pulled up a chair, and took her arm. His touch was warm. When she tried to pull back, he held her arm more firmly. She winced at the antiseptic's sting.

"Ach! That's enough!"

But he disagreed, repeatedly dabbing the dirt from the wound before kneeling and reaching for her knee.

"It's all right," she insisted.

He raised his head. His jaw was hard, his cheeks lean, but his eyes were surprisingly soft. Something stirred inside her.

"I'll do my best not to hurt you, but it should be cleaned." Very gently, he pushed the jeans past her knee. He applied disinfectant to the scrape there, blotting it to ease the sting.

Anne watched his shoulders flex as he worked, easy to see since his turtleneck fit him as snugly as each of his others had. This one was dark green. By contrast, the silvery-blonde of his hair was striking.

"There, now," he murmured. "That wasn't so bad, was it?" With both hands cradling her leg, he surveyed his work. His tone was gentle, his touch even more so, and when he raised his eyes, they were the gentlest yet.

Her breath faltered.

He curved a hand to her neck. His thumb feather-touched the soft swell of her lips. For an instant he hesitated, and Anne's breath held.

With eternal slowness, he raised his mouth to hers in a kiss that was little more than the tantalizingly light movement of his lips. When she made no protest, he deepened it, coaxing her mouth open with a gentleness that was worlds away from the first night's force.

Anne was entranced. She couldn't think, because this wasn't part of her plan. But she could feel, and what she felt was overwhelming, the purest pleasure in a meeting of mouths, a touching of tongues.

Abruptly he pulled away, and sanity returned.

With a gasp she bolted from the chair and, ignoring a twinge in her knee, went to the far side of the room. Mitch stood, keeping his back to her as his breathing steadied. When he finally faced her, he had his passion in check.

By that time, she was trying to understand herself. Because she couldn't, she lashed out at him. "You had no business doing that."

His lips thinned. "I don't seem to recall your objecting."

"You didn't give me much of a chance."

He approached, studying her eyes, the heat on her cheeks, the tiny quiver of her lips. He frowned. "It's been a long time, hasn't it?"

"I don't want your pity!"

"Pity?" His features tensed. "I don't deal in pity. I've seen enough of it in the past year to make me sick. No, Anne, if you can't recognize a basic physical need, then you're deluding yourself." His gaze narrowed. "Let's just say I took my reward for playing nursemaid to a bad-tempered tomboy."

She gasped in dismay, but he was on his way out of the room, which was probably just as well. That way she didn't have to eat crow, because he was right. She would be lying if she refused to admit that she liked his kiss. She had been physically roused by a physical act.

But it had been only a kiss, only a kiss in the midst of bizarre circumstances. Come next week, the cottage, the kiss, the man would all be memory.

Gradually, she calmed. She began paring and slicing apples, piling skins on a piece of paper towel, turning the slices into a large glass pie plate and sprinkling them with cinnamon. Her supplies were dwindling, but she found adequate amounts of flour, butter, and sugar for the topping. Once the pie was in the oven, she spotted the unused apples. She washed each, polished it to a high gloss, and set it in a dish in the center of the table. It wasn't until the dish was filled that she saw Mitch eyeing her from the doorway.

She was quickly defensive, "Is something wrong?"

"Just looking to see that you're all right."

"I am. I actually forgot . . ." She gestured toward her bruises with a sheepish grin.

"Glad to hear it." With a dip of his head, he left the room and, soon after, the house.

Anne immersed herself in the last of her work, while the scent of baking apples filled the air. The pie was delicious, by her immodest estimate, a perfect finish for the early dinner she ate alone. Again, dusk found her reading before the fire.

"Anything good?"

She looked up and blushed. "Just a romance." She was actually enjoying it without thinking of Jeff at every turn of the page. When Mitch set off for the kitchen, she called, "There's apple pie on the counter. Help yourself." She grinned when he looked back and arched a brow. "Even bad-tempered tomboys have their merits."

"Thanks."

"You're welcome."

"By the way, I put the peels out for the deer."

"I wondered where they'd gone, but I wasn't about to look a gift horse in the mouth. Do deer like apples?"

She learned the answer the next morning.

A warm hand shook her awake. "Come, Anne. There's something you have to see!"

She was disoriented only until she saw Mitch in his robe at the window, waving her along. Rolling out of bed, she joined him there and followed his pointing finger. Under a patch of mist in the yard, by the base of the old apple tree, a young doe was munching at the remains that Mitch had tossed out. As they watched, the lithe animal stood on her hind legs to pick a fresh piece of fruit.

"Deer do like apples, wouldn't you say?" His breath fanned her ear, its warmth enhancing the moment's pleasure.

"That was beautiful," she murmured when the doe finally moved off into the mist. "Thank you for waking me." She turned to find him very, very close, and she thought about that kiss. All he did this time, though, was to give her arm a gentle squeeze, then leave.

By the time she showered and went to the kitchen, he was dressed. As he gazed absently out the window, the freshness of morning gentled his features.

"Coffee?" she offered quietly.

"Ummm." He paused, slowly turning to look at her. "And a piece of that apple pie. My compliments to the baker."

"Apple pie? For breakfast?"

"Sure. Call it danish, if the thought disturbs you. But it was good."

She set to making coffee, somehow lost count and thought that maybe she added an extra scoop to the basket. She let it stand. "Swedish apple pie. My mother's recipe. Easy and good. Actually, now that I think about it, my dad used to have it for breakfast, too." Fearful that she'd spoken too personally, she quieted.

He must have wondered about that quiet, because he asked, "Is your father dead?"

"Oh, no. But it's been years since I lived at home."

"Do you live in the same place you did with your husband?"

"Yes."

"Does it bother you?"

"Sometimes." An understatement.

"Do you have children?"

"No." Regretfully.

"You're lucky."

Frowning, she lowered the gas under the perking coffee. "Why do you say that? I've often thought it would have been easier to have part of him left."

"It isn't," Mitch said tightly. "Take my word for it."

Anne heard vehemence enough to suggest personal experience. She wanted to ask more, but it seemed against the rules. When he didn't offer more himself, she figured he agreed. Anonymity was best. Definitely.

He finished his pie and coffee, tossed a playful, "Getting better!" over his shoulder in passing, and left her to add coffee to her own cuppa Joe. Soon after, he left the cottage.

Noise from the kitchen late that afternoon announced his return. Anne put the finishing touches on the piece she had translated, stacked her papers neatly, then paused. She sniffed the air. There was a new, vile smell.

"You went fishing!" she moaned from the kitchen door, staring in horror at the mess on the counter. She crinkled her nose in disgust.

"Now, now," he chided, "it may smell bad at first, but once this bass is fried, the end result will be worth it. You'll join me for dinner, won't you?"

The invitation sounded sincere. He looked sincere issuing it. This was her last night at the cottage. She'd had a week's worth of time, space, and her solitude.

Oil sizzled in the skillet. The sound oddly inviting.

"If you have enough," she said graciously and was rewarded with a smile.

"Oh, I have enough. More than enough, and whatever we don't eat tonight goes to waste. This is great bass. Trust me. I'm a champion fisherman."

"And an immodest one," she added, smiling back. She didn't doubt his ability for a minute. She half-suspected he would be good at whatever he did. He had an air of competence that went well beyond an arrogant jaw.

Indeed, the fish was delicious. As was the fresh-squeezed orange juice she found at breakfast the next morning. He was, it seemed, a handy man to have around.

This was Anne's last morning in Vermont. To her surprise, when she headed for the woods, Mitch fell into step beside her, and it was as peaceful a hike as any she'd had. There was silence, the soft sounds of nature, and Mitch's occasional comments. He was knowledgeable in the ways of the forest and had a wealth of information to share. He talked about species of trees and flowers, habits of woodland creatures, the history of the area itself, and did it all in an easygoing, unpretentious manner. He read Anne well, and knew when to speak and when to be still. She was almost sorry when they arrived back at the cabin, since her next chore was to pack.

Too soon that was done. With her luggage stowed in the trunk, she put her key in the ignition—and for a brief minute hoped her engine would fail. It was a possibility, wasn't it? She hadn't started the car once all week.

But it coughed to life at the first turn, and hummed smoothly as it warmed. Which left only one thing left to do.

She was about to climb from the car when that one thing rounded the house. "You weren't going to leave without saying good-bye, were you?" he asked, bending to talk through the open window of the car.

"I was just going to come and find you."

"Do you have all your stuff?"

"Uh-huh. I left the rest of the apple pie for you."

His eyes sparkled warmly. "Thanks. You do make a good one, even though your coffee is still too weak."

"Then you'll be glad to be rid of me." She smiled wryly. "When do you leave?"

"Later today."

"Oh." What else to say? His fingers curved over the window ledge. They were strong fingers, nice ones.

"Will you be back up here at all?" he asked quietly.

She shrugged. "I don't know. I haven't thought too far ahead. It's been a good week, though. I'm sorry to be leaving."

"It wasn't all that bad, was it?" He seemed suddenly hesitant. "Look," he began tentatively, "I'll be coming up the week before Thanksgiving. Kind of to give myself a boost before the holidays. Keep it in mind." He stopped short of an open invitation, but the implication was there.

It struck her that she would probably want a boost herself. "I'll remember." She cleared her throat. "Well, good-bye, then."

He smiled, hit the ledge once, and pushed himself straight. "Safe trip."

When he stepped away, she put the car in reverse, backed around, and headed for the road, all the time thinking that she might have liked a kiss. It was a whimsical thought. Not so whimsically, his lank image shrank steadily in the rearview mirror. When the car took a curve and he disappeared, she narrowed her sights on reality and New York.

3

How different the road looked this time around. Parched brown leaves blanketed the ground, forests of bare branches joined evergreens in a blur of gray-green on distant hills. Mountains stood stark, more harsh without greenery on their slopes. Leaf peepers had long since gone home to city heat and thoughts of Thanksgiving, barely two weeks away.

Those thoughts had precipitated Anne's trip, or so she told herself as she drove steadily north. On one hand, things had improved in New York. Her return trip had been uneventful, her apprehension at facing life and its memories eased by the onset of autumn and a renewed strength.

"You look marvelous!" her mother had said the first night of her return. "I like that pink on your cheeks. It becomes you."

Even after the long drive, Anne was full of energy, which was why she had stopped at her parents in the first place. "It was perfect," she said. "Just what I needed."

"Sit down and tell me all about it," the older woman ordered, and Anne had. Almost. She didn't mention Mitch. He played no role in her real life. She didn't even know his last name.

At first she gave little thought to the idea of returning to Vermont in November. The new semester had begun, and she was up to her ears in translation work. Friends still hovered, but she had more patience for it now. In turn, they sensed her calmer state and began to ease up.

She still refused to date. But she was excited enough about one professor's project to agree to sign on as a part-time assistant. Assured of steady work to off-balance incidental work, she faced the fall and winter seasons with confidence.

But Jeff was gone, and the holidays approached. These would be her first without him.

When she first heard low whispers in the back of her mind, she ignored them. After Halloween, though, they became a murmur. Go to Vermont go to Vermont go to Vermont, they said.

But how could she?

That first time had been an accident. Sharing the cottage with Mitch had been a makeshift solution to an unexpected problem. If she went this time, there would be nothing unexpected about it.

But Mitch was right. The closer Thanksgiving came, the more she dreaded it. She could use a boost, indeed, before facing them alone. Recalling with pleasure the land, the air, and the cottage, she figured that whether he showed up or not the week would be good.

This time her parents raised no objection. As a precaution, she made a reservation at an inn thirty miles from the house. It was the nearest one, but would assure her a place to stay if Mitch either didn't want her or wasn't there.

She didn't have a key, because she hadn't called the rental agent. What would she have said? Is Mitch going up this weekend? No, I don't know his last name, but we spent the week together there last time. Embarrassing!

She made the sharp turn off the highway onto the rutted road that lead up the hill to the house. The ruts were harder now, more jolting in the cold of a raw November than they had been in September. In that instant her thoughts jolted, too, up and down, in and out. She shouldn't have come—she had to come. What did she hope to accomplish—why did she have to hope to accomplish anything? What if Mitch wasn't there—what if he was?

She had deliberately waited until Saturday morning to leave the city. If Mitch had driven up on Friday night, like last time, she would reach the cottage just when he was waking up.

Her heartbeat quickened when she rounded the final curve and saw his sporty blue Honda parked in front of the house. It stood out clearly in the dusky November day, a bright and promising robin's egg in a dried twig nest. Her pulse pounded as she pulled in behind it, slid out of her car, and, pulling her navy pea coat closed, approached the door.

All was winter silent, such that the heels of her leather boots sounded abnormally loud on the flagstone walk. The grass bordering the walk was aged and dying, the lilac forlornly naked. But Anne felt alive as she knocked on the door.

When there was no answer, she imagined him in the kitchen, and knocked harder.

Still, silence.

But his car was there. She wondered if he had broken habit and gone for an earlier hike. She tried the doorknob, but it didn't budge. Finally, she banged on the door with a full fist.

It opened then, and she knew he'd been asleep. He was bleary-eyed, unshaven, mussed of hair, and rumpled-looking in an old shirt, tails hanging low over wrinkled jeans. He was as tall and lean as she remembered, though not quite as enthusiastic as she had hoped.

She swallowed down unsureness and a quiver. "Hi, Mitch."

"Where in the hell have you been?" he bellowed. "I was thinking of sending the troops out."

If not for his gruffness, Anne might have hugged him. Only then did she realize how much she had wanted to see him. "I'm sorry. I didn't leave the city until this morning."

"Why not? You knew I'd be arriving yesterday."

"No, I didn't."

Though his eyes were a deep, deep green, he continued to scowl. "I'm beginning to wonder if you're more trouble than you're worth!"

"Thanks a lot," she said, offended, and suddenly she remembered every little annoying thing about him. "I could say the same about you. I think I'll leave." Spinning on a heel, she took a single step before he caught her.

"No!" His voice softened. "Don't go." When she looked back, his eyes were gentler. "Come in. Please."

She had no choice when he drew her in. Not that she wanted one. Struck by his height and good looks, she was very glad she'd come, and suddenly shy.

For a minute, he seemed unsure. He studied her eyes, searching. Then he let out a sigh and drew her close for a hug. She returned it as though it was the most natural thing in the world.

His lips moved against her hair. "It's good to see you, Anne."

She smiled against his chest. "Same here, Mitch."

He drew back and framed her face. Tipping it, he kissed her softly. His mouth played, lightly, sensually. His tongue made the moment even sweeter.

When he drew back this time, his eyes smoldered. His voice was thick. "How about making coffee while I get cleaned up? You look a damned sight better than I do right now."

"You don't look so bad."

"Get the coffee? Please? I'll get your bags later." Putting her from him, he strode off.

Anne tossed her coat on a chair. She made coffee strong, and eggs scrambled moist. When the food was hot on the table, she went to the window. The backyard looked bare. A dull apple or two clinging stubbornly to lonely branches. The firs stood out, towering over trees that were de-leafed. They swayed gallantly in gusts of wind that sent shivers through the tall grass below.

But the chill was out there, and Anne was in here. She was warm and content.

"You're looking well," Mitch said from the door. "A little pale, but better than last time." He was groomed meticulously now and looking devastatingly fresh in an open-necked wool shirt and clean denims.

"There wasn't much in the fridge," she said. "I hope the eggs are enough."

He took a chair and helped himself from the platter. "I thought we'd go marketing today. Unless," he shot her a look over the rim of his coffee cup, "you brought groceries."

"Not this time. I wasn't sure I'd be staying here. I made reservations at an inn in Woodstock just in case."

He sat back. "Were you afraid I'd attack you again?"

"No," she said with care. "I wasn't sure you'd be here. It was tentative when you mentioned it, and since I had no way of contacting you in between—"

"You could have called Miles Cooper," he suggested lightly.

She looked him in the eye. "No, I couldn't. So there was no comfortable way of my learning your plans."

"Did that bother you?"

"No." She didn't look away. "I don't want to cope with identities yet."

"Then we agree on that. No more said."

"No more said." She felt proud of herself, if a little wistful, as she watched him eat.

When he finished, he ran a napkin over his mouth. Then he balled it up in his fist. "You can phone from the village later and cancel those reservations. But I think you should know that there are two conditions to your staying here."

Conditions? She arched a brow.

He leaned way back this time, until the chair was on its rear legs. "First, we eat together."

She had no problem with that. It pleased her, actually. She smiled her agreement.

"Second," he said, "I sleep downstairs."

Her smile vanished. "Uh, I . . . don't think so. I'm not ready for . . . that."

His eyes laughed. "I'm told that I'm a good lover. But hey," he relented, all teasing gone, "I'm not ready for . . . that, either. Maybe soon. But not yet. You aren't the only one dealing with ghosts."

Startled by that thought, she gathered up the empty dishes and went to the sink.

He was close behind her. "You're a beautiful woman."

"Last time, I was 'plain' and 'scrawny.'"

"Last time, I was wet and tired." Strong hands slid around her middle and drew her back against his body. His forearms brushed the underside of her breasts. Her heart thudded in response.

When he turned her to face him, her lips parted. He kissed her then, possessive but gentle, and she responded with a fervor she had forgotten was possible. Wrapping her arms around his neck, she opened her mouth, and he moved right in. After her mouth he kissed her cheeks and her eyelids. Then, hotly, he sought out her tongue.

They weren't ready for this emotionally, but there was no problem physically. Mitch was rock-hard against her. His hands moved restlessly on her back, her waist, her hips. They found her breasts and explored in detail, and Anne was every bit as active. She touched him everywhere to make sure he was real, and he was, real and ready. While their mouths tangled hungrily, her fingers spread over his thigh and moved upward, upward and inward.

With a strangled sound, Mitch pulled away.

Anne felt instant loss, then acute embarrassment. Mitch's ragged breathing was small solace for her aggressiveness. "That shouldn't have happened," she said in a faltering whisper.

He made a sputtering sound and pushed a hand through his hair. "Yeah, but it did. Damn it, this was a crazy idea!"

She averted her eyes and tried to edge away from the sink, but he had her pinned there. Taking her chin, he forced her face up. His voice was rough as sand. "You try my patience, Annie. One part of me aches to pick you up in my arms and carry you out to that bed, but the last thing I need right now is to hear you calling for another man in the throes of passion. You're still mourning your husband. Your clothes, your hair, your eyes all tell me that. And I have a past, too. The last thing you need is to hear me call out another woman's name."

Anne's eyes filled with tears. When she pushed at him, he let her go. She went to the window, wrapped her arms around herself, and looked out. "Why do you lead me on?"

There was silence, then a begrudging, "I can't seem to help myself. What's your excuse?" When she didn't answer, he approached her and goaded, "Hmm? Are you that frustrated?"

She spun around and sent the flat of her hand against his cheek. He caught it on the rebound and had her arm behind her, drawing her hard against him, in an instant.

"Don't ever do that again!" he muttered and, as suddenly as he'd seized her, let her go. He took long steps toward the door before stopping short.

Anne was stunned, short of breath, wondering what was coming next.

One lithe stride brought him back. To her astonishment he framed her face with his hands, placed a hard kiss on her lips, then walked off again.

"What was that for?" she cried.

"Moist eggs and strong black coffee." He half-turned at the door. "I have a couple of things to do. Find something to keep you busy for an hour, then we'll leave for the village."

It wasn't a question, and he didn't wait for an answer. That was what kept Anne busy while she unpacked her bags in the attic bedroom. She brooded. She agonized. She wondered why she had come and why she ever wanted his kiss. Mitch whoever-he-was was stubborn and self-centered. He was the exact opposite of gentle, caring, generous-to-a-fault Jeff.

But Jeff was dead.

An art teacher had once told her that a painting was successful when it evoked a reaction, be it positive or negative. For Anne, the months since Jeff's death had been devoid of reaction, until Mitch.

So where did she go from there? Into bed with the man at the very first chance?

Unsettled by that thought, she exchanged her city skirt for a sweater and jeans, grabbed her heavy parka, and ran down the stairs. She needed fresh air and a long walk.

She barely got out the back door when she spotted Mitch in the yard splitting logs for the fire. Bundled in a sheepskin jacket with its collar raised, he didn't see her. Time and again he raised the ax and struck, time and again splitting each new log with a single sweep of the blade, and all with his right arm. She wondered how the left had been injured. It was none of her business. Still she wondered.

She joined him in the yard and sat quietly on a pile of logs while he finished his work, then as quietly helped carry the wood into the house and stack it by the fireplace. Shortly after that, they left for the village.

In the confines of the car, he was more imposing than ever. His hands were strong on the wheel, his thigh strong when he braked. In profile, his hair was a thick silver-blond, his eyes alert, his nose, lips, and chin classically chiseled. Everything about him spoke of command, of a man with a mind of his own. But she knew that already.

They bought food. They drove home. They did fine right through dinner, sticking to general topics like politics, the economy, and the oncoming winter in the mountains. They disagreed on some things, but could listen to the other's point of view.

They didn't run into trouble until the last of the peach melba disappeared. Then he asked, "Why did you decide to come up here this time, Anne?"

It was inevitable that the talk would turn personal on some level, and she had nothing to hide. "I realized that you were right. The holidays are closing in. I'm hoping to take home a little extra strength. They'll be tough."

His voice was quiet. "You still miss him a lot?"

"Yes. It isn't as bad as it was. I can accept that he's gone now. I'm used to waking up without him. The people around me are having more trouble. They're sometimes so solicitous it'd make you sick. Thanksgiving's apt to be one long let's-cheer-up-Anne ordeal."

Mitch blew out a breath. "Oh, boy. I know what you mean there."

"How so?" she asked, not letting it go this time. "Are you married?"

Lips pursed, he studied his hands. "No."

"Have you ever been married?"

"Yes."

"Are you divorced?"

"No."

"Separated?"

"No."

There was only one other possibility. It made sense on many different levels.

"My wife died," he said, looking at her now.

Anne saw the pain in his eyes. "I'm sorry. You must have loved her very much."

"I did."

"How did she die?"

His jaw clenched, and anger joined the pain. She was wondering if the anger was directed at her, when he grew mellow again. "I'd rather not go into it. That'd be getting more personal than we planned."

"But it helps to talk sometimes. Doesn't it? I mean, if you're angry—"

"Who's angry?"

"I thought I saw—"

"What about your anger? I've heard it, you know. Do you talk about it?" He pushed his chair back but didn't rise. Both hands clutched the edge of the table. "You don't know what I'm feeling. You don't know anything about me, about my work, my responsibilities. How can you be so sanctimonious?"

She recoiled. "Sanctimonious? I was just trying to help. After what I went through not so long ago, I may be feeling some of what you are, and yes, I may want to talk about it. I may want a little help, myself."

The confession startled her. She was wondering where it had come from, when Mitch sat back and asked quietly, "How did Jeff die?"

She glanced around the room, but there was no avoiding the issue. So she studied her wedding band. "He was in an accident."

"I know that. But what kind? Were you with him?"

She shook her head. "No."

"Tell me."

"He was on a business trip. The plane went down."

In the silence that followed, she raised her eyes. Mitch looked pale. "When did it happen?" he asked.

"Last January."

He flinched. It was a while before he said, "It's been nearly a year. Do you date at all?"

"No."

"You should."

"Now look who's being sanctimonious. When did your wife die?"

"Last winter." He held her gaze.

"Do you date?" It was a foolish question. She knew it the minute she saw the wry twist of his mouth.

"I'm not sure you'd call it dating. When I want a woman, I get one." He took a breath, paused on the verge of saying more, then dropped it. "At any rate, I have other obligations."

"Female-related obligations?"

He watched her closely. "Yes."

"I see."

"No, I doubt you do. But maybe that's better for now."

She didn't know what he meant, but she wasn't asking. She had too much pride. Besides, questions weren't part of the deal. If she hadn't asked that last one, she wouldn't be feeling suddenly low.

Mitch stirred. "Do me a favor?" His eyes were softer. "Take those pins out of your hair and put a red ribbon in it."

"I don't have a red ribbon."

"Anything bright will do."

"Am I that depressing to be with?"

He left his seat then and circled the table. "No, Annie. I've never found you depressing." He began removing the hairpins and didn't stop until he had her hair spread over her shoulders. Then he hunkered down so that he was closer to eye level. "But I think you overdo the starkness. You don't have to punish yourself for your husband's death. Losing him is ample punishment all by itself."

She had to hand it to him. He was perceptive enough, but she assumed that he spoke from experience. So what was his punishment? His arm? Those other obligations he mentioned?

But he didn't appear to be thinking of other obligations just then. He was fingering her hair, seeming entranced by its sheen. "You look so pretty with your hair down, Anne."

When his eyes rose, her stomach flipped over. They could talk all they wanted about not being ready for this, but when they were close, it just happened. His eyes fell to her lips. He rubbed them with a thumb, then leaned forward and touched them with his tongue. The tip of his tongue. Tracing her mouth from corner to corner with devastating leisure.

Anne liked what he did. She closed her eyes and sighed, enjoying each small touch for the pleasure it brought. When she began to tremble, she clutched Mitch's shoulders. They were made for that, for clutching. They were large, solid, and warm.

But part of being pleasured was pleasuring back. It was instinctive, and no hardship at all, because she was hungry. What he did satisfied her for only a short time. She moved her mouth and found more, moved her tongue and found even more, and above it all were the throaty sounds Mitch made, telling her that he was getting hotter.

When he murmured, "Christ," there was awe in his tone. Incredibly, though, he backed up. He sat down hard on the floor, draped his forearms over bent knees, and his forehead on his wrists. *"Christ,"* he whispered, then raised his head. His eyes were filled with amusement and sex.

It was a minute before the sex part faded. Then he threw back his head, dragged in a long breath, and hauled himself to his feel. From a safe distance, he said, "About your hair. You'll need to wear something red or orange if you're going to hike with me tomorrow morning. It's deer-hunting season."

They spent the better part of the next morning in the woods. It was cold, but Mitch kept her moving, leading her over trails she had never explored, through gullies she had never seen. A red wool cap kept her head warm, mittens warmed her hands.

With the trees bare of leaves, vistas were open as they hadn't been in September. Mitch led her from hilltop to hilltop, one view more far-reaching than the next. The land was quiet. Forest creatures were hidden away. The doe that had stood on her hind legs to chomp on a crisp apple now hid from the hunter. Chipmunks and squirrels were burrowed in their dens. There was the rustle of evergreen boughs in the wind, the icy gurgle of the brook as it charged downstream, the crunch of their boots on the near-frozen ground.

Anne's cheeks were as red as her cap when they returned, tired but exhilarated, and it was a harbinger of the days ahead. They settled into the comfort of easy companionship, sharing not only meals, but most every other time of the day. Mitch read when Anne did, his eye occasionally catching hers. They played backgammon in front of the fire, and worked together on a jigsaw puzzle. The weather held, offering pleasant days with clear skies, and an invigorating chill to the night. They walked together and worked together, Anne on her translating, Mitch on papers dug from an overstuffed briefcase. They lived in the here and now, avoiding talk of the city like the plague.

All too soon, Anne loaded up her car for the return trip to New York. Slinging an arm across her shoulder, Mitch walked her from the house a final time. The silence had been heavier that morning than at any other point in the week. Anne knew its cause.

"Will you be spending Thanksgiving with your family?" he asked quietly.

"Yes." She took in his handsome features, studying, memorizing. "And you?"

"The same." He held her just a little closer. "Plans for New Year's Eve?"

They had reached the car. She faced him, smiling sadly. "Funny. I used to worry about New Year's Eve. Would I have a date? Would I not? Would he be tall, dark, and handsome? Now it doesn't seem to matter." She sighed. "No, I don't have a date. I may just plant myself on my sofa with a bottle of Chablis and a book."

"Why not do it here?" His eyes were deep green, the color of saying something important.

Her pulse raced. "What?"

"Spend New Year's Eve here."

"Will you?" she asked without premeditation.

He pulled her close, into the warmth of his sheepskin jacket. "Yes."

"What about your other obligations?" Unpremeditated also, but the answer mattered.

Mitch was a minute in answering. "She goes to bed too early for my tastes, certainly too early to make it to midnight. No," he grinned, "she wouldn't be much fun on New Year's Eve. Besides, she's not a fan of Chablis."

Anne didn't know what to say to that, but his good humor was infectious. She relaxed in his arms and rested her hands on his chest.

"How about it?" he coaxed softly. "New Year's Eve here?"

"I don't know, Mitch. This thing is so bizarre."

"Are you afraid?" His hands drew light circles on her back.

"A little."

"Of me?"

She was acutely aware of the swell of his broad chest beneath her palms. "No." She eyed the ribbed pattern of his sweater, and whispered, "Of me."

"You have nothing to fear, Annie," he assured her gently. He took her chin with his fingers and tipped up her face. It was the closest physically that they'd been since that first day. "I know what my own needs are right now, and they don't include making things harder for you. By helping you through New Year's, I may just help myself, so there's a selfish motive involved."

She nearly drowned in the deep, deep green of his eyes.

"So, what do you say?" he asked.

"I say this is starting to sound like a Neil Simon script." She wanted reassurance that meeting again was right. She wanted him to say, *There's reason why that script made millions for the guy, it's a damned good plot, it makes a whole lot of sense.*

But Mitch only shrugged. Dropping his arms, he moved back. "It's your choice. I'll be here anyway."

She hated the sudden sound of indifference, but it made it easier to leave. When he opened the door, she slipped behind the wheel.

"Drive carefully," he said.

"I will." Backing the car around, she straightened the wheel. She gave Mitch a last, longing glance before putting a foot on the gas. The car had barely moved forward when his voice echoed in the winter wood.

"Hey, wait!"

She braked. His long-legged gait quickly brought him alongside the car. His breath misted the air when he leaned into the window.

"Don't forget to pack a dress. We'll be going out." He grinned and popped a featherlight kiss on the tip of her nose. "Now, go, before the snow gets here."

She went.

4

Thanksgiving wasn't nearly as bad as Anne had expected. She spent it at her parents' house with their usual crowd, and, yes, she missed Jeff. But there were interesting people to talk with, and chaos enough to pretend that Jeff might just be off in another room. Her major discomfort proved to be a stomachache from eating more heavily than she had in a year, but an antacid and a long walk with her father eased that pain.

Work kept her busy, as did, to her dismay, unfinished business relating to the plane crash. The FAA had finally come through with its findings, and Anne's lawyer had filed suit against the airline—a small, privately owned one—for the inadequate upkeep and safety-check procedure of its craft.

Anne had always known that the suit was a possibility, but her appetite for it had waned. Not so Jeff's parents' appetite. They kept the lawyer on the case even after Anne asked them to stop.

Now the wheels of justice were turning. The lawyer called her in for meeting after meeting. Rarely did a day go by when he didn't phone her with one question or another. The latest word was that there would be a hearing in early April. Anne cringed at the thought.

She was tired of reliving the accident, tired of the horror, the helplessness, the anger. She would love Jeff until the day she died, but she needed to live until then.

And there was Mitch. Something had begun to change—in her life, in her outlook, in her attitude toward him. He was becoming real. When she was low, she thought of him and felt better. The prospect of seeing him for the New Year's holiday became part of her daily routine.

It worried her a little. She wondered if she was building him up to be something he wasn't. She remembered him as being smart, solid, and strong, as offering protection and comfort, stimulation and challenge. At times he seemed larger than life, too large for a plane crash to kill. She half-suspected he would look at the burning debris and walk away unscathed.

It occurred to her that after building him up, she might be in for a letdown when she saw him again. She figured she had until New Year's to get a grip on herself.

As it happened, she was wrong.

Alexander Robie, the professor for whom she did the ongoing grant work, organized a dinner for the seven people involved with the project. There were two secretaries, three research assistants, Alex and a colleague of his, and Anne. Thumbing his nose at the usual budget restraints, Alex reserved a long table at one of New York's finest restaurants. Only because she had refused him on so many other occasions, Anne agreed to let him pick her up and drive her to the dinner.

She was self-consciousness when they arrived together, but the awkwardness faded. No one seemed to think twice about it. Besides, she knew these people and liked them. This was the kind of dinner with friends that she and Jeff had always enjoyed.

And Mitch? Did he like spending time with friends? There were other groups in the restaurant. Her eye skimmed one or two, then went to a third, and her pulse tripped. A man there had Mitch's hair and good looks. He wore a dark suit and tie, and a crisp white shirt. He was with a woman. In all the time Anne watched, he didn't take his eyes from her face.

Funny, but the possibility of their bumping into each other hadn't entered her mind. New York was a big place, and she rarely went out. The man in the corner couldn't be Mitch. It would be too much of a coincidence.

She refocused on her friends. Shortly before dessert was done, though, the maître d' materialized beside her and slipped her a folded piece of paper.

"What's this," Alex teased. "A secret admirer?"

Anne unfolded the paper. There, in a bold black script, was the short message. UNTIL DECEMBER 31ST. Her eyes flew toward where the man and his date had been seated, but the table was empty now, reset with fresh linen and silver.

Biting her lip, she reread the message.

"What is it, Anne? Any problem?" Alex's concern made her aware of the others' attention.

Embarrassed, she refolded the paper. "It's nothing. An old friend was in and saw us." With a feeble smile, she tucked the note in her purse.

"Must have been some old friend," Alex whispered. "You're blushing."

"I am not," Anne replied. "It's the wine."

But her cheeks grew red more than once in the following days. Sometimes it was with annoyance that Mitch had embarrassed her in front of her friends, sometimes with frustration that he hadn't approached, sometimes with anger that he hadn't made his note more personal. One or twice, it was even with jealousy. He had been with a woman. His "other obligation"? Anne couldn't recall anything about her, not her looks, her age, her dress, or her expression. She wished she could, but she'd had eyes only for the man who looked so much like Mitch.

Thinking about this faceless woman, she had second thoughts about returning to Vermont. If Mitch wasn't free, what was the point? Already she thought about him far too often. Better to cut her losses and make a clean break.

But she did think about him a lot, and she needed Vermont. No matter that it would be safer spending New Year's Eve home alone, she found herself driving to the cabin.

The landscape was snow-covered and bleak now. Ice hung in spikes from the boughs of trees and the eaves of tidy farmhouses and cottages along the familiar route. Everything in sight was either gray, ash-green, or white. With the superhighway far behind, her small car slid often on patches of ice.

Anne drove as fast as she dared. The midafternoon sun cast a feeble shadow through bare trees lining the road. She was mesmerized by the grid it formed, so much so that she lost track of her speed, until the loud blast of a car horn from the village road on her right brought her back.

She recognized the light blue Honda instantly. With a smile of delight, she pulled up on the shoulder of the road. The Honda stopped just behind. When Mitch climbed out, Anne's heart throbbed. Any doubts she'd had about coming vanished on the spot.

Smiling more widely than ever, she rolled down her window and called a breathy "Hi!" even before he reached the door.

His glower took her by surprise. "What are you trying to do, get yourself killed? You can't speed on this road."

"I was only going forty."

Anger and all, he was a sight to behold. Looking her fill through dark glasses, she kept right on smiling. His hair was more blond than silver in the dull sun, making him look younger and, for a tall, hard man, oddly soft. Then she realized that despite the show of anger, he was glad to see her again.

As though he sensed she had him figured out, he blew the anger off with a misted sigh. "Look, Annie, you stay behind me for the rest of the trip. Okay?"

She humored him. "Did you get everything at the market? All the per-ishables? Plenty of wine?"

"Behind me!" he repeated.

"Hot chocolate? And whipped cream?"

He wiped the smile from her face with a hard, fast kiss, sucking her lips to his for just an instant before straightening. Shooting her a watch-your-self-lady look, he returned to his own car and pulled out in front. He drove at a sedate thirty miles per hour. It was deliberate, and too slow for the road. Anne smiled and simply adjusted her foot on the gas.

Shortly, they reached the cottage. When the cars were parked in a line on the snow-packed drive, Mitch carried her luggage inside. She took the attic room without a word, because it hadn't been at all uncomfortable, warmer if anything than the larger room downstairs. And she didn't have to listen to him over her head. It was bad knowing that he had once slept in this bed. Hearing things would have driven her imagination wild.

She was in the process of storing groceries when she felt him at the kitchen door. He looked her up and down. She still wore the gray wool pantsuit that had been warm and comfortable for driving. But its white cowl-neck sweater was a switch from the somber navies and blacks he'd usually seen her in. And then, her hair was loose.

"Well?" she asked, growing self-conscious when he just kept looking.

"Come here," he said in a low, deep voice.

She didn't hesitate. Within seconds, she was across the room and in his arms. They were warm and intimate, very dear in a way that said friend before lover.

"You looked beautiful that night in the restaurant," he said against her hair, then drew back enough to smooth a loose strand from her cheek. "Did you enjoy yourself?"

She looked up, leaving her hands locked behind his back. "I didn't re-alize it was you until I got the note. Why didn't you come say hello?"

"That's off limits, isn't it? Socializing in the real world?"

In that instant, Anne sensed she didn't want it that way, not anymore. But she needed to get used to the thought, so she blocked out words by dropping her head to his chest. Her arms told him that she'd missed him. The speed of his heartbeat said he'd missed her, too. Okay, so they didn't use words. That was fine for now.

Mitch shifted her to his side and, with an arm over her shoulder, led her to the living room. He drew her down beside him on the sofa, tucked her head in the crook of his arm, and stretched out his long legs. "Tell me about Christmas."

She spoke tentatively. "It wasn't as bad as I'd expected."

"No downs?"

"A few. Jeff and I always went from house to house on Christmas Day. It was more simple this year. Dinner with his parents."

"Who were your friends that night?"

"At the restaurant?"

"Uh-huh."

"People I work with."

"Tell me about your work."

He hadn't ever asked her that before, but his eyes said that he wanted to know. So she explained her interest in languages and described the evolution of her career. He asked thought-filled questions, clearly catching on to what she did. When she was least expecting it, he said, "That professor—what did you say his name was, Alex?—looked interested in you. Have you gone out with him?"

"I told you that I don't date," she chided.

"Ah," he drawled. "That's right. I forgot. He's asked you out, though, hasn't he?"

Anne saw no point in denying it. "Several times. I'm not interested in dating him, though. That dinner was a group get-together." When she saw him relax, she made her move. "What about your date that night—excuse me, your companion?" Jealousy was a tough thing to hide.

Mitch played it up with a knowing grin. "What about her?"

"Who is she?"

"Her name's Liz."

"Do you see her often?"

"Yes."

"Oh."

"Aren't you glad you asked?"

"Not particularly." She pried herself away from him and slid to the far end of the sofa. He didn't seem bothered, simply lifted her feet to his thighs. He slide a lazy hand under the wool of her slacks to massage her calf. It felt too good for Anne to object.

"Jealous?" he asked.

"Yes."

"That's good." He was grinning more broadly than before.

Anne scowled. "You're an arrogant brute," she began and turned the discussion around. "So tell me what you do. You must have some line of work. Is it in the city?"

He answered her calmly and clearly. "My corporation has headquarters in the city, but we operate all over the country."

"Your corporation?"

Strangely, where it might have been appropriate, the arrogance vanished. "I head a corporation. Does that bother you?"

With a sudden, irrational anger, she asked, "Why would it bother me? It has nothing to do with me."

He leaned forward and pulled her again to his side. "All I meant," he said, teasing, "was that—well, to be perfectly honest, I've been told I make a good catch. Being the president of a large corporation doesn't help to discourage overeager women."

Anne snorted. "Any woman who'd want your strong black coffee and your long hot showers has to be crazy. As for me"—she put her nose in the air—"no amount of money can compensate for your squandering my macadamias."

He gave her middle a playful squeeze. She was acutely aware of the arm beneath her breasts. More breathlessly, she said, "So. What does your corporation do?"

"We develop real estate—office parks, shopping centers, and so on."

"Define 'and so on.'"

"Oh, we have . . . other interests."

"Confidential ones," she surmised.

"For now."

"The mystery of the year."

He responded to that by shifting her sideways and down. He followed, holding himself on his elbows. "You talk too much." His eyes caressed her face, but it wasn't her face he was talking about when he said, "You not only look good, you feel good." His body inched over hers, giving her a good feel in return.

If Anne hadn't been breathless before, she was now. She wasn't fighting him, because she realized that the attraction wasn't only physical, at least on her part. It had gone beyond that.

She wrapped her arms around his neck and exerted the slightest pressure at his nape. It brought him in for a kiss that held all the passion missing from the earlier hug. She shivered when his tongue slid into her mouth and their breath mingled. With his shoulders flexing under her palms, her head began to spin. He intoxicated her. But she didn't want him leaving her, and said so with a cry when he angled his body off, then cried out again, differently now, when his hand found her breast.

He trailed kisses from her eyes, down her cheeks to her neck, while she unbuttoned his shirt. His bare chest was an Eden of sinew and fuzz, a potent aphrodisiac. She was ready to burst when his hand left her breast and held her neck so that he could kiss her harder. She welcomed it, needed it.

"Annie, Annie, Annie," he groaned, ragged against her lips, "what am I going to do with you?"

She held his head, then dropped her fingers down his throat and, again, into the tawny hair on his chest. "Look who started it," she whispered but she was fascinated by the bunch of muscles under her hand. She moved her palms around, then over his nipples.

He made a frustrated sound and sat up, hauling her along with him. Abruptly he released her and leaned forward. He put his elbows on his knees and his head in his palms.

Everything about him cried of sudden distress. Anne rubbed the taut muscles at the back of his neck. "What is it?"

He gave her a sidelong glance. "You don't know?" When she didn't answer, he shrugged off her hand and pushed himself into a far corner of the sofa. "I thought I'd be able to chalk what we have here up to a vacation thing, but each time I go home, I can't put you out of my mind. I want you, Anne. Want you bad."

She was dizzy with pleasure. "Why does that upset you?"

He stared, then came forward. "Do you know what I'm talking about here?"

"Yes. I'm not stupid. You're asking yourself the same questions I've spent hours asking myself. What am I doing here? Why did I come? What do I want to happen? Where's my sense of propriety? The list goes on and on." She caught a breath. "What do you want me to say? I know what you're saying, but I don't know what to do either!"

Mitch sighed and drew her back to his chest. "It's gone past that, Anne. I'm asking myself whether I'm ready to see you in public, in New York, and whether you're ready for that. I'm asking whether I'm ready for more of a commitment than just a physical one, and whether you're ready for that." He tipped up her face. "I want to sleep with you, Anne, but I can't do that and then walk away when it's done. For the first time in so long it's not just a physical need."

He had echoed her thoughts. Anne was more interested in him than in anyone else since Jeff's death, but she wasn't ready for a full-time, open relationship. There was still that loose end to tie up in court, still that emotional barrier.

He pressed her cheek to the beat of his heart. "I wouldn't want to hurt you for the world, Annie. You deserve the best. You need a guy's full attention and devotion. I have too many other responsibilities right now."

It was the right answer, still she felt discouragement and loss. She held on, and was held for long seconds. When she looked up, he brushed a tear from her cheek.

"I won't ask much," she whispered falteringly. "I'm not sure what I want any more than you are. The only thing I ask is that you be here for me to come to every once in a while."

He tightened his arms around her. "I will, honey, I will."

* * *

The New Year arrived with a surge of high spirit that neither of them, weeks before, would have imagined possible. They ate at a small inn where the restaurant was elegant, intimate, and quaint. For Anne it was like a first date. She wore her favorite navy knit, which she had packed for the occasion. Its softness offset her darkness, its gentle wrap showed curves that had begun to return. She wanted to look sophisticated, and to that end, wore makeup for the first time here.

Mitch rewarded her with a glow in his eyes. He looked gorgeous in his fine wool slacks and tailored blazer. They made a stunning duo, drawing the attention of more than one pair of curious eyes.

He avoided intimacy beyond a light hand on her waist when he escorted her to their table. Later, back at the cabin, they rang in the midnight hour with champagne toasts.

And the light-hearted tone held through the week. They took daily walks in the crisp, cold air. The woods were an enchanted place in winter, a safe harbor from winds that whipped across the meadow but couldn't penetrate the evergreens. Bundled in woolen and down, they hiked over ponds of solid ice and followed the crusty line of the brook from mountaintop to valley. The snow squeaked under their boots, but, aside from their voices, it was the only noise in the forest.

Shielded by spruce, pine, and cedar, they walked for hours through the blue-shadowed land, returning to the cabin only when their hands and feet were numb. More often than not then, they settled in at the kitchen window to watch chickadees at the feeder that Mitch had staked into the ground.

It was a time of quiet serenity. Anne did little reading and even less work. Rather, she spent hours in calm reverie before the fire, a triumph in and of itself. She was happy. She wasn't brooding or mourning. She didn't want to be anywhere else, with anyone else in the world.

During one of these relaxing moments, on the last evening of their stay, Mitch suddenly went to his bedroom and returned with a small box. It was wrapped in white and had a pale blue ribbon.

"What's this?" she asked in surprise.

"Open it."

She pulled at the bow with unsteady fingers. "When did you get this?" She hadn't expected a gift. His presence was enough.

"I was in Brazil right after Thanksgiving. It was made by one of the local artisans in a small village in the interior."

The top of the box fell back to reveal a ring, a rectangular piece of enamelware framed in gold and mounted on a fine gold band. Anne gasped at the beauty of the intricately painted design, a semiabstract portrait of sand, sea, and sun, all woven together in blues, greens, yellows, and creams.

"It's beautiful," she breathed. "You never should have—"

"Put it on," he said.

The ring fit perfectly on the third finger of her right hand, and gave her pale, slim fingers even greater delicacy.

"There," he said with a satisfied sigh. "That's a little color for you. Maybe next time a bright sweater to wear for me."

Next time.

The words thrilled her as much as the ring. "I will. And . . . thank you, Mitch. The ring is beautiful. I'll cherish it." She put both hands up to frame his face, to trace the powerful line of his cheeks, his jaw, his chin. Then she leaned forward and gave him a soft and heartfelt kiss.

"I wish I had something to give you," she whispered when it was done.

In a trembling breath, he said, "You already have, Anne. And I thank you."

5

Anne drove north again on a Friday afternoon in the second week of February. As the first flakes of snow began to fall, she sniffled and pulled another Kleenex from the glove box. For the better part of the week she'd had a cold. If she had known Mitch's number, she might have called to cancel their meeting. But she didn't know it, and she wanted to see him. She was counting on feeling better in the clean country air. What she hadn't counted on was the snow.

As she crossed the border from New York into Vermont, the flakes grew larger and more feathery. They were sticking to anything and everything in sight. Traffic had slowed with the decreased visibility, but that was a double-edged sword. Yes, it was safer driving slower. But it meant the trip took longer, and the longer she was on the roads, the worse they became.

She was impatient to reach the cottage. Even aside from a hacking cough and the accumulation of snow on the windshield, she wanted to be in a place that had become, in some ways, more real a world than the other. The past six weeks in New York had been a way of passing time between trips. She was happier here, more relaxed and alive with Mitch than anywhere else.

Traffic slowed another notch. She glanced at her watch. Two hours behind, already! It was late afternoon. Darkness would be here before long. She didn't relish driving through the storm in the dark.

She thought of stopping at an inn for the night, but feared that tomorrow wouldn't be any better. Besides, she had no way to contact Mitch. He would be worried if she didn't show up.

Her snow tires clung tentatively to the road as she turned off the highway at last. There were still miles to go, but at least the road was smaller. Unfortunately it was also deserted. She pushed the small car through a blinding rage of white. Vistas were obliterated. Only the low fencing at the side of the road kept her on course, though how long it would be before they were covered by drifts, she didn't know.

Her hands were white-knuckled on the wheel. The snow was a thick wall behind her, so there was no turning back. She peered nervously through the windshield, praying for a plow. With each passing mile, she drove more slowly through accumulating depths.

When her pace was down to fifteen miles an hour, and she couldn't see more than a single car's length ahead, she felt a wave of panic. The sense of isolation was utter and intense. Fighting a sudden dizziness, she kept her foot on the gas.

Dusk had fallen by the time she reached the cottage cutoff. She was so relieved to see it, that she took the turn a hair too fast. The car skidded and fishtailed before coming to an abrupt halt several yards into the private way, lodged firmly in a snow bank at the side of the road.

Swearing under her breath, Anne worked the gear shift, alternating between forward and reverse in an attempt to free the car from the drift. Her nerves were already taut. Now she cursed her luck as she fumbled with the door handle, tripped out of the car, and promptly sank in snow nearly as high as her boots. Even through rose-colored glasses, hopes for the car were low.

She peered up the hill in the direction of the house. In ideal weather, the walk was a mile's mild uphill challenge. But in this blizzard? And then there was the possibility that Mitch was stuck somewhere, too. But he was the one with the key.

She sneezed and raised a parka-covered arm to her face. If the door was locked, she would just have to break in. There was no other choice. She couldn't go back, and she couldn't stay here.

Packing her pockets with Kleenex, she closed up the car. She zipped the parka all the way, pulled its hood over her wool hat, pushed her hands into gloves, and set off. She trudged as fast as she could through the mounting snow, lifting one leg high, then the other. Her muscles began to ache. Tucking her head deeper into the hood of her parka, she plodded on.

Thirty minutes passed, then another fifteen. Exhausted, she looked around for something to rest against. But all was white, lonely, uninviting, and bleak. Looking back, she saw nothing but her own footsteps. Looking ahead, she saw nothing at all. She pushed on, absolutely, positively refusing to believe that she may have taken the wrong road.

Bone-weary and weak from coughing, she grew more frightened as the minutes passed. Signs of life were nonexistent. The cabin had to be somewhere. For another half hour, she pushed herself forward, pausing occasionally to blow her nose, huffing hoarsely at the exertion, ignoring the heat on her cheeks.

Snow continued to fall, creating a fairyland that, to Anne's bleary gaze, was nightmarishly grotesque. She imagined being lost and freezing to death. The road had never been this long.

Her senses blurred black with the onset of night. Dizzy, she fell to her knees, then forced herself back up and struggled on. Tears of fear mixed with melting snow on her fevered cheeks. Her clothing chafed against her sweaty body. Still she moved on.

Finally, though, she was too weak. She collapsed on her knees and sank into a billowing drift. Head bowed, panting with exhaustion, she fought hysteria and swayed in the gusting wind.

"Mitch . . . Mitch . . . please help me . . ." she whimpered.

"Annie!"

Mirage or reality, she didn't care. When a large form knelt before her, she fell against it, aware only of the support it offered, the warmth it held.

He lifted her from the snow. "Hold on, Annie. It's not far to the house."

"Mitch?" she cried against his jacket as she shielded her face from the driving snow.

"It's me, honey. Quiet now. Save your strength."

The light from the house filtered through the snowy darkness like a beacon. Once inside, he kicked the door shut with his boot and gently lowered her feet to the floor, only to catch her up again when her knees buckled. Without a word, he carried her to the downstairs bedroom. Depositing her on the edge of the bed, he began to quickly remove her wet clothing. He paused once to throw off his own jacket and pull back the bed's quilt, then returned to undress her.

Anne didn't protest. Chilled to the bone, she trembled uncontrollably.

"Lift your arms, like a good girl," he said softly and, one at a time, drew the sleeves of her heavy sweater off and pulled it over her head.

"I thought I was lost, Mitch. I walked for so long and I couldn't find the house."

"Shhh. You're safe now."

She clutched at his shoulders for support when he knelt to pull off her boots, then her socks. "Lie down, honey. Your jeans are drenched." With infinite tenderness he eased her back and pulled them off, tugging impatiently only when the sodden denim resisted his hands.

"I feel so sick," she said in a hoarse whisper, throwing an arm over her forehead.

In an instant he was bending over her. "I know, Annie. But you'll be fine now. I just have to warm you up. Okay?" She didn't answer, not even to protest when he drew off her cold, drenched panties. He tucked the lower half of her body under the weight of the quilt before turning to remove her turtleneck and bra. With the covers bunched around her shoulders, he crossed the room to his suitcase, pulled out a clean cotton shirt, and returned to the bed.

Sitting beside her, he pressed cool lips to her burning forehead. "You'll be fine," he repeated and quickly dressed her in the shirt, then covered her up again.

Anne sneezed. "You shouldn't have taken off my sweater."

"Forget modesty. You were soaked to the skin and freezing."

"That sweater . . ."—a fit of coughing interrupted her, but she managed to catch her breath—"I wore it for you. Did you notice?"

His lips twitched. "I did notice, Annie. It was pink." He brushed a strand of hair from her forehead. "Thank you." With the back of his hand, he felt her forehead, then her cheeks. "I'm going to heat up some soup for you."

She shook her head. "No. I can't eat. Just stay here with me for a few minutes."

He drew her, quilts and all, into his arms and rubbed her all over to warm her up.

"I was so frightened," she whispered. "It was cold and wet. And dark."

"You should have known I'd come looking for you."

"I wasn't sure you were here. There were no tire tracks—" She broke off, coughing again.

He waited until she quieted. "I arrived before the storm began. Snow can be pretty dramatic up here. It should be beautiful come morning."

The thought of wandering through the snow with Mitch was a lovely one. She smiled then sneezed.

"I'll get that soup now."

"No. Really, I'm not hungry."

"You need something warm inside."

"I don't think I can keep it down."

"You will." He set her down. "Just rest. I'll be back."

She rolled to her side and tucked up her knees. The warmth of the bed burned, still she felt chilled. Turning over, she huddled in a ball and dozed. She woke up when Mitch returned with a bowl of steaming broth. He helped her sit, and he fed her himself. When she couldn't take in another drop, he let her sleep.

She awoke an hour later feeling even worse. Mitch was bathing her face and neck with a damp cloth. "That's quite some cold," he muttered.

"It just hung on. I thought it'd be better by now."

"Why did you leave New York in the first place? You should have stayed in bed."

He was annoyed with her. She thought that was unfair. "It wasn't snowing at home," she argued. "I had no idea I'd run into this mess, or that it would get so bad so fast."

"Forget the weather. You should have been in bed anyway, with a cold like this."

"Good God, Mitch, I can't put my life on hold every time I get a cold."

"Yeah, well if you don't take better care of yourself, you may put your life on permanent hold. Colds can turn into pneumonia, and people die from pneumonia."

She teared up. "I just wanted to be here with you." She turned onto her side, away from his glower, and pulled the covers up around her ears.

She was startled when Mitch lifted her, covers and all, and held her tightly. From time to time he dipped his head, touching his lips to her hair, her brow, or her eyes. His voice was softer when he finally spoke. "Don't think I didn't want to see you as much. I did. But we could have come next week."

"Someone else may be here next week."

"No one will be here."

"How do you know?" she cried with a touch of indignance.

Looking suddenly resigned, he shifted her in his arms and ran a hand back through his hair. "Because this is my house. Miles Cooper works for me. He rents it out when I'm not planning to be here."

The puzzle piece fell into place. Hoarsely, she said, "Oh, my. It figures, I guess. Helps explain the original mix-up. And why you prefer this bed. It's yours."

"There won't be any more mix-ups, Annie. I've taken the house off Miles's rental list. From now on we'll be the only ones who use it."

Before Anne could grasp the full implication of that, a new shudder shook her. She burrowed against him, seeking warmth for her extremities.

Gently, he laid her down and disappeared. He returned moments later and lifted her head. "Aspirin," he explained before she could ask. "Open your mouth."

She was a docile patient, too weak to protest his pampering, too pleased by it to want to protest. He kept her pumped with broth and aspirin for most of the night, dozing beside her under the quilt. One part of his body always touched her. She couldn't so much as turn over when he was up on an elbow, concerned. In other circumstances, the sleeping arrangement would have been heady. But Anne's senses were blunted by fever.

The next day was a mass of hours blurred together. Her fever stayed high despite the medicine. Increasingly, her whole body suffered when she coughed.

"What is the matter with me?" she cried in frustration, when she awoke late in the afternoon feeling no better.

Mitch took her hot hand in his. "I'm not sure. As soon as the road is plowed, I'm taking you to the doctor."

"Has it stopped snowing?"

"Finally."

"How much is on the ground?"

"A little over a foot. It makes the plowing slower, though the folks up here are well-equipped."

"Mitch?" She rolled onto her back to see his face, as he sat beside her on the bed. Her voice was weak, but something had been nagging at her.

"Yes?"

"If you own this house, then you have access to the names and addresses of the renters. Yes?"

He looked amused. "Yes."

"Then you know who I am."

"No."

"But you have that information."

"Miles has that information. I suppose I could see it if I wanted to, and I've been tempted a time or two, but I haven't peeked."

Anne wasn't sure whether to be relieved or hurt.

He laughed.

"What's so funny?" she grumbled.

"You. Your face hides nothing!"

"I'm that transparent? It's not fair, y'know."

"What isn't fair?"

"Me . . . here . . . at your mercy. With my transparent face and all, I feel naked."

"Except for the good graces of my shirt, darlin', you are," he drawled.

"That's not what I mean, and you know it," she scolded and broke into a spasm of coughing. When she quieted, he ran cool fingers across her hot cheek. It felt good.

"You talk too much, Annie. Rest your voice now."

At the silence that followed, a sound filtered in from outside. "The plow!" Mitch was on his feet, stopping only at the bedroom door to call, "Don't move until I get back!" Then he was gone.

She lay there for what seemed hours. Finally, she struggled out of bed to use the bathroom. Her reflection in the mirror appalled her—pale skin, red cheeks, dark and sunken eyes. Her hand trembled as she sorted through Mitch's toiletries for a comb. Halfway combing her hair, her knees began to knock. Dropping the comb, she clutched at the edges of the sink for support. That was when the bathroom door opened.

"What are you doing out of bed?" He scooped her up and carried her back, and the bed felt like heaven, the quilt even more so. "Next time," he taunted, "you might just pass out in the middle of the floor. Will you stay in bed?"

"I just went to the bathroom."

"Good. You should be set for a while. Where are the keys to your car?"

She tried to remember. "I think I put them in the pocket of my jeans."
He vanished and returned moments later with the keys in hand.
"I'm hitching a ride with the plow down to your car. It may take me a little
while to dig it out. Does it have snow tires?" When she nodded, he said,
"Good. I'll be back as soon as I can, then I'm taking you to the doctor."

"Mitch—" Her hoarse call caught him at the door. "Your arm—is it all
right to shovel?"

She heard a sharp intake of breath, then a grunt. "It'll do."

While he was gone, she suffered. Her head hurt, her sinuses hurt, her
throat hurt, her chest hurt, her legs hurt. Curled up in misery, she prayed
for sleep.

She must have dozed off, because it seemed only minutes before Mitch
returned with a gruff foot-stamping at the front door. Lacking the strength
to call out, she waited until he appeared by her bedside, ruddy cheeked
from the cold, but eager to pack her up and leave.

He did it without a fuss, simply snatching her up, quilt and all, and carrying her out. He stopped short at the front door. Swearing softly, he
back tracked and deposited her on the sofa, went into the kitchen, and
returned with her wool hat, which was now warm and dry. He put it on
her head, scooped her up again and didn't put her down until they
reached his car.

She wheezed heavily for most of the trip into the village. Between darkness and the new walls of snow lining the roads, there wasn't much for the
headlights to pick out.

He parked in front of a tiny clinic, ran around the car, and hoisted her
up. He had had the driver of the plow call ahead. A doctor was waiting inside.

Thirty minutes later he carried her back to the car. "Bronchial pneumonia. Good show, Annie," he teased gently as he tucked her into the pas-
senger's seat again.

Weary, she caught his eye. "Do you have my pills?"

He patted the spot where the upper-left breast pocket of his shirt would
be. "Right here. Are you comfortable?"

"Comfortable?" she shot back hoarsely. "I've been poked, X-rayed,
stuck with needles, and carted around like I had no feelings at all." She
scowled. "I feel hot and cold and achy. And you ask if I'm comfortable?"
She looked away. "Don't ask."

Mitch chuckled. Slamming the door, he circled the car to the driver's
side and slid behind the wheel with remarkable ease, given his length. "At
least your good humor is intact," he teased. "Let's go home. The doctor
ordered warmth, rest, and lots of hot liquid. We'd better get to it."

* * *

For the next three days they followed the doctor's orders to a tee, with Mitch in command, dictating when each pill was to be taken, when she was to eat and sleep. She felt miserable for another full day before the medication began to take effect. Only then did she dare to balk at the strict regimen.

"I'm going to turn into a chicken if I drink one more drop of this soup. It's awful," she complained when he appeared on Tuesday morning with another mug of broth. "I feel better today. Honestly I do." She was sitting up against the headboard of the bed, dressed in her own flannel nightgown.

"You still sound lousy," he informed her, as though that settled that, but she was impatient.

"If you don't want to hear my noise," she croaked, "don't goad me into conversation. Isn't it about time I went upstairs to the other bedroom?"

He grinned. "You don't like sleeping with me?"

"I'm not 'sleeping' with you, as the expression goes. It's more like sleeping in spite of you. You may think that I'm out of it, but I feel you beside me. I know you're there . . . all night! You touch me just enough to make sure I'm all right, but that's all. What fun is that?"

She broke into a fit of coughing from which only Mitch's firm slap on the back saved her. He stayed to gently rub her neck and shoulders, his touch growing more seductive by the minute. She hadn't been aware of his other hand on her midriff until it moved upward. Her breast tingled at its touch. She gasped, but couldn't pull away. His palm passed around and over her nipple, teasing it through the soft flannel. She gripped his arm, as much to hold it there as for support.

"It isn't much fun, is it?" he said, "but you'll stay down here for now, where I can keep an eye on you. In a few days you can go back upstairs."

"In a few days I'll be going home." A sad thought, indeed.

At his urging she lay back on the pillow. Her eyes held his. She waited.

"Something has to give," he said. "You know that, don't you, Annie?"

She nodded. They were nearing the point where a kiss alone wasn't enough. Same with the occasional week together.

"Are you ready for more?" he asked.

"Are you?"

"I asked first."

"I can't answer until I know more. Tell me about your family."

His eyes held hers. "There isn't much to tell. My parents are alive and well in Manhattan. My father is retired. He has been for several years now. It's nice. Gives him time to spend doing other things."

"What did he do?"

Mitch grinned. "He was a concert pianist. I'm sure you'd recognize the name if I told you." He didn't offer it, nor did she ask. That part of the bargain held.

Anne was intrigued. "That's quite a switch—from concert pianist to business tycoon in one generation. Was the musical ability passed on at all?"

He smiled. "Can I carry a tune? Fairly. Can I play the piano? No. My sister does, though."

Her eyes widened. "You have a sister? Is she older or younger than you?"

He gave the ceiling a one-eyed squint. "Older by . . . let's see . . . three, no four, minutes."

"Years," she corrected quietly.

"Minutes," he reasserted, laughing.

"Twins?"

He nodded.

"Oh, Mitch!" She was delighted. "That's marvelous! You must have had fun growing up!"

"Not really. She was always taller, smarter, and faster than I was."

"And now?"

He grinned. "I've caught up."

"There must have been some advantage to being the runt of the litter," she teased.

"Oh, there was. My mother pampered me more. She felt sorry for me." A mischievous gleam danced in his eyes. "I suppose that's why I still have the need to touch and be touched." He took her hand between his two.

Anne refused to be distracted. "Are there other twins in the family?"

He shook his head. "Just Liz and me."

"Liz?" A bell rang. She smiled when Mitch realized his slip. "Hmmmm . . . Liz," she repeated with an accusing lilt.

He grew sheepish. "Now you know my secrets."

"That was Liz with you at the restaurant before Christmas."

"Uh-huh."

"Is she married?"

"It didn't work out. But lately she's been seeing a nice guy."

"What does she do with her music?"

"Actually, she's more a harpist than a pianist."

"Beautiful!" Anne exclaimed.

"Not while she was first learning," he muttered.

Anne gave him a nudge. "You're jealous of her talent."

"Maybe." He raised her hand and kissed her fingers in true continental style, then left her alone to rest.

* * *

That night Anne had a nightmare. It was more frightening than any she'd had since she'd been a child. Bolting upright in bed, drenched in a cold sweat, she struggled to catch her breath until Mitch's arms came around her.

"What is it, honey?" he asked in alarm. The room was dim, bathed eerily in the blue light of the moon as it spilled over the snow in the yard.

"A nightmare. Oh, God, it was awful." She trembled in spite of his steadying hold.

"Want to tell me about it?"

"It's that court case hanging over my head."

"What court case?"

"The accident. My husband's family has been pushing me to sue for negligence. I agreed at first because I was as angry as they were and we were all so helpless. Now I'd rather put the whole thing behind me."

Mitch was silent for a time. "And the nightmare?" he asked quietly. His arms were exquisitely tender as they held her to his chest.

She took a shuddering breath. "I dreamed I was on that plane with Jeff when it crashed, but that I wasn't injured and had to stand by and watch while he burned to death. There were no doctors, no medics, nothing but flames and smoke and debris and people's screams." She buried her face in his chest. "It was awful."

He spoke softly against her hair. "I know, honey, I know. But it was only a dream." His nearness comforted her. "Only a dream," he repeated and said it on and off, between gentle rocking, until she fell back to sleep.

Mitch seemed preoccupied. She sensed it from time to time and guessed that he had work on his mind. On the last night before she was to leave, though, she looked up to find him brooding at the flames in the hearth. He was sitting on the floor by her chair, with his legs stretched toward the warmth.

She touched his shoulder. "Is something wrong?"

Snatched from some distant place, he jerked his head around. "Hmm?"

"You look bothered by something. I'm back to normal, and you haven't begun to fight with me." She gave him a teasing smile.

His smile was oddly sad. "I seem to have lost my taste for the fight."

"This must have been a boring week for you."

"I haven't minded. It's been restful."

"Too restful. Tomorrow is my last morning here. Will you go walking with me, or do I sneak out alone?"

He looked back at the fire. "I'll go with you."

She had expected an argument, something to the tune of *You're not well enough for a walk.* When he said nothing, she knew something was definitely wrong.

But he wasn't the only one who had lost his taste for the fight. She didn't want anything to mar their last night. So she let it go.

With the snowfall still fresh on the deserted mountain, the sight greeting them the following morning was one of blinding splendor. The sky was a deep blue, the air cold and still. Days of warm sun and freezing temperatures had created a crust of ice. The crunch underfoot echoed as they made their way across the hillside. Bits of the brook that weren't frozen ran through crystalline palaces of branches and weeds. The only other signs of life were those frozen in the snow, the tracks of the snowshoe rabbit or the packed path of the deer.

It was a scene of rare beauty, all the more beautiful for the week-long wait to see it. But time was short. Too soon, afternoon arrived and the moment of parting.

"Are you sure you won't stay the weekend?" Mitch asked. "You shouldn't be driving so far yet." Her car was packed. They stood beside it.

His wistfulness added to Anne's regret. "I wish I could. But I promised my folks I'd attend a hospital benefit with them tomorrow night. I can't let them down."

He wrapped an arm around her. "Even if you're letting me down?" His eyes dropped to her lips. Seconds later he kissed them. It was a gentle caress, sweet torture to Anne's reawakening body. She wound her arms around his neck and felt him tighten in response. She was well now. Her departure was imminent. If ever there was a time for ardor, this was it.

The kiss deepened and the fire grew hotter. With a wildness borne of desperation, he thrust his tongue deeper into her mouth, and Anne reeled at the sensation. She would have happily returned to the house, to that same bedroom, that same large bed if he'd asked just then. But he didn't.

With a shaky breath, he drew back. He took her hand, pressed something in it, and closed her fingers. "I want you to take this. It's a key to the place. I have a few hectic weeks ahead, but I'll be up again at the end of March. If you want to come at any time, I want you to."

Anne was deeply touched, but that wasn't the only reason her eyes filled with tears. Frightened that she would make a fool of herself, she whispered a soft thanks against his cheek in a final hug, pulled away, and got into her car. She headed down the sanded road without a look behind. Parting was getting harder and harder.

6

March in Vermont was the time of unlocking, that period during which the frozen ground gradually yielded one frigid layer after another to the power of an ever-stronger sun, when the brooks and ponds, rivers and lakes lost their ice to the rush of the downstream current. It was a time of the loud thrashing of formidably cold waters against their banks. It was a time of mud.

Anne hadn't expected that when she left New York. Taking Mitch up on his offer and using his key, she arrived several days in advance of him. The excitement was in being there, in these hills, in Mitch's house. Nothing could have kept her away longer.

"You're going again?" her mother had asked in surprise.

Anne was prepared for the question. She had done her homework. "It's maple-sugaring time. I wouldn't miss it for the world."

Her father had remarked, "I wouldn't be surprised if you turned around and bought that place. Pretty soon you'll be spending more time there than you do here."

It was an exaggeration, of course. Still, Ann blushed. The cottage already had an owner, a hale and hearty one, who appeared to be in no way interested in selling. Fortunately her parents had never learned of the stranded car or the pneumonia fiasco, and they still knew absolutely nothing about Mitch.

Anne was starting to feel guilty about that. She had always been close to her parents. They had been understanding and solicitous during her grief. It occurred to her that they would want to know when she was happy.

For she was happy. Knowing that Mitch would be with her in Vermont, she could face just about anything else that arose. His giving her the key was a significant gesture. Now she had a steady tie to the place.

Since returning this last time, she had changed. For one thing, she had finally been able to pack up Jeff's things. For another, she was smiling more, laughing more, eating more. For a third, she was going out more with old friends.

Strange. For so much of the last year her apartment had been her private retreat, her sanctuary when she couldn't face the world. Lately, though, it was nearly as lonely as it had been in the dreadful days following the crash.

She missed Mitch. The longing grew with each day that passed, until her only refuge was in work and the company of others. Even then, he was never far from her mind.

Now, with mud streaks covering the bottom half of her once-bright yellow car, she turned onto the familiar private road. Twice her tires began to spin in the muck; twice she was able to back down and charge forward around the offending mud hole.

It was early Wednesday afternoon. Mitch wasn't due up until late Friday. Everything seemed larger, emptier, and more silent without him, but she wasn't lonely. His mark was in every room of the house, surrounding her in a promising cloak.

In his absence, she applied herself to menial tasks like dusting, mopping, scrubbing sinks and the top of the stove. Oh, she had brought several translations to do, but she didn't touch either. She wasn't in the mood to concentrate.

During those two days, she did more baking than she had in the past two years. She baked bread. She baked muffins. She baked cookies. Something about the rural life was conducive to it.

Same with hiking. Despite the mud, she did it daily. Without a motor humming, she could better hear sounds of the world emerging from winter. The first of the geese honked as they flew in formation through a pale blue sky. The tallest of the tree branches stretched and flexed in the gusting wind. Squirrels scurried. Woodpeckers pecked. The ground squished.

The snow was gone, and the woodland hadn't leafed out. But naked boughs stood straighter, heralding their resurgence. Even the leggy lilacs by the cabin's front door stood proudly in promise of fragrant blossoms.

Friday night came and went with no sign of Mitch.

Anne was devastated. She had cooked a chicken dinner and opened a bottle of wine. The house was spotless and polished. She had showered and dressed in a pair of soft wool slacks and a paisley print blouse, had brushed her hair to a high luster and draped it over her shoulders. Though the soft pink glow on her cheeks needed no help, she had carefully applied a sheen of lavender to her eyelids and a coat of mascara to her lashes. On the third finger of her right hand was the exquisite enameled ring he had given her.

Well after midnight, she wrapped the food and cleaned up the kitchen. At two in the morning, she went to bed, but she barely slept. One ear listened, always listened for the sound of a car. It never came.

Saturday morning, she was heavy-eyed and disturbed. She went through all the possible explanations for his failure to appear. He might have been hung up with business and unable to reach her. He might have forgotten that she would be waiting. He might have decided not to come at all. Now that she had a key, she didn't need him to let her in.

The minutes crept by, one after another, after another. By late afternoon, when there was still no sign of the Honda, Anne was convinced that she had simply blown the relationship into something it wasn't.

Then came the blare of a horn. She ran from the window seat in the kitchen to the front door. But it wasn't his horn—she had known that instantly. While everything about Mitch oozed of charm, this sound carried the rough edge of a local pickup truck.

"Mrs. Boulton?" barked a gruff voice. The stocky form of a farmer, clad in heavy wool jacket, baggy overalls, and aged work boots, stepped from the cab of the truck and strode toward her.

"Yes?" She didn't recognize the man.

"Gut a message for ya. From a fella named Cooper. Phoned the police station. Sorry for the delay." He handed the crumpled paper into Anne's outstretched hand, touched a callused hand to his cap's bill, climbed back in his truck, and was gone.

Nervously she unfolded the paper. The scrawl was nearly illegible. "Unavoidable delay. Mitch arriving Sunday night. Miles Cooper."

With a tired sigh she cast a glance down the empty road. Another whole day to wait. Unavoidable delay. She wondered what that meant— but it didn't keep her awake that night. Exhausted from the night before, she slept deeply.

Sunday brought rain, and a dark, gloomy day. Anne went out for a walk anyway, did a crossword puzzle, sat at the window for what seemed hours. By mid-afternoon, she was champing at the bit. With neither cleaning nor baking left to do, she did some translating. When she finally heard a distant car, the dim light of day had long since yielded to night. But the growing purr was familiar. Without doubt, it was the Honda.

Excited, she opened the front door. It seemed an eternity before he finally climbed from the car, wrested his bags from the trunk, and bolted through the rain toward the house. When he brushed past her without a direct glance, she knew something was wrong.

She closed the door on the rawness of the night, and turned to see him drop the bags, throw off his overcoat, and head for the fire, all without a word. Unsure, she sank down on the sofa and waited.

The man reached out to her both physically and emotionally. He wore a beige sweater and brown corduroy slacks, and looked as strong and fit as ever. But it was the fatigue, suggested by his bent head and the limp hand in his pocket, that made the greatest impression on her. She ached to help, but she feared rebuff. So she remained silent.

For a time, frowning at the fire, Mitch seemed oblivious to her presence. Needing to make some small gesture, she went quietly to the kitchen and returned with a mug of strong black coffee.

"Have something hot, Mitch. It was a long drive."

He looked at her so suddenly that she knew his mind had been miles away. Without a word of either greeting or explanation, he accepted the cup and returned to his brooding. Again Anne waited, fearing what was wrong, but needing to be there.

Finally, he put his head back, drew in a great breath, straightened, and turned. His eyes were tired, his face more drawn than she remembered it. He drank the last of his coffee and set the mug on the mantel. His smile was wan, but it was a smile. "You're looking well."

She rested her chin on her knees, which were drawn up and held by her arms. "I have been, thanks to you. The antibiotic did the trick."

"No more trouble?" When she shook her head, he said, "That's good," and looked back at the fire.

"What's wrong, Mitch?"

He shot her a dry look. "Don't ask. I wouldn't know where to begin."

"Was it a bad drive up?"

"The usual."

A silence followed.

"I received the message," she tried. "Thanks for sending it."

"I didn't want you waiting."

Or worrying, she added silently, bitterly. His aloofness scared her. It suggested he hadn't wanted to come at all. Perhaps he even regretted having given her the key.

"Would you like me to leave, Mitch?"

He looked at her like she was daft. "Of course not. Why do you suggest that?"

"Because you're two days late, then you walk in here like a zombie and stare at the fire. It occurs to me that you might just want your house to yourself."

"If I had wanted that, I'd never have given you a key to the place."

"Why did you? I keep asking myself that, but I can't come up with a good answer."

"I wanted you to have access to the place whenever you wanted."

"Why?"

"That's a crazy question."

"And this is a crazy situation."

He went to the front window and stared out at the darkness. "I never promised you more."

Well, he was right. A heavy weight settled in Anne's stomach. Head bowed, she rose from the sofa, reached for the empty mug, and headed for the kitchen. At the door, she stopped, but she didn't turn. "Have you had any supper?"

"No."

"I'll make something."

"That's not necessary."

"I'll do it."

Five minutes later, she sat across from him and watched him down the club sandwich that she had made with the chicken that had gone uneaten on Friday night. Conversation was sparse and cryptic, compounding her frustration.

"Thank you," he said when only crumbs remained. "That hit the spot."

"I'm glad I've finally done something right," she murmured, standing to clear the dishes.

He caught her hand. "What's that supposed to mean?"

"I think you know." She freed her hand and she continued to the sink.

Suddenly he was directly behind her. "You've been vague about something for the last hour. What is it?"

Fiercely, she scrubbed at the dish.

"You're angry because I showed up late?"

"No."

"What else could it be? I sent word. I even did it through Miles so you wouldn't worry that I knew your last name."

"That's not bothering me."

He turned her around. "Look at me, Anne."

Her hands dripped of soap. She held them out to the sides.

"I want you to tell me what's wrong," he insisted, and she was suddenly angry.

"Why? I don't owe you an explanation for my behavior, any more than you owe me one for yours!"

His eyes held hers for long minutes. "Ah. That's it. You want an explanation for my lateness, like this is some kind of a business meeting."

"I don't want a thing!" she cried, whipping out of his grasp to dry her hands on the towel. She thrust a damp rag into his hand. "Here. You finish cleaning. I'm going to bed."

She held off tears until she was safely up in her attic room and sure of not being followed. Then they came with a vengeance. She had loved Jeff and lost him, through powers that were beyond her. Now it was happening all over again with Mitch.

Oh, yes, she loved Mitch . . . Mitch, whose last name she didn't even know. She knew that she had missed him desperately, that his brooding upset her, along with her inability to console him. She knew that she wanted an explanation for his delay.

For long hours she agonized. Leave here tomorrow, a tiny voice said, protect yourself, you don't need this pain. But a louder voice told her to wait. Mitch made her feel. She wanted to be with him. There was always hope.

On that optimistic note she fell into a deep sleep, long after all sound of life from downstairs had ceased. The rain continued to pound the windows, but it was the smell of strong coffee that finally woke her up.

Even before she opened her eyes, she knew he was there in her room. The weight by her right hip, a distinct depression in the mattress, the faint hint of after-shave—all told her so. She opened heavy eyes and focused on him. Through a sleepy haze, he looked soft, gentle, and caring. Freshly shaven, showered, and dressed, he was powerfully male. His face was one big tender smile, broken only when he sipped coffee from the mug he held.

"Good morning," he said. "I'd begun to wonder whether you'd ever wake up. A real sleeping beauty."

Anne was relieved enough that his mood had improved to muster a smile. "I had trouble falling asleep."

"Tell me about it."

"Hmph. Got a taste of your own medicine?" Pushing higher up on the pillow, she moved her hair off her cheek.

As the quilt fell away, Mitch's eyes lit. "What's this? Bare arms? A negligee? Where'd the long flannel nightgown go? It's not that warm yet."

Anne scowled. "It's not a negligee. A negligee is something daring. This is just a nightgown." Primly, she pulled the quilt to her throat.

"We're arguing semantics, Annie. The fact is, you look like a woman should look first thing in the morning."

"I look awful," she grumbled, picturing ratty hair, swollen eyes, and bare features and suddenly wishing she could hide.

"If you could bottle up and sell what you call awful, you'd make a million."

"Well, I'm sure you'd know. You must have seen dozens of women first thing in the morning."

"Ah. I think you need coffee." He slid an arm behind her and drew her up. "Jealousy isn't your usual style." Though a smile played around his mouth, his eyes were serious.

"I'm not jealous," she said, but she drank his coffee. The intimacy of it made a lie of her denial. She wanted to know who occupied Mitch's time and thoughts when he wasn't with her. Oh, yes, she was jealous.

"Better?" he asked and took another drink himself. He placed the mug on the nightstand when she lay back against the pillows. "Is the nightgown symbolic? Like the pink sweater last time?"

She lifted a shoulder, self-conscious. "I suppose. I'm getting out more now. I feel better." Except when she thought about the upcoming trial, which she desperately tried not to do. "What about you? Any symbolic recovery gestures?"

He gave an evasive smile. "Some."

Anne waited. After a minute, she said, "Like what?"

"It's better told at another time. I have something more important in mind right now."

"What?" she asked with total innocence, until his eyes fell to her breasts. The nightgown was sheer. Blushing, she crossed her arms over the pale yellow bodice.

He took her wrists and pulled them away, then murmured a husky, "I haven't properly said hello," and drew her forward. His lips found hers unerringly, and proceeded to do all the things Anne loved until she was dizzy with pleasure.

Had she actually been angry at him the night before? The only thing she felt now was love. She kissed him as deeply as he kissed her, and when he shifted her, cradled her, she pushed her hands into his hair.

He was everything Anne had waited for and wanted. His kiss set her afire, his arms fed the flame. By the time he set her back, her cheeks and lips were rosy with heat.

She opened her eyes wide. "That was a nice hello."

To her delight, he wasn't done. When he reached for her again, she went willingly. Her hands slipped around his waist, fingers burrowing under his sweater to brush his skin. She was barely aware that he had pushed off the slim straps of her nightgown, until he drew back to release her arms and let the silky fabric fall to her waist.

His gaze caressed her breasts, which tingled and swelled. "How lovely you are, Annie," he said hoarsely.

"You've seen me before." She felt vaguely self-conscious.

But his eyes were deep green with passion. "Then, you were sick with a fever and a hacking cough. The beauty was there, but I hardly had time to admire it. Now's different. You are lovely. I'll say it again and again, every time I hold you, every time we make love."

Her insides quivered, all the more so when he stroked her breast. When his fingers rubbed her nipple, she grabbed at his shoulders for support. "You're cruel."

She felt a grin by her ear. "You bring out the worst in me," he said and kept up the torment.

The flames in Anne burned hotter, threatening to reduce her to embers. Small, unfamiliar sounds came from her throat when he eased her down on the bed and took her breast in his mouth. He sucked it in, bringing her arching off the bed. Clutching handfuls of his sweater, she was thinking she couldn't bear any more, when he released her and whipped the sweater over his head. Her hands were all over him, then. She couldn't touch him enough.

He ground out her name through gritted teeth and crushed her to him to stop her. She gasped at the press of his chest against hers, the texture against her softness, the rapid thunder of his heart.

"I need you," she cried, looking up at him. This wasn't enough, just wasn't enough. "Please?"

"Do you know what you're doing?" he asked huskily, and sucked in his breath when she pulled at the snap of his jeans. Seconds later her fingers were inside, against his abdomen. "My God, Annie!" For long seconds of indecision he stared down at her, and she was an open book, she knew. But she wasn't ashamed. She might not be ready to say the words aloud, but the depth of her love, her longing, brought tears to her eyes.

Then something went wrong. Suddenly his eyes grew hard.

"Damn it!" he swore and released her abruptly. Bolting from the bed, he strode to the window, where he stood with his hands on his hips, his legs apart, his head hung low, his shoulders heaving. Then, swearing again, he stalked past her and left the room.

7

Anne sat in stunned silence, unable to move, to think, to feel. Finally the chill in the air drove her under the quilt, but even then the trembling hit her hard. There was only one explanation for Mitch's behavior, and it had to do with the "obligation" to which he had once referred. He wasn't free.

So again she wondered, Do I leave, or do I stay? And again she reached the same decision. Self-destructive or not, she was staying. She had to be near Mitch.

But she wasn't being humiliated again. She wasn't begging for love until it was freely offered first.

Needing to make a statement to that effect, she slipped from bed, went to the dresser, and pulled on a pair of corduroys and a turtleneck sweater. Then she went downstairs with her head held high.

But her show of confidence was wasted. Mitch was nowhere in sight. He had eaten. She saw dishes in the sink. And the blue Honda was parked outside. Deflated, she guessed that he was out in the woods.

Resigned to spending the afternoon alone, Anne built a roaring fire and settled before it. She had a short essay to translate, and a new novel, of the bestseller type, to read. She set to it.

Late afternoon became early evening without a sign of Mitch. More restless than bored, more concerned than angry, she wandered into the kitchen. But she didn't have it in her to make dinner, so she returned to the fireplace.

Not long after, the back door opened and shut. Heavy boots crossed the kitchen floor. A slicker-clad figure appeared.

Without a word he approached, shucking the slicker along the way and draping it over a chair. Then he hunkered down near her and added another log to the fire. When it had begun to sizzle and smoke, he swiveled to face her.

"Angry?" The fire behind him threw a halo around his head, but his face was in shadow. Unable to tell whether he empathized or taunted, she went with the truth.

"No. I have no right to be angry."

"I needed to walk. Even wet, it was good. I needed to think."

About her? About another "obligation"? "You sound like you have the weight of the world on your shoulders," she teased.

"It sometimes seems that way." His voice was softer, more rueful. "It's been a bad week."

"Work?" she asked with caution.

"No. Work's fine. I have good backup there. They keep things running when I fade out."

Anne sat quietly, waiting for him to say more. If his problem wasn't business, it had to be personal. Suddenly, she didn't want to know.

She stood with a start. "I'll go make dinner."

He caught her wrist. Suddenly gentle, he said, "It's my turn. You did it last night. This time I'm cooking for you."

His gentleness threw her, as did his eyes, which begged her to let him do this. It wasn't exactly the begging she wanted, but it was something.

Trying to be as nonchalant as she could, she sank back into the chair and held up both hands. "It's your house."

He chuckled, in a suddenly lighter mood. One agile movement brought him to his feet, another brought him to her. He planted a kiss on her cheek before she had time to pull away.

"What was that for?" she asked.

"For being a saint," he said and set off.

Dinner was so companionable, that when Tuesday morning brought bright sun, Anne wasn't surprised to see Mitch up early to join her for breakfast.

"It's a perfect morning to set in the spouts," he said, wiping the dishes as she washed.

"Spouts?"

"We've had cold nights and warm days. The sap should be flowing like water."

Anne laughed in delight. "Maple-sugaring? We can do it ourselves? I'd planned on visiting a local farm to watch."

He gave a satisfied grin. "Why go elsewhere when we have everything we need right here?"

"Do you know what to do?"

"Do I know what to do? Since when have you had cause to question my expertise?"

She grunted. He was all too appealing when he was in good humor. "Modesty seems to have escaped you entirely."

He gave a short laugh. "No one's perfect."

In Anne's biased judgment, Mitch was as close to it as anyone could be on that day and the ones that followed. Though they hiked, read, and rested, the bulk of their attention focused on the maple-sugaring, about which he did indeed know almost everything.

"The best trees have to be big, forty years old or more," he explained, when they left the house carting the tools he had produced from a shed. "We're using metal spouts. This is the old-fashioned method of tapping trees, but it works for me."

"You've done this before?"

"Many times."

At the first maple that fit that bill, he drilled a small hole and inserted a metal spout that extended several inches beyond the bark. He did the same at each large tree.

"The sap generally flows between mid-March and mid-April. I do this whenever I'm here then." With a shove, he pushed a spout into place, then inserted one on the back side of the same tree.

"More than one per tree?"

"With a tree this size, there'll be enough sap for two. Here, you slide this one in, while I get more buckets."

By the time he returned, she had done as he asked. He fit a bucket on the spout.

"A sliding lid?" she asked, studying it. "I've never seen lids on sap buckets, period."

A smile touched the corners of his mouth. "Then you've never seen a stray horse or a field mouse drink the sap as it collects."

She laughed. "No, I haven't."

"This lid doesn't always keep them out. A persistent animal can get what he wants. But it helps."

They picked up the equipment and moved on to the next tree.

"How much sap will we get?" she asked, but she was distracted watching him as he debated where to drill. He was a sight to behold, larger and more rugged-looking than ever in a high-collared sheepskin jacket and faded jeans.

He knelt before the tree and applied the drill. "On a good day the bucket will fill and overflow. On a poor day we'll get only a few inches." He grunted as he pushed the bit forward into the tree. "If we were to continue for the entire length of the sapping season, we might get ten or twenty gallons from each tree."

She was startled. "That much? Whoa. What would we ever do with all that sap?"

The hole drilled, he straightened and motioned with his finger for her to insert the spout, which she deftly did this time with the aid of a hammer.

"'All that sap,'" he said, "boils down to very little. To get one gallon of syrup, you have to boil down anywhere from thirty-five to fifty gallons of sap."

"Ah. That explains why genuine maple syrup costs so much."

Mitch went on with the lesson as he continued to work. "New York and Vermont produce the most syrup in this country, though the province of Quebec yields more than the two states combined. Today, most of the commonly used syrups are actually a combination of maple syrup, cane sugar syrup, and corn syrup. If you ask me, though, there's no contest. The straight stuff, the real thing, beats all."

Anne couldn't argue with that.

For a while they proceeded in silence, but it was a friendly silence, an intimate one. She noted that he favored his right arm, cranking the hand drill around with it, while the other held the shaft in place. When she offered to take a turn, he indulged her, enjoying her struggle with a smug smile. When she finally gave up and turned the chore back to him, he said, "That's okay, Annie. I could never have cleaned the house the way you did this time."

"You noticed?"

"How could I help it," he teased with a rewarding grin. "I was nearly blinded by the sparkle."

Anne knew the feeling. She was nearly blinded now by the sparkle in his eyes. When he pushed two spouts into her hand, she was temporarily disoriented.

"In the tree?" he prodded with a cockeyed grin, leaving her to recover while he went for more buckets.

That first day, they drilled holes, inserted spouts, and hung buckets on the largest of the maples near the house. On succeeding days they collected the sap that had flowed. It was no mean feat, carting heavy buckets from tree to house and back.

"If we had the most modern equipment," Mitch teased as she massaged the nagging muscles of her shoulders, "we'd have used plastic spouts attached to plastic tubing that would take the stuff directly from the tree to the sugarhouse. It's much more efficient in terms of time and labor."

"That's all okay," she reasoned. "We don't have a sugarhouse. Besides, I'm gaining weight. The exercise will do me good."

He looked her over. "Well, you're not scrawny anymore, but . . . in danger of being overweight? Not a chance."

"Fine for you to say. You did most of the work this week." And he had.

He had cooked nearly every meal, in addition to doing the lion's share of the sugaring work.

He threw an arm across her shoulders and drew her to his side. "I owed you for being such a bastard when I first got here. Most women would have packed up and left."

She managed a gruff, "The thought did cross my mind."

"I'm glad you stayed," he said with affection.

There was a gleam in his hazel eyes, a softness in his smile, gentleness in the fingers that cupped her shoulder, and a velvet edge to his voice. All in all, it was a warm moment. Anne committed it to memory.

By Friday morning, there was enough sap in the large vat to begin the boiling process.

"They usually do this in long, shallow pans called evaporators," Mitch explained. "The one we're using is a little deeper than we need, but it'll have to do. When all the water has evaporated, we'll have pure maple syrup."

No matter that he had done this before, his enthusiasm and genuine enjoyment of the process were in no way watered down.

As for Anne, she was enchanted watching the thin, colorless liquid bubble and thicken to a dense golden brown. On impulse, she slid an arm around his waist, happier in that moment than in any in recent memory. Regardless of what the future held, she would cherish this memory.

He grinned down at her. "What?"

She sighed her pleasure. "It's been a fun week. This is a great finish to it." She was leaving in the morning. As it was, she had stayed a day longer than she'd planned, but he had asked her to.

"I'd rather a more personal finish," he said now. "Better still, I'd rather no finish at all."

She basked in the tenderness of his expression, loving him and aching to say it. But she wasn't setting herself up for rejection again. And anyway, just then the sap gurgled wildly.

"It shouldn't be long," he said, lifting a large wooden spoon to stir the solution and test for its thickness. "Should we have pancakes or French toast for dinner?"

"For dinner?"

"I don't know about you, but I don't have the willpower to wait until breakfast for this."

Anne drew a finger across the back of the cooling wooden spoon and licked the sweet syrup from its tip. "Mmmmmm. You may be right." She paused. "French toast."

"French toast, it is." Following her example, he tasted the syrup, then ran his finger over the spoon and held it to her mouth. The syrup was as rich and sweet as the moment itself. Anne thought she could go no higher.

Suddenly, a faraway gleam entered his eyes. His voice was filled with gentleness. "Rachel enjoyed this taste-testing stage the most last year, too."

Anne froze. Rachel? His "obligation"? She frowned, then stood straighter, then backed away from the arm on her shoulders. Rachel? With that faraway gleam, and such gentleness? Oh, yes, he loved Rachel. Anne didn't doubt it for a minute.

He was frowning. "What is it?"

"How could you?"

"How could I what?" His innocence riled her.

"How could you do that to me? How could you mention her name at a time like this?" She felt eviscerated, as though he had become part of her and was being cut free.

"Her name?" Then he realized what he had done, and his frown gentled. "I mentioned Rachel, didn't I?"

The softness in his voice at the mention of her name ravaged Anne. "How could you?" she repeated. Tears welled. When he reached out, she flinched and took a step back.

"Annie, listen—"

She took another step, then another. "I don't want to hear about your love life."

"You're wrong—"

"Yes, I'm wrong. I'm wrong to want to stay up here with you, when I should be back in New York trying to build a new life. I'm wrong to think that you really wanted me here, when in one careless minute you go wimpy over another woman. How could you, Mitch? Can't you see that I love you?"

Whirling around, she ran from the kitchen, taking the steps with reckless speed, stopping only when the door to her bedroom was slammed and flush to her back. Trembling hands covered her eyes and grew wet with tears. The pounding of her heart drowned out the sound of footsteps on the stairs.

He rapped on the door. "Open up, Anne."

"No." She was mortified by what she had said, and heartsick that it had come to this.

"There are things I have to tell you, Anne. Open the door."

Weeping, she only shook her head.

"Anne . . ."

"Go away!" she pleaded. She couldn't face him. Nothing he said mattered.

"I love you, Annie." His voice filtered soft and sensuous through the ancient wood of the door, and suddenly it did matter, very much. If this was a cruel hoax, she would never forgive him.

Turning, she laid her wet cheek against the door. Afraid to listen, afraid not to, she waited.

"Did you hear me, Annie?" Again the velvet sound, too dear to be dismissed, too real to be denied. "I love you."

Her pulse raced. She wanted to believe that he did, wanted to believe it more than anything in the world. But there was a crucial question still to be answered.

Slowly she turned the knob and drew open the door. Fearful, she raised her eyes to his. And she saw love, surely she did, unless she wanted it so bad that she was imagining it.

"Do you love Rachel, too?" she asked in a faltering whisper.

When he reached for her arms, she didn't resist. Neither did she melt toward him, but held her line, waiting, waiting for his answer.

His smile was sad but tender. "Yes, I love Rachel." His hands tightened when she would have pulled free. "But I love her in a very different way from how I love you, Annie. Rachel is my daughter."

Anne was shocked. His daughter? She had been jealous of his *daughter*?

"Why didn't you tell me?" she cried, wanting to hit him but slipping her arms around his neck instead.

He held her tightly. "I've wanted to so many times. But it never seemed appropriate. At the beginning, there was a part of me that wanted—God forgive me—that wanted to forget her existence while I was up here. Fatherhood has its merits, but it's been my greatest challenge since Bev's death."

He had a daughter. Anne could only begin to imagine that, much less the challenge of going it alone. "Maybe I could have helped."

"You've had enough to face without having to cope with a child."

"How old is she?"

"She turned six last week. And she came down with the chicken pox the day after her birthday. It's the first time she's been sick—really sick—since her mother died."

Anne understood. "That's why you were late arriving last weekend?"

He nodded against her head. "My parents have been wonderful, taking her for weeks at a stretch. They're often more cheerful than me." He looked down at her. "But I couldn't leave them with a sick child who only wanted her mother to hold her." His voice broke at the last.

"Why didn't you bring her up here with you?" Anne scolded.

He studied her closely. "I wasn't sure how you felt about kids. We've never talked about that, you and me. I only know you have none of your own."

"Not through choice, Mitch, not through choice."

"But to foist a sick child on you? How could I do that?"

Anne spoke from the heart. "I would have loved to have met your daughter. I'd have loved helping you take care of her. She's your daughter." Her voice fell. "And I love you."

He crushed her in his arms. The force of it said all that he didn't, but seconds later he was kissing her. If she hadn't already gotten the message, he did then. There was a vow in his kiss, a declaration, a promise.

"I love you . . . love you . . . love you," she whispered at the very first chance, loving being able to say it at last.

When his hands moved down to frame her face and tip it up, she savored the devotion she saw. His eyes asked a question; hers answered. Then he lifted her into his arms and carried her back down the narrow staircase to the room with the large bed, his bed.

This time, when he lowered her and reached for the hem of her sweater, she caught his hands and stilled them. "Let me," she said. "I need to know you."

He searched her eyes for a minute. Then, silently, he sat back on the bed and let her undress him. When his big body was bare, she could only marvel at its beauty, at the beauty of the love she felt. She explored his every sinew, touching him with innocent wonder from his shoulders to his thighs, skimming lean planes, tracing manly swells, delighting in his arousal.

When his patience was exhausted, he made a gutteral sound. "That's it, honey. That's it." With bullet speed, he flipped over her and removed every stitch of her clothes.

They lay naked then on the cool sheets, facing one another. Their breathing was heavy with need and want, but he held her off for those last few infinitely trying seconds. His eyes ran the length of her once more before searching her soul.

"Are you sure?" he asked softly.

"I love you," she replied.

"But it's different for a woman, isn't it?"

"Not when she's in love."

"Then you'll be mine?"

She grinned. "If you keep me waiting much longer, I may attack you."

The waiting ended. He possessed her as the pale purple of early evening bathed them in its glow, and it was good from the very first. Good . . . better . . . all-consuming . . . exhausting . . . absolutely, positively mind-blowing.

Arms and legs entwined, they slept, the deep and satisfied sleep of two who were spent and content. Long forgotten was the maple syrup on the stove, cooling to a thick amber perfection, and the French toast that was to have showcased it. They were oblivious when dusk faded to a dark and moonlit night.

When Anne awoke some time later, the only things she cared about were the warm chest pillowing her head and the lean hip under her palm. Her first movement brought a tightening of the arm across her back and the reverent caress of a hand. Smiling, she kissed the matted hair on his chest, then tipped her head to see him. His chin was strong but relaxed, the angled jaw likewise. His hair fell in waves over his forehead, lending a boyish charm. But his eyes—his eyes held hers, speaking of love.

"How are you?" he asked gently.

She traced the line of his jaw. "I've never been better."

"I love you. You know that now, don't you?"

She nodded. He could never have made love to her the way he had if it hadn't come from the heart. But he repeated the words as the night passed, reassuring her again and again, and Anne had never known such a night. She would collapse, breathless, weary of limb and shuddering in the aftermath of passion, only to discover before long that Mitch had a new way to say it.

The sun was high in the late-morning sky when they finally awoke. They lay in bed, face to face, studying, marveling, smiling.

"How am I going to drive back to New York today?" she finally asked. Forget her heart. Her body was done in.

"You're not. When I go to make my phone call later today, I'll make any you need to make. I'm sure the O'Gradys won't mind."

"The O'Gradys?"

"Our neighbors, about two miles to the east. I found them by accident once, but they're used to me now. I always call Rachel from there."

Anne smiled. "Rachel. You're daughter. That's so special, Mitch. I'm glad you keep in touch with her while you're away. I feel guilty that you left her at all to meet me, especially when she was sick."

"She was better by the time I left. But don't worry your pretty head about that. What you need to worry about is whether I'll let you out of this bed before Monday."

She feigned shock. "You wouldn't keep me here that long."

"No?"

She took another tack. "You couldn't."

"No?" His eyes held a naughty gleam. Then he slid over her and proved her wrong.

*　*　*

Saturday night they had cause to celebrate, toasting each other by first and last names, making merry despite the fact that they had both decided to leave the next day. Mitch had a Monday morning board meeting, Anne needed to deliver a promised piece of work. The real world waited.

She dreaded the moment of parting. What they had was so new, so fragile, so precious that she would have liked nothing more than to stay in the cottage forever.

But Mitch grew preoccupied as that moment of parting drew near. Finally, cautiously, he said, "The next few weeks are going to be impossible for me, Annie. I have some business matters coming to a head, and I'll want to spend extra time with Rachel. Let me call you as soon as things clear up. Is that okay?"

Given their intimacy and the number of times he'd said he loved her, Anne might have been puzzled by his unsureness, but she was starting to grow preoccupied herself. The court hearing on the matter of her law suit was only a week and a half off.

She took a resigned breath and gave him a hopeful smile. "I'll be waiting."

8

Wait she did, day after day, night after night. The knowledge that Mitch was suffering through a busy spell was small solace. Only the belief that he loved her carried her through to the evening before her court appearance, when the phone finally rang.

"How are you, Annie?" He sounded caring, but a little guarded.

"Fine. But I miss you." She had no pride.

"Same here, honey. Are you all set for tomorrow?"

She was touched that he remembered the date, touched that he was calling to give her last-minute encouragement. "I don't think I'll ever be ready," she answered honestly. "But my family and Jeff's will be coming to get me first thing in the morning. I think they're not sure that I'll show up on my own."

"They'll all be there?"

"Most of them. I'll have plenty of emotional support."

"I'm glad."

A silence fell. To lighten it, she asked, "How's Rachel?"

"Fine. Thanks for asking. A few scabs still left, but she's back at school." Again a pause, even heavier this time. "Anne?"

"Yes?"

"I love you very much." His voice was melancholy. Anne wanted to believe that he was as bothered by the separation as she was.

"I love you, too. When will I see you?"

"Soon, honey, soon. I'll talk with you again soon. Just remember that I love you."

Tears filled her eyes. Something felt wrong. But he said he loved her. She had to hold on to that.

The next day was warm by April standards, but Anne woke up feeling chilled. At nine o'clock sharp, Jeff's father rang her bell.

She kissed him, feeling the same fondness she always had, and reached for her coat and purse. "Are the others downstairs?" She was eager to be gone. The sooner the day was done, the better. She had been unable to touch any breakfast, and her stomach continued to knot.

"Actually, no. There's been a slight change. Our lawyer got the call this morning."

"What kind of change?"

He took her arm and directed her back into the room. "Sit for a minute and I'll explain." When they were seated on the sofa, he said, "The hearing has been called off."

"What?" After dreading the day for so long, the last thing Anne wanted was to have to go through the agony of anticipation all over again. "Why?"

"It's good news, really. There will probably be an out-of-court settlement."

A wave of relief swept her. "You mean, there won't be a hearing at all?"

He shook his head. "I doubt it."

"Then today?" The first thing she could think of was changing out of her suit and into jeans, and putting the whole matter behind her at last.

"Today we go to the lawyer's office. The lawyer representing the airline, that is. It seems that SouthEast American Air has counter-filed a suit, one against the manufacturer of the aircraft itself." He waited for her nod, just as Jeff would have done. Then he went on. "The latest investigation points to a weakness in the design of the craft as the cause of the accident, rather than pilot error or substandard maintenance procedures. SouthEast American Air has a fine reputation on those scores."

Anne didn't understand. "Then isn't this the end between the airline and me? Why do I need to do anything more?"

Theodore Boulton took her cold hand. "They need a deposition from you, a statement of what you suffered and will suffer in the future because of the accident. The lawyer asks questions and you answer under oath. You see," he explained, "in order to arrange a settlement, there has to be some assessment of damages, of losses. Not only will our lawyer, the airline's lawyer, and its president be there, but there will be similar representation by the airplane manufacturer."

She sighed. What he described sounded less threatening than a court hearing. Still, the prospect of a question-and-answer session was less than pleasant. "What will I be asked?"

He gave a negligent shrug. "They'll want to know about you and Jeff. How old you were when you met him. How long you were married. Where he worked. How much money he earned."

"But aren't those things matters of record, already?"

"Yes, but a deposition is a sworn statement of them. It's legal and binding. It's just a formality, but an important one."

Anne rested against the back of the sofa. "I see," she said when there seemed nothing else to say. "Are my parents meeting us at the courthouse?"

"My wife will have called them by now. There's no need for them to be there, not at a meeting like this."

She nodded, then searched the room for memories of Jeff that were warm and treasured, memories that had finally found their place. When her eyes completed the circle, they fell once more on her father-in-law. "Shouldn't we be going?"

He glanced at his watch. "We don't have to be there until eleven. Was there something else you wanted to do first?"

She laughed sadly. "I'd pretty much chalked off the day, not to mention the next few."

"Do you have much work to do?"

"Right now? No. I was expecting the worst from this hearing, so I gave myself a week's vacation."

"I hear you got a good rest in Vermont the week before last."

"You've been talking to my mother," she accused lightly, astonished at how the mere mention of Vermont could cheer her.

"We all worry about you, Anne. But you've been looking more yourself lately. Something is working for you."

It was the perfect opening, but she couldn't get herself to tell him about Mitch. It seemed so soon, and, in light of the day's happenings, inappropriate.

She blushed—but her father-in-law couldn't know why. "I've accepted Jeff's death, which is why this whole legal thing is so hard. It helps spending time away from it all in Vermont."

"I suspect you'd like to be there now."

Her grin was sheepish. "Oh, I wouldn't mind it, no offense to present company, of course."

"Have you started to date yet, Anne?"

She took a breath the wrong way and coughed. "Not . . . really." She and Mitch had never actually "dated."

Theodore Boulton was sober. "We think you should, Anne. You're young and beautiful. I know how much you and Jeff loved each other, but he's gone. Dot and I have accepted that, too. He was our son. Not a day goes by when we don't think about him. But it's been over a year now, and life has to go on. You're only twenty-eight. You should be enjoying yourself and your friends, finding someone else to love, having babies." His cheeks reddened. "Come the day you do have a baby, I'll think of it as my own grandchild."

Anne's eyes filled with tears. Reaching out, she hugged him soundly. "Thank you." He had lifted a burden from her shoulders. She felt better knowing that when she told them about Mitch, they would support her. She prayed that that day would come soon, particularly once this one was over.

The midmorning traffic was heavy. Sitting in it on Manhattan's residential side streets, Anne looked around for a distraction from the upcoming interview. Her eyes fell on the first of the flowers that had appeared in window boxes, then, when the car reached the wider avenues, on trees that were beginning to bud. They were tall, thin, and pale, compared to her memory of the trees in Vermont.

Those Vermont trees, being farther north and later to blossom, would be barely swelling with buds now, but those buds held promise of a rich and fruitful spring.

Soon, Mitch had said. Soon they would talk again. Soon they would see each other, and the waiting would be done.

Her father-in-law touched her hand as they waited for a traffic light to change. "Such a wistful look."

She sighed. "I'll just be glad when this is over."

He smiled Jeff's warm and reassuring smile. "It's going to be fine, Anne. Just fine."

Within minutes, he pulled into a parking lot and guided Anne into the posh skyscraper that housed the offices of the attorney for SouthEast American Air. The elevator ride to the sixty-eighth floor seemed endless. Her palms were moist and her stomach jumpy by the time they finally reached the law firm.

The Boulton family attorney, Terrence Carpenter, met then in the outer waiting room. He spent several minutes explaining the types of questions Anne would be asked, then led her through the double doors. They walked down long corridors of secretaries' stations, past open doors of office after office to one at the very end of the hall.

It was a conference room, dominated by a long, rectangular table of a rich wood, surrounded by large leather chairs. On the opposite side was the window, but the city seemed far away from this height. The wall to her left held oil paintings of past partners, the one to her right offered blackboards and panels, a television set, and a bar.

Others were already in the room, a woman and several men talking intently, but they quickly grew silent. Anne felt every pair of their eyes turn her way.

"Coffee, Mrs. Boulton?" her attorney asked, gesturing toward the percolator at the side of the room.

"Yes—ah—no," she whispered. Caffeine was the last thing her jangling nerves needed. But her mouth was very dry. "If I could have some water, that would be fine."

Moments later, when she had her water and a seat on one side of the long table, a man from the other group approached her. "We'll be ready to start soon, Mrs. Boulton. My client should be here momentarily."

Terrence Carpenter, who sat on her left, leaned in when the man left. "That was Peter Simmons, counsel for SEAA. He'll be deposing you. He'll introduce you to the others, but I believe the tall dark fellow is the attorney for Jet-Star Aircraft, the manufacturer, and the man with him must be its president."

Anne nodded and took a sip of water. She wasn't sure she could do this. It had been bad enough in the instant when they had looked at her. She had felt like the guilty party, rather than the one who had been wronged.

A professional-looking woman entered the room, whispered something to Peter Simmons, then left, closing the door behind her.

Simmons cleared his throat, "Ladies and gentlemen, let's begin. My client is delayed and will join us shortly."

The others took their seats. Formal introductions were made, ending with the stenographer, who would be making transcripts of the meeting. She was the one who put Anne under oath.

The next fifteen minutes passed harmlessly enough. Peter Simmons posed questions; Anne answered them. It was much as she had been told to expect, straightforward questions so innocuous that she was actually feeling a sense of security.

Then the door opened quietly and Simmons' client slipped into the room. The lawyer said, "For the record, this is the President of SEAA, Mitchell D. Anderson, Jr."

The only thing Anne could even begin to appreciate was that all eyes in the room were momentarily somewhere else. She felt her color drain and her stomach twist, felt a shaking, then shock, pure shock.

It was Mitch. Wearing an immaculately tailored blue suit. Groomed impeccably. Tall, well-built, and handsome. Hair neatly brushed, jaw firm and confident, eyes looking everywhere but at her.

It was Mitch. Head of the airline that she was suing. What had he said, that he had "other interests" beside real estate? When she had prodded, he evaded her. Then he had known all along? Had he planned the whole thing? How naïve she had been!

She fought a rising nausea when he crossed the room and took a seat beside his lawyer, who proceeded to introduce him to the others in the room. When her name was given, he nodded politely, for all indications a total stranger meeting her for the first time.

The situation was so unreal, so horrific, that she actually distanced herself and found the strength to go on. Her voice was more unsteady, and she didn't dare take a drink of water lest her trembling hand spill it, but she managed. She kept her eyes on the lawyer, completely blotting out the man to his right.

When did she meet Jeff? How long had she known him before their marriage? How long had they been married? Where did his family live? Her family? How many members in each?

The questions grew more personal. What had Jeff done for a living? How long had he done it? Annual income? Rising or steady? Did their parents help them financially? Did they travel? How often and where to? How much rent did she pay each month?

Had Anne been herself, she would have been annoyed with the questions. When, after an hour of questions, they took a short break, her lawyer explained, "He has to establish a lifestyle. He needs to determine the way you live in order to estimate the value of your loss."

"I lost Jeff! How do you put a dollar sign on that?"

The lawyer shrugged, and when they returned to the table, Anne was on the hot seat again. Had she loved her husband? Had they been faithful to one another? What had she done when he was away on business? Did she have friends? Did she have male friends?

Anne responded in a low voice, willing it to be steady, but she couldn't hide the shake of the hand she used to wipe away tears.

Mitch whispered something to his lawyer, who shook his head and went on with a vengeance.

Had Jeff been generous with her? Did he buy her gifts? Did he call her when he traveled? How often? Did he ever invite her along on business trips?

Anne had broken out in a cold sweat, but the questions went on.

"Mrs. Boulton, you were married for seven years. Did you have any children?"

"No," she whispered.

"Why not?"

She was mortified. "We just—didn't have any."

"Did you want a child?"

"Yes!"

"Did your husband want a child?"

"Yes." She brushed at more tears.

"Then why—"

Mitch cut in. "That's enough, Peter. She's upset. Is this necessary?"

The lawyer called for a short recess and led Mitch from the room.

Anne bowed her head and put a hand to her forehead. Inhaling deeply, she tried to steady herself.

"Are you all right?" her father-in-law asked.

Her plea was a barely audible whisper. "I have to get out of here. How much longer can this go on?" She reached into her purse for a tissue to wipe her eyes.

"Not much longer. Try to hold up, Anne. Once this is over, you'll never have to face it again."

In her heart Anne knew that the agony was just beginning, but she had no time to dwell on it. Mitch and his lawyer returned to their seats.

The lawyer said, "My client feels strongly that we have all the information we need. I have no further questions."

"Excuse me," broke in the man who had been introduced as counsel for the manufacturing company. "If you have nothing more to ask, I do." His tone was ominous. Clearly, he wasn't having his client go down without a fight.

Simmons spared Mitch a glance before saying, "Certainly, Mr. Parks, but try to be brief. Mrs. Boulton is under a strain." To Anne, he said, "Are you up for a few more questions?"

Anne dared a look at Mitch, but his expression was masked. Angry at him, angry at the world, she turned back to the lawyer and nodded.

Parks picked up where Simmons had left off. "On the matter of children, we want to know why, after so many years of supposedly wanting them, you never had them."

Anne stared at the man in astonishment. She couldn't imagine any greater invasion of her privacy than this.

Terrence Carpenter leaned sideways to explain in a low voice, "They want to know the extent of your loss in terms of future parenthood. If you and Jeff wanted a child and he's no longer here to sire it, the loss is greater. Do you understand?"

She nodded. Yes. She could understand that.

She took a breath. "We wanted to have a child, but it just never . . . happened."

"You mean, you never conceived?"

"I did conceive. Twice. I miscarried both times." In the silence that followed, her father-in-law took her hand.

"Did you see doctors?" the lawyer prodded.

"Of course!" Her voice rose. As if the memories weren't painful enough, the humiliation of airing them before this hostile group was traumatic. "They couldn't find a cause. They insisted that another time the baby would be fine."

"And you kept trying?"

"How could I, Mr. Parks? My husband died."

Her words brought silence to the room. Anne sat stiff, clenched her jaw, and looked nowhere but at the lawyer, who quickly redirected the discussion.

"Do you date, Mrs. Boulton?" When she frowned, he rephrased the question. "Have you begun to date since your husband's death?"

The sudden hammering in her chest threatened to rob her of breath. She refused, absolutely refused to look at Mitch. "No," she whispered.

"I'm sorry, I couldn't hear that, Mrs. Boulton."

She raised her voice. "No." It was a technicality, she knew, but she didn't care.

"That's hard to believe, if you'll excuse me for saying so. You're an attractive young woman. Aren't you planning to date?"

"Not now," she said with a bitter laugh. After what Mitch had done, she was a wasteland inside.

"Wouldn't you like to marry again?"

"No."

Disappointed at not ferreting out information that would help his client, Parks made a final stab. "You mean, there have been no men in your life—"

"The woman answered you once, Mr. Parks," Peter Simmons broke in forcefully. "Unless you have anything different to ask, I suggest we let Mrs. Boulton go. There are other depositions to be taken, from my client and yours."

Reluctantly the other lawyer agreed. "Very well. Thank you, Mrs. Boulton. I have no further questions."

Anne heard nothing of the remaining exchange. Feeling hollowed out, she let her father-in-law guide her from the room and the building, then drive her home.

"There, now, that wasn't so bad," he said when they were back at Anne's place, but her silence must have tipped him off. He went to the liquor cabinet and returned with a glass of amber liquid. "Drink this. It'll help."

She downed the liquid quickly, sputtering in reaction to the flame that seared her throat. Unable to think, much less speak, she let her head fall back against the sofa and closed her eyes to the world.

"Let me call your mother, Anne. She'll want to be with you."

Anne shook her head once, then again.

"Are you sure? Would you like me to stay awhile?"

She forced her head up and her eyes open. "No. I think I'd like to be alone."

He looked torn, but he bent and kissed her head. "It's over now. Keep telling yourself that. It's all over." With a reassuring pat to her shoulder, he let himself out.

Over. Well, it certainly was that. Anne's heart might have grieved for what had been lost that day, but her mind simply shut down. Exhausted and in need of escape, she dozed off within minutes right there on the sofa. The harsh peal of the phone brought her awake with a jolt.

It was her mother, filled with concern. "Ted just called and explained what happened. Are you all right?"

"Yes. I'm fine."

"You don't sound it."

"I was sleeping. I'm worn out."

"Would you like me to run over and take you out . . . for a late lunch, perhaps?"

Anne shot a startled look at her watch. It was nearly two-thirty. Lunch had fallen by the wayside, along with her appetite. The thought of food turned her stomach.

"Anne?"

"Yes, Mother. No, thanks. I don't feel like eating."

"Was the deposition that bad?"

It couldn't have been worse, she thought. "It was . . . difficult."

"Are you sure there's nothing I can do?"

"I'm sure." She forced a smile into her voice, for her mother's sake, but it vanished the instant the words were out.

The older woman sighed. "All right. I'll call you later. Get some rest."

"I will. And thanks for calling, Mom."

"You're welcome, darling. Bye-bye."

She hung up the phone thinking that, more than anything, she needed a shoulder to cry on, but the tears refused to come. For a time, she wandered aimlessly from room to room, window to window. Eventually she changed into jeans and an oversized shirt and, barefoot, returned to the living room. She felt every bit the hollow shell she must have looked. The view from the window held nothing for her. Nor did a glance at the day's mail. Unable to muster energy, she stretched out on the sofa.

One hour passed, then another, and the enormity of the day's happenings sank in. Mitch had deceived her. Oh, it might have started innocently enough in September, but in time she had mentioned the crash, even its date, and the upcoming trial. He might have spoken up then. He might have spoken up last night.

She held her stomach tightly. If only she could cry. If only she could scream. Instead she felt drained, heartbroken, half whole.

The telephone rang again. She tried to ignore it under a layer of pillows. When it kept up, she realized that if it was her mother again and she didn't answer, the woman would be on at her door in no time flat.

With an effort, she dragged herself from the sofa and went to the wall phone in the kitchen. "Hello?"

"Anne?" His voice was deep and, in spite of everything, dear.

Stunned, she quietly hung up the phone.

Wobbly legs took her back to the sofa. She doubled over there, hugged her knees to her chest, and waited for him to call again. In a matter of seconds, the phone began to ring. She let it ring and ring and ring. She rocked back and forth, suffering with the sound. She tried covering her ears with her hands, but the ringing seemed to grow louder and louder, more and more harsh, crueler and crueler.

At last, it ceased. Only then did she break down and weep.

9

The days that followed were pure hell for Anne. After tears, came self-recrimination. She had been naïve, she had been irresponsible, she had been wanton. She should never have returned to the cabin after the first week. She shouldn't even have stayed there then.

Self-recrimination gave way to anger, and she railed on at Mitch for a while. She didn't understand how a person could do what he did. And he kept calling her! She cringed each time the phone rang and answered only to avoid visits from her family. When it was Mitch, she hung up.

Her seclusion was more total than it had been after Jeff's death, because no one, but no one, knew about Mitch and her. If her parents sensed that her reaction to the deposition was extreme, they attributed it to the final pain of losing Jeff. She let them believe that, rather than having to tell them what a fool she'd been.

She couldn't begin to think of the future. Once again, it was a frightening void. Each day was a challenge. Her only hope was in wiping Mitch from her mind, and it was easier here in New York. They hadn't spent time together here. There were no memories of him here, other than of the deposition, but, there, he hadn't been the man she loved.

On occasion she thought of Vermont. Spring would be coming there. She would have liked to see the lilacs bloom and smell their fragrance. So there was a loss in this, too.

He stopped calling after the first few days, but, try as she might, she was never able to push him far from mind. Her father actually mentioned him one afternoon.

"I received a call from Mitchell Anderson the other night. You know, the head of SEAA?"

Did she know him? Did she know him!

"Seems like a nice fellow. He wanted to make sure you were all right, since you seemed so upset at the deposition."

"Wasn't that considerate of him," she snipped bitterly. *Guilt feelings. Good. Let him suffer.* "How did he know to call you? He doesn't know my maiden name." But, of course, he could find it out. He could find out anything he wanted. Powerful men got what they wanted without batting an eyelash.

"He called Ted first," her father explained. "He hesitated to call you directly, for fear of upsetting you more."

"Wise man." *Upsetting me more. That was cute.*

Anthony Faulke eyed her with gentle reproach. "It was considerate. After all, his airline's been found innocent in the matter. Technically, it's no concern of his any longer."

Anne didn't care that his airline was innocent. In her mind, Mitch was still a deceiver.

She was angry with no one to yell at, heartsick with no one to hug, and if she moped about for the better part of each day, the nights were no better. She was obsessed by a living nightmare, waking and sleeping.

By the middle of the second week, she was at the end of her rope. So she lined up several fast interpreting jobs that would get her away from paper translations and out into a people-oriented mainstream again. And it worked. She got a handle on her emotions.

Then she was thrown a setback. Her doorbell rang one evening when she wasn't expecting anyone. Leaving the chain latch in place, she opened the door the several inches allowed and peered out to find Mitch there. She closed the door with a slam. The bell rang again and again. She went to the most remote corner of the apartment, crossed her arms on her chest, and vowed to let it ring.

She wasn't prepared for the loud pounding that followed. He was making a godawful racket.

Fearing that he would have her neighbors out in no time, she returned to the door. "Go away!" she yelled, hoping that her voice would carry through his ruckus.

It did. His returning call was muffled, but she heard every word. "Not until I've spoken with you, Anne."

"Go away! I don't want to talk!"

"You'll have to."

Irate, she reopened the door those few allotted inches. "I don't have to do anything. Now, please leave, or I'll call the police." It took very ounce of restraint for her to remain calm when she would have liked nothing more than to run him through with a carving knife.

He looked agitated. "I'm trying to be patient, Anne, but you refuse to take my calls. We have to talk. There are things I have to explain."

She seethed. "Sorry, bud, but you had your chance, and you passed it up. You had all those days and nights to tell me who you were and what your business was, but you didn't. You were so cagey. *I'll see you soon, Annie, soon.*" She contorted her voice to mock him. "But you didn't bother to tell me when, did you, Mitch? Well, I don't want to talk now." She leaned against the door to shut it, only to find he had a foot in the way.

"Move!" she ordered hoarsely. She was wearing down in more ways than one.

He swore. "Hell, Anne, but you can be stubborn. If we were back in Vermont, I'd know just what to do."

"We're not in Vermont!" she screamed, uncaring that others might hear. "I'll never be there again. Now, leave!" Every muscle in her body quivered.

"Fine," he gave in. "I'll leave, but I'll be back. If not here, I'll catch you somewhere else. On the street, in a restaurant, even at your parents' house, if need be. I can be devious. You can't stay holed up in this place forever. And I won't give up!"

When his foot slid back into the hallway, Anne slammed the door shut then, she turned and ran, trembling, toward the bedroom, where she huddled against the headboard like a hunted animal. He could be devious; that was putting it mildly! She *would* see him again, and the thought filled her with dread.

Determined not to be made a prisoner in her own home, Anne booked even more jobs. She was all over town, with varied and interesting people, but the diversion she wanted came only in bits and snatches. Ever on guard against running into Mitch, she found herself looking over her shoulder wherever she went, half expecting to find him ready to pounce. It was nerve-racking, to say the least. After more than a week of running from place to place and feeling haunted, she grew discouraged.

The worst of it was that that she didn't see him, and that deep inside, in a place she didn't want to know about, she was disappointed because of that. The pain went on.

Relief came from her parents in the form of an invitation to spend time with them at the shore. Yes, they tended to smother her, but she could use a little smothering now. She wanted to be pampered and loved. She wanted to be protected from Mitch. The change of scenery would be good. She planned to make the most of it.

The first of May found her dressed in a bright yellow sundress, waiting beside her bags at the front entrance of her apartment building. She checked the street, then her watch. Her parents had promised to be there at one. It was one-fifteen now. They weren't usually late.

With a brief word to the doorman, she returned to her apartment, dialed her parents' home phone, waited through ring after ring. Assuming they were on their way, she went back downstairs. What she found there stopped her cold.

With the doorman's ready assistance, her bags were being loaded into the trunk of a shiny brown Audi that she didn't recognize. But she did recognize the man who stepped from its far side. He was sun-bronzed and gorgeous in a pullover and white ducks, looking as handsome and masculine as could be, and very, very smug. Before she could find her tongue, he opened the rear door of the car and leaned in. When he straightened, he was carrying the most beautiful child Anne had ever seen.

Her breath faltered. How *could* he? He wasn't playing fair, wasn't playing fair at all—and he knew it, if the mischief in his grin meant anything.

"Hi, Annie!" He greeted her as though nothing was wrong. "Hope we didn't keep you waiting too long. Traffic was a bitch. I think we have all your bags. Is there anything else inside?"

Anne may have been thick in the past, but she wasn't thick now. He had known she would be waiting. He had known what time to come. He would never have brought the child, if he hadn't been sure of the outcome. That meant her parents were in cahoots with him.

Had it been Mitch, alone, she would have turned and run. But when she looked at the child, she was lost. The six-year-old wore pink bib-topped shorts, a white jersey, and clean white sneakers. Her limbs were tanned, long legs dangling around Mitch's thighs. Golden cascades of curly hair fell halfway down her back, held off from her face by gaily painted barrettes above either ear. But the barrettes were small and couldn't quite hold all her hair. Short wisps escaped into tendrils that framed her face. And that face? If Anne hadn't been in love with the rest, that face would have done it. It was softly rounded and rosy cheeked, with a swarm of bright freckles over the bridge of a button nose, and eyes that were chocolate-colored and soulful—and staring at her.

"Oh, my," Mitch said. "I've almost forgotten introductions in my rush to get going. Anne, this is my daughter, Rachel Anderson. Rachel, this is Anne Boulton."

With more poise than Anne could seem to muster, the child extended a small hand. "Hello, Anne. I'm pleased to meet you. Daddy's told me all about you."

Anne held her hand, loving its fragility and its warmth. "Only the good things, I hope?"

Rachel's eyes rounded quickly. "Oh, my daddy would never say anything bad about you. He—"

"That's enough, pumpkin," Mitch cut her off with a squeeze. "You can't give away all our secrets, now, can you?"

The child broke into a wide grin, displaying a mouthful of small white teeth with a wide gap smack in the middle of the top.

Anne was enchanted. "That's quite some hole you've got there. Did the good fairy bring you something nice for those teeth?"

Again the grin, along with owl eyes. "I got a whole dollar for each of them. Daddy says he only got a quarter when he was a little boy, but that the good fairy was afraid I might swallow a coin, so she gave me paper. I'm really glad," she bubbled and lowered her voice in confidence, " 'cause you can't buy much for a quarter."

Anne laughed. "You're a perceptive little girl."

Mitch appeared to agree. Pride was written all over his face, and he had a right to that pride where the child was concerned. Not where his own behavior was concerned, though. For starters, he should be ashamed of himself for using her as a shield.

"Uh, perhaps you ladies are ready to go. The sooner we leave the city, the sooner we'll reach the cabin."

The cabin? Her heart stopped. She couldn't go to the cabin.

But Rachel's eyes were glued to hers and Mitch's held clear warning.

"Rachel," she began softly, checking back over her shoulder, "do you think you might wait here while your father helps me out with one last thing upstairs? Maurice, the doorman, will keep you company."

The child looked to her father for permission. He kissed her and set her back in the car. "We'll be down in a jiffy." He spoke gently, repeating the same for the doorman. Taking Anne's elbow, he escorted her inside.

As soon as they rounded the corner and were out of the child's sight, Anne turned on him. "You arranged this with my parents, didn't you?"

He grinned. "They're wonderful people. When I explained the situation, they were more than glad to help out."

"Well, that's just fine, but I'm not going! For all your smugness and your crafty little plans, I'm not going!"

His grin died. "I told Rachel that you'd be spending the week with us."

"You had no right to do that."

"But it's done. She's counting on your being there. Would you disappoint her?"

Anne was exasperated. "How can you use her like this? You know I can't hurt her."

"I was counting on that."

"So you're going to go out there"—she pointed a shaky finger toward the street—"and tell her I can't go."

"But you can. Your bags are packed and loaded. Your work has been cleared for the next two weeks. There's nothing left to hold you here."

Anne felt trapped. With a tired sigh, she slumped back against the wall. "Why don't you leave me alone? Can't you see that I don't want to be with you?"

He was sober then. "That's because you won't listen to reason. I've tried to explain, and more than once, but you wouldn't answer my calls or let me in when I banged on your door. You wouldn't give me the courtesy of hearing me out. So now I'm asking you, for Rachel's sake, to come with us. Just this once. At the end of the week, if you still feel this way, I will leave you alone."

Anne wondered if it was the only way out. She couldn't bear the thought of hurting a child who had already been so badly hurt in life. And the little girl would be a chaperon of sorts. What harm could there be?

"Is that a promise?" she asked cautiously.

"Yes."

There was no point belaboring the matter. With a defeated sigh, she pushed away from the wall and returned to the car with Mitch.

10

Within the hour they left the traffic of the city behind and sped northward. "When did you get the new car?" Anne asked, groping for conversation with Mitch as Rachel knelt on the backseat, studying the receding skyline.

"About a week ago. This is her maiden voyage. The Honda was a bit small for three." The eyebrow that arched her way was subtle, but Anne had to marvel at his presumption. If the three included her, he had paid a whole lot for a single trip.

Rachel poked her golden head between the bucket seats and rubbed her cheek against the soft velour. "I like this car. Daddy says the color matches my eyes."

"It does, at that," Anne said with a warm smile. How not to smile at a child who exuded sweetness like this one? She prayed there would be pouts, crankiness, and temper tantrums as the week progressed. Otherwise, she could be in big trouble.

There weren't any pouts, crankiness, or temper tantrums, and Anne grew more and more attached to the child. Even knowing that Mitch contrived it didn't detract from the pleasure Anne took in simple custodial things like bathing her, combing those long blond curls, helping retie the shoelaces that came undone after Rachel laboriously tied them herself. There were substantive things to cherish, like cookie baking, hikes in the woods, and reading stories before the fire at night.

And if Anne was in love, she felt it coming right back from Rachel. Such innocent, heartfelt, freely given affection was the most precious thing in the world.

Staying indifferent to Mitch was a problem, but she did her best and, to his credit, he didn't push. She slept upstairs, he slept downstairs, with Rachel in a sleeping bag on the floor of his room. By Wednesday morning, though, Anne felt she was walking a tight-rope of conflicting emotions, with Mitch watching from morning to night to see which way she would go.

Memory nagged. She remembered beautiful times here with Mitch, innocent times of fulfillment and love. She might put them aside in New York, but they were more real here and harder to flee.

Still she tried. "I'm going for a walk," she announced after a post-breakfast bit of brooding.

"That's a good idea," Mitch said without mockery, but then, his gentleness was part of the torture. "Take your time. I think I can manage Rachel for a few hours."

Despite the little girl's protest, Anne left. It was the first time she had been alone since they had arrived, and she needed it badly. She was feeling frayed at the seams, but there were still two days left in the week. She had to find a way of surviving.

Spring was everywhere. What had been damp and gray a month before was now a fresh, vibrant green. The scent was of rebirth, spreading upward from the lush carpet of new grass and through the lime leaves that clothed long tree branches. The sounds were enchanting ones—the chirping of birds from nest to nest, the rustle of forest creatures in the newly spreading undergrowth. Water ran freely over rocks and silt, rushing with the force of the snows that melted higher up the mountain. The pasture glowed yellow with dandelions and pink with crab apple blossoms. It was the countryside at its gayest and most promising.

Not so her heart. Its sadness was all the more poignant by contrast. Pebbles scattered before her shuffling feet. She kicked a boulder or two. When she finally buried her head on her arms, the tears flowed as fast and free as the brook beside her. But while the brook's course was one of liberation, Anne's was the opposite. She was in an emotional prison. Loving Mitch did that.

In time, she knelt on the stones and splashed her face. The water was so cold that she gasped, but the pain felt good, and the invigoration was welcome. She headed slowly back toward the cottage, winding in and out among the forest paths, physically relieved from the cry, if no closer to a solution.

Under the warmth of the high noon sun, she arrived at the house to an unexpected silence. Assuming that father and daughter were out in the woods themselves, she passed through the kitchen to the living room, only to stop short at the sight of Mitch, standing tall and lean at the front window. His hands filled the pockets of his jeans in a pose that was more idle than she would have expected, given the presence of a vivacious six-year-old.

"Where's Rachel?" she asked.

He faced her. "She's gone."

"Gone." But he wasn't upset. "What do you mean *gone*?"

"My parents came by to pick her up. They're continuing on to Montreal for a few days."

"You mean, she's gone?" The implication of it was only slowly seeping in.

"Yes." His eyes held hers. "You've been crying."

"No." She felt justified lying. He had tricked her again!

"Your eyes are red," he challenged softly.

"I have hay fever," she snapped, feeling a growing fury. "You planned this, didn't you? You had it all arranged with your parents. You orchestrated the whole thing, using Rachel to get me up here, then conveniently having her vanish." Every muscle in her body had tensed.

"Yes," he admitted and offered no excuse.

Anne's eyes blazed. "And you really think I'm staying, now that she's gone? Hell, she was the only reason I agreed to come up here in the first place!"

He began to move toward her. "Was it, Anne? Was it really? Be honest with yourself."

She was suddenly afraid. "I am! That was why I came up here." She put up a hand to ward him off and took a step backward. "Don't come any closer. Don't you dare touch me—"

"Or what? Haven't we been through this before? We're right back at the beginning, Annie. Face it. No child. No deposition-taking. No other pretense. Just you and me."

"It's not that simple!" she cried and took another step back. He was too tall, too attractive, too near. "I can't forget those things. They're all here, even if you try to deny them, and nothing can change the fact that I didn't want to see you, that I don't want to have anything to do with you!"

But her body was trembling. It remembered how he felt and responded the closer he came.

He continued his advance until she was backed against a wall. "I don't believe you," he informed her smoothly. "I think you want the opposite."

She shook her head in denial. "Don't, Mitch. Get away from me." But her warning was a whisper, and a faltering one at that. She was between Mitch and the wall, between a rock and a hard place. She was wondering where to go, when he flattened his hands on the wall by either shoulder.

"This has gone on long enough. I'm going to talk now, and you're going to listen. My patience is wearing thin."

"Your patience?" she cried, raising her eyes to his. "What about mine? And what about my feelings? But then, you never were all that concerned about what would happen to me after you'd taken everything you wanted! You are the most selfish, arrogant, ruthless—"

The list of scathing expletives would have gone on if he hadn't stopped them with his mouth. She tried to pull back, to twist her head away, to push him off. But he was bigger, stronger, and determined.

He drew her from the wall and into his arms, kissing her so vehemently that her breath was cut off. At the instant she would have collapsed, he eased his grip, breathing raggedly for a moment before capturing her lips again.

This time was different. His mouth was more persuasive now, moving with gentleness and sensual sureness. Anne might have been able to resist force, but a caring kiss was something else. Her body was weak, her mind muddled. While her arms continued to apply a token pressure against his chest, her lips betrayed her. Gradually they softened, then opened, then drank helplessly of his kiss.

When he finally raised his head, she bowed hers and dissolved into helpless tears.

"Don't cry, Annie. Please." Sounding tormented, he held her tightly until she gradually quieted. "I won't hurt you. Please believe me, honey. I've never meant to hurt you. I just want you to listen to what I have to say."

"Do I have a choice?" she finally whispered.

He smiled. "No."

She remained docile as he led her to the chair before the cold hearth. The same wings that had once been blinders against the dark, now blotted out all but Mitch.

He raked a hand through his hair. "I know what you must be thinking about me, but you're wrong. It's unfair of you to blame me for what happened to Jeff."

Anne had *never* blamed him for the crash. But before she could tell him that, he said, "It wasn't until February, when you were so sick and had that nightmare about the accident and mentioned the court hearing, that I began to wonder if there was a connection. Contrary to your assumption, I did not run right back to New York to check it out." He turned away and approached the hearth. With an arm on its mantel, and a foot on the ash-strewn grate, he was silent for several minutes. "I didn't want to know," he finally said. "My guilt feelings about that accident were bad enough, without having to bear your scorn."

But he was missing the point! She didn't blame him for the accident! That wasn't the problem!

He went on without turning. "I was tortured coming back here in March. I knew I had to be with you, but I also knew you might hate me even more afterward." He pushed a hand through his hair. "You were bound to learn the truth sooner or later. I wanted to tell you myself. I just . . . couldn't."

Slowly he turned to face her. His eyes held unfathomable pain. "When we made love, Anne, it was magnificent. We might fight about little things, but when we came together that day, it was heaven. I kept thinking that if you knew how much I loved you, you'd forgive me. If I could have prevented that accident," he said on a note of defeat, "I would have, believe me, I would have."

"I never blamed you for that crash!"

"The guilt has been unbearable," he said as though he hadn't heard her. "It's irrational and unjustified, but it's real. You have no idea. Between the plane and the car . . ." He shook his head.

Anne was missing something. Quietly, she said, "What car?"

He turned away, took a shuddering breath, straightened in resignation. "My wife was killed in an automobile accident three weeks before that plane crash. It was late at night. The roads were icy. Our car was hit head on by a man who'd had too much to drink." He looked back over his shoulder. "I was at the wheel."

Anne stared dumbly at him, and suddenly she was the one overwhelmed with grief. She hadn't asked how Mitch's wife had died, because that was against the rules. But she should have known that the death of a young woman would be tragic no matter how it occurred.

"It wasn't your fault," she reasoned.

His eyes flashed. "I was driving! If only I'd driven slower or faster, or taken a different route." He hung his head. When he raised it again, his anger was spent. "Remember the nightmare you had? Mine was no dream. I was able to pull Bev out of the car, only to watch her die in my arms. There was nothing I could do. A battered arm was the least of my punishment. The plane crash seemed an extension of it. Then"—he pressed his lips together and nodded—"then I found you."

Anne swallowed hard. He wandered across the room, seeming aimless, as though it didn't matter where he went. She had never seen him like this, had never heard his voice so bleak or so sad.

"I had fallen in love with you long before I made the connection between Jeff's death and my airline. In an odd way, I felt you were my only chance at happiness, at building a new life. I was terrified of losing you. I didn't know what would happen when I told you what I knew. I wanted to think you'd understand, but the stakes were so high."

He turned to face her, earnest now. "I never lied to you about the crash, Anne. I just didn't tell you the whole truth. It's tormented me for months. But the longer the deception went on, the worse my sin and the greater the risk of coming clean. I was afraid that once you knew, you'd despise me." For a long and heartrending moment, he stared at her. Then he cursed softly. "Ach, what's the use. It's happened, and I deserve it. I was too blinded by my own need to see to yours." He took a ragged breath. "I just wonder when the punishment will end." Turning on his heel, he stalked out of the room, leaving Anne alone and in shock.

The slam of the back door jolted her, but even then it was a minute before she could move. Bolting up, she ran after him out of the house, stumbling on the steps, catching herself and running on. The hammer of her heart made breathing difficult, but she didn't stop.

He was fast disappearing into the woods. Frantically she followed, running on through the low growth until she reached a clearing. He sat there with his back to her, brooding among the dandelions. The sun glanced off his hair in sparkles, but his hunched form was grim.

"Mitch?"

She crept nearer.

"Mitch, I'm sorry, so sorry." She tried to touch him, but pulled back when he flinched. So she hunkered down inches behind him and said, "I've been wrong. Please forgive me. It was cruel of me not to listen, not to even ask questions, but it hurt to know that there was so much I didn't know, after everything that we'd shared. *Because of* what we'd shared, I should have given you the chance to explain, but I loved you so much. Finding out who you were like that was awful. Try to understand."

This time when she touched his shoulder, he allowed it.

"I've always been naïve," she explained not to make excuses for herself, but so that Mitch would know more. "My life was easy and happy and charmed. Maybe I felt immune to tragedy. I'd never known any, not until the crash, and then I couldn't believe Jeff was gone. It couldn't happen to me."

She moved closer. "Then I found you. I love you, Mitch. I fought it for a long time. I was afraid of suffering the kind of pain I had suffered loving Jeff and losing him. When I saw you in that lawyer's office, the two worlds came together. I should have trusted you. I should have known that there was an explanation. So help me, I was afraid to listen. Maybe I was punishing myself. Maybe I was feeling guilty for finding happiness with you." Her voice broke.

His eyes met hers, then, and they were filled with the same vulnerability she felt. It gave her the strength to finish.

"My God, Mitch, haven't we both suffered enough? Isn't it time to end the punishment? I love you."

"Do you, Anne?" he asked unsurely, huskily, hopefully. "Do you love me enough to want to wake up in my arms every day, knowing that I make mistakes?"

"Knowing that you're human? It's a relief, y'know?"

A sound came from his throat, no, from his soul, it was that deep, and he pulled her around and crushed her in his arms. "I love you, Annie," he whispered with a rush of feeling. "Don't ever, ever turn away from me again. Don't shut me out. I can't survive it."

He kissed her, then pulled back and made a show of licking his lips. "Salt?"

She smiled through her tears. "That's happiness. You'll have to bear with me."

"I think I can manage it," he said with infinite tenderness and brushed the tears from her cheeks. "I do love you."

He showed her how much right there under the sun, worshipping her first with clothes, then without, making love to her on the soft carpet of new grass and dandelion puffs. It was hotter, harder, sweeter than it had ever been before, a preview of what it might be in twenty or thirty years' time.

When later they lay still and let the sun stroke their naked bodies, she nuzzled his neck. "This is heaven."

He patted her bottom. "Let's hope there's no poison ivy around here." When she bolted upright, he burst out laughing.

"Is there?" she asked.

He pulled her back to his chest. "No poison ivy. Just me."

"Will you give me a rash?"

He laughed again. "Hopefully one very special itch now and again; never a rash."

She stretching against him, so pleased to hear him laugh and know she was its cause. "You have no idea how I love you."

"Not as much as I love you."

"No? Wanna bet on that?"

"You're on," he said and rolled over her to settle the matter.

Through no lack of trying, it was far from settled by the next morning. Awakening with the sun in a happy glow, Anne crept quietly from his bed, pulled on his large shirt, and went to the front door. As it opened she caught the sweet scent of the lilacs. In the week's tumult she hadn't noticed them before. Now she smiled in delight at the shapely pink-purple clusters and the full, rich fragrance.

Snapping off a small cluster, she returned to his bed, dropped the shirt, and slid quietly between the sheets. She lay on her stomach and watched Mitch sleep, seeing the same peace on his face that she felt inside.

One sleepy hazel eye opened. He smiled lazily.

She moved the spray of lavender under his nose. "The lilacs are in bloom. Spring is here." As her lover's hand wound through her hair to draw her in for a good morning kiss, she knew that it truly was.